The Spy

CYNTHIA KEYES

Vinci Books

vinci-books.com

Published by Vinci Books Ltd in 2025

1

The publisher and the author have made every effort to obtain permissions for any third party material used in this book and to comply with copyright law. Any queries in this respect should be brought to the attention of the publisher and any omissions will be corrected in future editions.

A CIP catalogue record for this book is available from the British Library.

Paperback ISBN: 9781036702649

By Cynthia Keyes

Regency Romance

Chapter One

This late at night the wharf at London's harbor was not a safe part of the city, especially if you were a woman alone, and she was. She needed to find passage aboard a ship leaving for Lisbon, and she needed to find it tonight.

At the marine terminal, an elderly watchman peered out at her through the wicket window.

When she asked about a passage, the old man squinted at her suspiciously. "Oh, aye. We have a galleon leaving at dawn. The Refuge. Bringing fodder for our troops over there. She's docked down at the far end of the wharf—still loading, last I seen." He poked his head out the window and surveyed her from her boots to her bonnet. "You look like a lady. This is not a place or a time of day for you, ma'am. I got a boy working with me. If you wait here a few minutes, I can have him escort you."

Waiting here at the terminal was not an option. She would be easily spotted, dressed in her travelling cloak, and clutching her carpet bag and reticule. She could not risk it.

"Thank you. I will find my way," she said and with a glance behind her, started her walk down the dark passage.

After only a few steps down the wharf, she began to regret her choice. The docks were eerie this time of night. The fog had rolled in and swirled around her skirts as she quickened her pace. On her right, ships lurked in the shadows, their great hulls rising and falling in the dark as though breathing the reeking water of the Thames. On the left, the dark shapes of warehouses loomed. Occasionally, a rat scuttled past.

Thankfully, she met no one for the length of the long wharf. With her carpet bag tight against her body, she walked as briskly as her skirts would allow. All she could hear was her boots echoing on the planks of the dock.

At last, through the haze of fog, the yellow glow of lanterns bobbing up and down a gang plank became visible just ahead, as a crew busily loaded a ship near the end of the pier. She stood back from the action and peered up at its hull. She could just make out the faded letters 'FUG' near its railing on the bow. And as the watchman had said, they were loading her with cargo.

This must be her, The Refuge. It did not look like a very prestigious ship. Indeed, for a ship hauling goods to the Royal Navy in Lisbon, she seemed downright derelict. But beggars could not be choosers, she thought as she looked back towards the terminal to check if she had been followed. With the heavy blanket of fog, she could only see a few feet behind her. After waiting for a break in the line of workman, she took a deep breath and hustled up the gang plank.

The captain stood on the deck hollering orders to his crew. Beside him, a boy held a lantern, which did little to light the gloomy deck. As Alexis approached, she was struck by the shabbiness of the captain. It was too dark to make out much about his person except that he wore a plain sailor's flat cap and a tattered long coat. He was certainly not one of the crisp uniformed captains she had often met in her father's company. If she had not heard one of the sailors address him as cap'n, she would not have recognized him as the man in charge.

Alexis stood at the captain's side while he ignored her. Unsure of what she should say or do, she shifted awkwardly, waiting for him to acknowledge her. Fidgeting with her reticule and scanning the wharf below for any pursuers, she tried clearing her throat several times to get his attention. The captain steadfastly avoided her gaze.

"I am looking to book a passage," she said at last, raising her voice to get his attention.

The captain froze. Turning slowly, he leered down at her. As he leaned into the lantern's glow, his face illuminated an ominous amber. His lips broke into a nasty smile. Alexis noticed he was missing several teeth. She took a step back.

"Are you, missy?"

Alexis had to grip her toes into the soles of her boots to keep herself from heading down the gangplank and back to the relative safety of the wharf. She had never travelled on her own before. On her earlier visits to her father, she had always been treated with the utmost respect. Every detail of her journey had been arranged for her.

Her father was a general in the British forces, much admired and respected. Furthermore, he was a wealthy British peer. Henry Betcher, Lord Salsbury, was a man who demanded the best for himself and his family; he invariably got it.

But she needed to board this ship.

"I will give you thirty shillings for my passage." she blurted out.

The captain did not answer her immediately. Instead, he assessed her from top to bottom as though she was a piece of merchandise.

"I suppose I can put up with the likes of you for an hour or two," he said with a sneer, "but it will be forty, not thirty, and you'll stay below. I'll not have you pestering my crew. Wouldn't haul your arse at all, except that I'm keen to do the madam a favor."

"Of all the..."

"Or ye can get off my ship. I don't like carrying passengers to start with." He scowled at her. "I like women even less."

Her cheeks flared with shock and indignation. Never in her life had someone spoken to her so rudely. She fumbled with her reticule as she struggled to count her fare. Only the thought of the report she would make to her father, and imagining his retribution, gave her some relief from her chagrin.

She handed her coins over to the man and attempted her haughtiest voice. "My father is General Betcher of the Royal Guard. He certainly will hear of my treatment here, shoddy that it is."

The captain laughed.

"And my mother is the queen of Sheba." To her horror, he reached down and swatted her on the butt. Before she could recover from the indignity, he hollered to the lad at his side, "Take her below. Lock her in. I won't have her galloping about."

Once below, she paced the tiny cabin. Again and again, she rattled its locked door.

"I have made a mistake," she muttered to herself. "How

4

can I journey all the way to Lisbon locked in this disgusting hold? And the captain—"

She shuddered at the thought.

More than once, she reminded herself she was escaping a worse fate. Whatever indignities she suffered here were minor compared to what she would face at home. There was simply no choice. She wished she had lived a more adventurous life back in London, that she had been more than a society belle. All the skills she had so painstakingly learned to negotiate a soiree were of no use here.

Taking a deep breath, she decided to settle into her cabin and make the best of her situation. *I have done well so far. At least here in this cabin, I am hidden and safe.*

Only minutes passed before she felt the ship begin to move out into the harbor. She propped up the single pillow on the bunk and, lying on top of the covers, resigned herself to her fate.

The ship lurched as its sails filled. Already they were on the open sea. She closed her eyes.

When she awoke, the ship was still. Rising to her knees, she peeked out the porthole above the bunk. There was not much to see. They appeared to have docked but it was still too dark to make out much of anything.

We must have stopped at an English port along the coast. Good. I will jump ship here and board a proper vessel. Everything will work out for the best.

The rattling of her door caught her attention. It squeaked open a crack, just wide enough to allow the cabin boy from last night to poke his head into the room.

"Cap'n says you are to head out now before you get in the way of the loaders. You're to hurry, ma'am," he said, stepping into the room.

"I had hoped to wash up. Could you please fetch me a basin and some water, young man?"

"Nah. No time for that. Cap'n wants ye off and gone before we unload. The boys are already in the hold. We best hurry." He grabbed her arm.

She barely had time to snatch up her belongings before he shoved her out of the room and onto the deck. In moments, she was heading down the gangplank. She paused and adjusted her bonnet. Several locks of her red hair had loosened from her bun and straggled down past her shoulders. She tried to tuck them back under her hat but was only partially successful.

This is ridiculous, she thought, still only half awake and battling her confusion. Her father would hear of all the degradation she had suffered. She managed to balance her reticule and carpet bag as she negotiated the gangplank.

"There ye go," the boy hollered from the deck when her feet hit the dock. "Gravelines in record time."

She looked up at him where he held his lantern at the top of the gangplank. In faded letters on the hull to his right, she made out the letters of the word Fugitive.

She had boarded the wrong ship.

Gravelines was a smuggler's port on the coast of France, just across the channel. Napoleon had cordoned off the walled town to exclusively accommodate the illegal trade.

She had heard her father and his cronies speak often of the town. It was said to be inhabited by the worst element of British society: thieves and traitors to the crown. They had even debated pulling into the harbor and using their canon to level the place.

"Oh no," she moaned, her stomach rolling with panic. This was not Lisbon. She had been dropped at Gravelines, of all places.

The wharf was busy this time of night. Unlike legal ports, the cover of darkness was prime business hours for the sailors here. Men hefting tubs or crates scowled at her as they pushed past her to the docked ships.

Needing a moment to think and fighting the fear gnawing at her belly, she worked her way across the busy wharf to a well-lit area just off the docks. She had no idea where to go or what to do. Perhaps her aunt was right, and she was helpless and inept, incapable of managing even her own life. Her mind revolted at the thought. Now was not the time to wallow in self-pity. She resolved to find a solution to this fiasco.

Up ahead, a lane circled the loading area. It was cluttered with carts being loaded either directly from the boats or from a series of warehouses banking the wharf to her far right. She found a clear place beneath a streetlamp and, clutching her carpet bag, she began to contemplate her predicament.

Moving to the streetlamp was a mistake. Under the light, she was clearly visible to the sailors who were heading for the rowdy taverns up the street to enjoy a much-needed drink or even a tumble in the bawdy house at the end of the lane.

A group of sailors, five or six of them, left the wharf and walked towards her. She looked down, pretending to examine the clasp on her case, hoping she would go unnoticed.

The men circled her; she was surrounded by the scurvy crewmen.

"What have we here?" A sailor in his pea jacket grinned at her. "Looks like some fresh produce for Madame's hot house."

She whirled around, thinking to escape his attentions,

but found that several more men had come up from behind her. They stretched their arms out as though herding cattle, barring her way. Wherever she turned, she saw only their faces, laughing.

"Leave me be," she said, trying to use her haughtiest voice. She hung on tight to her carpet bag. It held her jewels and the money she would need for her journey. Convinced she was about to be robbed, she hollered, "Help! Help me, please!"

"Mayhap we should be the first to sample the goods, eh boys?" an older man with a scarred face said.

"Get away from me, you swine!" She tried to force her way through the human barricade but each time she lunged forward, she was caught and shoved back to the center.

The men laughed and jeered at her. One of them ripped her bonnet from her head. A round of cheers went up when her red-gold hair tumbled down her back. She was flung back once more. Someone grabbed at her cloak, and it was ripped from her body.

"That is enough. Keep your hands off me," she sputtered, beginning to panic. Filled with sickening dread, she realized it was not only her money they were after. "Leave me be. Let me go!"

Her cries only incited the men to further violence. One of them got a firm grip on the shoulder of her gown.

"Let's see what you got to offer, girl." He sneered into her face, ripping her sleeve from her shoulder to the top of her bodice. The skin on her pale shoulder shone in the lantern's glow. The men shouted out their raucous encouragement.

"Come on, girl, give us a little taste of strawberry tart. The coin here is as good as it'll be at the Madame's."

The men laughed.

Alexis held the carpet bag against her breasts and began to scream in earnest. For a moment, the shrieks gave the men pause.

"It's only a tumble or two. No need to behave like this," one of the men mumbled.

A man forced himself through the ring of rowdy sailors. "Enough, boys. As you can see, this girl is not enjoying the game. Get off with you."

"And who are you to captain us?" one of them snarled.

The stranger pulled a knife from his belt and flashed it at the men.

"I am just the man to do it." He shook his cutlas. "I may not get you all but one or two of you will get a wound for sure. Where's the trouble? If you want her, I am sure you will be able to head down to Madame's a little later and have her."

She held her bag against herself to protect her modesty and watched the smugglers mutter their disappointment as they sauntered down the street. Before they had gone ten steps, they burst into loud laughter, obviously unaffected by the encounter.

"I am not a whore," Alexis managed to gasp out to the stranger. Hot tears came to her eyes and rolled down her cheeks. "I am not a whore," she repeated.

He said nothing. Instead, he sheathed his knife, and reaching down, retrieved her cloak and draped it over her shoulders. She pulled it in tight around herself.

"I am supposed to be in Lisbon," she blurted out, wiping away her tears with her cloak. "To visit my papa. General Betcher. But I have made a mess of the whole thing."

She looked at him hopefully. He at least appeared to be a gentleman. His face was shadowed by a brimmed felt hat, but his great coat was draped around a fashionable suit and trousers. Maybe she could get some much-needed assistance here.

He looked at her speculatively. "Then what, my dear, are you doing here in Gravelines?"

"I don't know. I thought I had boarded a ship to Lisbon. That scoundrel of a captain charged me forty shillings for an hour's ride across the channel," she replied. She took a deep breath and attempted to control her growing hysteria. "And now I have no idea what I am to do. I need to find a ship bound for Lisbon."

"Well, you won't be finding it here," he answered calmly. "This is a smuggling port. It serves only the English traders. You best board and return to England."

His use of language marked him as an upper-class Englishman. Perhaps a merchant.

"But I cannot return to England. That is impossible," she replied. Desperate to get his assistance, she decided to change tack. She rose to her full height and raised her chin. "I'm afraid I must insist you find me a ship to Lisbon, not England. My father will be happy to reward you when he hears of your service."

To her astonishment, the man laughed. "No, my little princess. Even if I wanted to, I would not be able to find a ship here bound for Lisbon."

For the first time in her life, Alexis was unable to rely on her father's position to achieve her ends. Indeed, tonight it seemed as though it was a hindrance.

He looked at her and grinned. She decided he had an engaging face. He might be French, judging by his swarthy skin. If he was, he spoke perfect English. Whoever he was, somehow, she had to convince him to help her.

"Please—"

"It is back on board with you, and if you're lucky, London bound."

Tears burned her eyes. "But I cannot go back. I must find a way to get out of here and on my way to meet my papa."

He sighed, and repeated, "There is no way to Lisbon from here."

He indicated several wagons stacked high with fleece.

"I have my own job to do. I'm ready to leave this mud hole and return to Paris. Come on." He nudged her shoulder, taking her arm. "I'll do you the favor of getting you safely abroad and you can thank me for that."

He pulled her forward.

She had little choice but to follow along as he led her to an old lugger and left her on the dock in the shadows while he had a conversation with its shaggy captain. She stood holding her carpet bag, scowling at the situation. She absolutely could not board a ship bound for England. Not tonight.

She looked towards the merchant's caravan of goods and began to hatch a plan. She would not go back, and she certainly could not stay here. This man was her only option. Taking her chances with him was her best choice.

The merchant walked toward her where she stood with her carpet bag held snuggly against her belly.

"There you go, princess." He grinned at her. "You're all set."

He patted her on the shoulder and walked away without a backward glance.

I can do this. I'll not give up now, she thought, watching as the man disappeared behind his caravan of carts, each heaped with wool.

She edged towards the side of the wharf, standing

directly opposed to his wagons, eyeing the piles of fleece. When he and his other drivers were mounted, and the wagons began to inch forward, she made a run for them. A shout sounded from behind her, but Alexis ignored it in her determination to reach her goal.

She flung her carpet bag onto the last wagon, grabbed its end gate, and swung herself into the load, just as the driver signaled his horses with a, "Hup, hup," and the caravan began to move down the muddy street. Once safely atop the load, she burrowed down into the wool, making a neat hole for herself and her case. She pulled sheeves of wool on top of her and settled in for her trip.

After a brief pause at the village gates, the wagons began their overland trek on their journey to Paris.

She felt proud of herself as she pushed aside the mound of fleece covering her face and breathed the cool night air. For the first time, she was truly independent—and she had managed her escape alone. She grinned, imagining her aunt's reaction back at home, when she checked her room in the morning.

I am not so helpless, after all.

Even the stars from the night sky winked at her, appreciating her resourcefulness. She tucked her carpet bag in at her side, slid her reticule under her head, and prepared for a much-needed sleep.

Being in France, a country at war with England, was not a concern. She thought only of how pleased she was to escape her home. A sojourn in Paris while on route to Lisbon sounded like a romantic holiday. And as to the gentleman, he had proven himself the chivalrous sort. Surely, he would help her find her way to her papa.

What could possibly go wrong?

Chapter Two

When Alexis woke, it took a minute to get her bearings. For a moment, she thought she was still on board a ship. All was still. They must have stopped.

When the wagon lurched forward again, shaking the sleep from her foggy consciousness, the previous day came flooding back to her like a bad dream. The sun shone down on her face from directly overhead. She was hot and perspiring. And she was itchy. She was riding in a bloody wool wagon. She pulled back the fleece that covered her body and began to squirm out of her cloak, wrinkling her nose in distaste. She smelled strongly of sheep dip. Better that than ticks, she thought grimly, rubbing her itching skin.

Alexis looked toward the front of the wagon. Thankfully, she was sheltered by the heavy load. The merchant would not be able to see the end of the wagon over the heaps of wool unless he stopped and walked around it to check the load. He would have no idea what went on here at the rear. She felt secure for the time being.

She maneuvered the wool into a makeshift chair,

covering it with her cloak, then sat back in its soft seat, dangling her legs over the end gate. Envisioning the reaction of her London friends to her appearance, she chuckled. She was an heiress. Amongst her many acquaintances, she was the one with the best prospects.

She tried to run her fingers through the snarls of her coppery hair and grinned. She was far from the proper young lady now. How her society friends would gasp and gossip to see her here this way.

Yesterday morning seemed a lifetime away. The disaster had started with her aunt demanding her son Lionel take her for a turn around the garden. Alexis shuddered. The problems had actually started earlier than that. Two months ago, her uncle Max had died suddenly of heart failure, leaving his wife of only a year, Aunt Enid, as her temporary guardian. Lionel, Enid's son from a previous marriage, arrived on the day of the funeral and never left. Besides being decidedly dull, Lionel's body reflected his obtuse personality. He was a massive man, with a chin so burdened with fat his neck was invisible.

Lionel had glued himself to her side. It seemed the only time she could escape him was when she kept to her rooms, which she did as much as humanly possible. To make matters worse, the family was in mourning—she had not attended a soiree or a ball since her uncle's passing. Confined to the house and grounds, she was easy prey for her persistent suitor.

At first, she had politely attempted to dissuade Lionel, but he refused to take no for an answer. The harder she tried to escape him, the more persistent he became. When she approached Aunt Enid with the problem, her aunt became offended and angry.

"How dare you discard Lionel! He is the perfect mate

for you! I am your guardian now, Alexis, and I demand you change your behavior." Enid took a breath and spoke again, this time in calmer tones with a forced smile. "Lionel is a strong young man, with fine prospects. Get to know him, Alexis. With a little courting I am sure you will change your mind."

Trying to address the problem had made it worse. Her aunt joined Lionel in taking every opportunity to force her into his company.

And yesterday, when Aunt Enid pronounced, "You must take Alexis for a little walk on the grounds, Lionel," she'd bit her lip to avoid being rude.

Once clear of the house, Lionel took her arm despite her protests. She tried to yank it away from him, but he held firm, using his other hand to hold her at his side. She shot him a resentful glare, gritting her teeth to keep herself from scalding him with her words.

He'd grinned at her stupidly, holding tight to her arm as they walked.

"I've excellent news for you, Alexis." For a big man, he had a squeaky, whining voice. He nodded, his heavy jowls shaking above a tight neckcloth. "Aunt Enid has decided it's time you married. We're going to be wed."

Alexis could only look at him and gasp. To her horror, he pulled her to a stop, using his beefy arms to yank her in for a kiss. She turned her head from side to side, frantic to avoid his grinning mouth. But he only squeezed her more tightly and jerked her against his sweating torso. One of his hands firmly grabbed her by the back of the head, anchoring it, while he forced his slobbering lips on to hers. He reeked of cooked onions. Alexis felt her stomach heave.

She managed to free her arms and beat against his back to no avail. When he finally released her, she swung with all her might, slapping his face, first on the left and then on the right.

"You filthy oafish pig! I will never marry you!" She took the back of her hand and wiped her mouth clean from his kiss. "And don't you ever touch me again."

He stood there, looking stunned.

Recovering, he sneered at her. "You will regret those actions, girl." Leaning in close to her face, he added, "And you'll marry me whether it's to your liking or not."

She backed away from him. "Never! Do you hear me? I will never marry you. I hate the sight of you! You disgust me."

Turning, she ran toward the house, but the thought of having to face her aunt made her pause. Enduring another lecture on the positive attributes of the loathsome Lionel was not something Alexis could tolerate after the incident in the garden. She whirled around and headed for the back garden to sit in peace and calm down.

A full thirty minutes passed before she made her way inside through the kitchens. She was still revolted by Lionel's behavior. That he expected a marriage between them made her nauseous. Determined to settle the matter, Alexis approached the library in search of her aunt. As she neared the room, she heard Aunt Enid screeching, "She will damn well marry you."

Alexis stopped, shocked by the bitterness of her aunt's words. The door was slightly ajar; she leaned in to listen.

"But Mama," Lionel's voice whined, "she said she hates me. She will never agree."

"Oh, but she will. She will have no choice."

There was a pause. Alexis heard a drawer slide open.

"See these letters. I have convinced her father the two of you are madly in love." Aunt Enid gave a bitter snort. "He has replied that though the match is not what he had hoped for her—imagine the arrogant bastard!—he will give his approval if it is what his precious daughter wants. We have his consent. It is enough to force the marriage."

She chuckled. "If she refuses, we will have her committed to the nut house until she faces reality."

"Can we do that?" Lionel asked.

"I am her guardian. I can have her committed at a moment's notice on a charge of female hysteria. We will claim she is unruly, risking her reputation by not following the rules. Female hysteria is not an unusual affliction."

"But Mama, if she is to be my wife—"

"Don't worry, Lionel. She is a spoiled and pampered girl, and naïve enough to be quite helpless. The girl is incapable of resisting. No, it won't take Alexis long to change her mind. A week or two locked up without all the niceties she is accustomed to, and you shall have your bride." She made a strange growling sound. "And she is a girl alone here. There will be little she can do about it. We have her at our mercy."

She cackled again.

"I hope you're right. I want her, Mama."

"And you shall have her, my love. She has enough money to keep the two of us living in style for our lifetimes. God knows we will need it after the pittance Max left us," Enid said.

"You promised there would be plenty after Max died. It's still hard to believe he had so little. I counted on that inheritance. I need the money."

"Yes, you do. And Alexis has enough of it for both of us. I made sure of it this time. Her mother left her a fortune. There is even the promise of more when her father dies." She laughed again. "With his arrogant self at war, it will surely be sooner than later. It is only too bad the title cannot be transferred." There was a pause. "Hmmm, we shall have to see about that."

Alexis's mind reeled. She had heard enough. Tiptoeing past the door, she ran up the stairs to the safety of her room, locking the door. She paced the length of her room while she attempted to grasp her predicament. Aunt Enid had her trapped. Alexis knew her aunt was right; having her committed to an asylum would not be a difficult process. As her guardian, Enid's accusation that she was suffering from female hysteria would be enough to have her confined. She thought of opting for the asylum, but she had heard horror stories of the conditions in Bedlam. It was not an option.

Since the death of Alexis' uncle, Aunt Enid had been adamant about limiting her social life. She had not been allowed to go out, and no callers had been admitted. Assuming the increased restrictions on her movements had to do with mourning Uncle Max, Alexis had grudgingly accepted them. Now she saw it all in a new light. She had been purposely isolated.

Alexis had closed her eyes and wished her father were home. If he were to arrive, Aunt Enid and Lionel would be tossed out and everything would return to normal. But wishing did not make it true. With a sinking feeling, Alexis realized if she were to foil their plans, she would have to do it on her own. Her cheeks burned as she remembered her aunt's words: spoiled, pampered, and helpless.

There was no alternative; she would escape at once.

The afternoon and early evening had been consumed with her frantic struggle to find a solution. Nowhere in town would be safe for her. She could be hauled home from any of her friends' homes. The incident might even add evidence for the case of hysteria against her, should her aunt and Lionel need it. She had remained in her room, trying to plan her future until there was an abrupt knock at her door.

"Are you not coming down for dinner, Alexis? Lionel and I are waiting."

She had not realized how late it had become while she formulated her plans. She glanced at the packed carpet bag at her side and her reticule beside it. She had chosen her largest purse, one with a shoulder strap to allow her to carry what few items she could more easily. On the dressing table, she had left a scathing letter for her aunt. In it she told her intentions to go to her father and report to him the humiliation she had suffered. It was her small attempt at vengeance.

"No, Aunt Enid," she replied through the closed door, "I will just have the tray I ordered. I have one of my headaches."

Enid replied with a snort.

Alexis waited until Enid's footsteps receded before she opened the door. Tugging off her boots, she stuffed them into her bag and tiptoed down the stairs to the library. There was one more task she must do before leaving the house. Luckily, Enid and Lionel would be eating; it was their favorite avocation. She would be quite safe for an hour at least.

In the library, she first went to the wall safe and removed all the money it contained, then emptied every box holding her mother's valuable jewels, carefully leaving the few paltry pieces belonging to Enid. The money was her father's and there was plenty of it. Alexis felt no pangs of conscience as she slid both into the bottom of her case. Next, she searched the drawers to find her father's letters. They were at the back of the bottom drawer. Beside them, tied with a neat bow, was every letter she had written to her father since

Uncle Max had died. Swearing softly at her aunt's villainy, she stuffed these too into her satchel.

She slipped from the house, put on her boots, and walked to the end of the lane. Now all she had to do was flag down a hansom cab to take her to the docks.

And here she sat, less than twenty-four hours later, riding in a wool cart, stinking of sheep dip. Her hair was so snarled she had no idea how she would ever get a brush through it, even if she had remembered to pack one. Her sleeve was ripped to her bodice and dangled off her shoulder, revealing a wide expanse of white skin. She itched. Alexis was sure her face was covered in dust from the bumpy roads. But for whatever reason, she felt completely happy for the first time in a long time. She had managed to escape her aunt's clutches all on her own. Whatever her future, she was confident it was far better than what awaited her in London.

The sun felt warm against her face. The fleece made the most comfortable chair. She pulled up her legs and removed her boots and stockings, then tucked them into the load. On an impulse, she reached beneath her dress and struggled out of her hot petticoats. She might as well be completely comfortable. She sighed, leaning back against her cloak.

She grinned to herself, proud of her accomplishments. Her escape had begun to feel like a grand adventure. Never could she have imagined herself in these strange circumstances. There was a delicious triumph in defeating her aunt, while thumbing her nose at society's strict rules for a young lady of her class. She had to stop herself from laughing aloud.

Alexis's smile wobbled slightly as she considered the merchant's reaction when he discovered she had stowed away on his cart. She would definitely need a plan. First, like any stow-away, she would have to be certain they were too far into the journey to turn back. Then, she would simply have to convince him she would be no trouble. Once in Paris, she would make her way to a port and sail to Lisbon. The man would be free of her in no time at all.

She decided she would try to be her most charming and hope to placate him. Maybe if she played the damsel in distress, he would assist her. She would praise him and compliment him. He had helped her once; surely, he would help her again.

Everything would work out perfectly. She hoped.

Chapter Three

Aran leaned back on the bench of his wagon. He looped the reins together and hooked them over the horn on the seat's railing. Reaching down, he grasped his canteen and took a long swig of water. It was almost empty, which was not a problem. Just a few miles ahead there was a water stop for the horses. It was just a pail which could be slung up and down into the canal to fill a trough, but it worked. There was a well near the canal where travelers could fill canteens for their journey. Because it had become a popular resting place, merchants from the nearby village and gypsies often gathered at the site to sell their wares.

He thought about his recent message from Admiral Hews and frowned. The admiral had forced him to become a spy in Napoleon's Paris. Every day, he cursed the evening when the revenue officers had boarded his small lugger, designed for smuggling, and took him aboard.

He knew now he had been set up. Hews himself had been waiting for him on the deck of the King's ship. He had been given the option of entering France in the guise of a wealthy wool merchant to gather information as a spy or having he and his crew put under arrest as smugglers. There had been little choice.

To add insult to injury, Hews had clapped him on the back saying, "You were my first-choice, young man: well-educated, fluent in four languages, and a lord to boot. You'll know the drill over there. You'll fit in well, lad. I even knew your father. Fought with him in Portugal, I did. Quite a patriot he was, and I expect the same from you."

Aran had given him what he wanted and more. Last night, he had sent a copy of Napoleon's codebook to England. After almost two years, he had expected his assignment in Paris to be over. Instead, he had received word the English had become aware of Napoleon's increasing antagonism towards Russia. Relations had begun to deteriorate when Czar Nicholas had refused to allow Napoleon to wed his sister. After divorcing Empress Josephine, Napoleon, who longed for the legitimacy of royal blood for his budding dynasty, was forced to take an Austrian princess as a second choice.

Napoleon's delicate ego had been slighted. He was no longer willing to tolerate Russia's underhanded breach of the trade embargo against England. Russia, in Napoleon's mind, needed a well-earned lesson.

It was the spring of 1812. England was tiring of the constant struggle to oust Napoleon, while dealing with her other battles in the Americas. The wars in Portugal and Spain had been particularly costly in every way: money, lives, and time. If Napoleon withdrew troops and supplies from other parts of Europe for a battle with Russia, England could not be happier. She would be able to attack Napoleon when and where he was most vulnerable.

Aran had been sent back to Paris. He was assigned the

task of finding out if indeed Napoleon was planning a major attack against Russia. And if he were, Admiral Hews wanted to know how many troops he would send, and where he might be pulling them from.

It was a daunting assignment. Aran had no choice but to continue to befriend his connections in the French military and dig for information. At least the admiral had supplied him with funds. He would need them.

He would also have the money from this latest shipment, he thought with satisfaction. The one thing that endeared him to his military friends was that he provided them with lavish parties, complete with beautiful society women. Aran had worked hard to make his connections in Paris, using all his charm, and much of the Admiral's funds to create the illusion of a Parisian playboy.

Aran sighed. This was to be his last job. For two long years he had been in Paris. The admiral had promised his term of duty would be over before winter, perhaps sooner if Napoleon made his move. It was March. In six months, he would be able to return to his beloved Yorkshire coast. After the decadence and corruption of Napoleon's Paris, Aran longed for the purity of his wild Yorkshire home.

The wagons approached the water stop. Aran pulled on the reins, aligning his cart with three others in his caravan. He hopped down from his bench seat and stretched his stiff legs. It had been a long night. With their heavy loads the wagons had made slow progress. And there would be at least another grueling day of travel, perhaps two, before he reached his home in Paris.

He walked around the wagon to check his load and stopped dead in his tracks. Seated on the back of his cart was the young woman from Gravelines. She was leaning back in a thronelike indentation in the wool. Her startlingly bright red hair was sticking out at odd angles with bits of white wool clinging to it. Her bare calves dangled over the end gate and her feet were flipping back and forth like a child's.

"Good afternoon. Such a pleasure to meet you again." She gave him a grin with a beautiful but terribly dusty face.

He was unable to respond. He could only stare at her open-mouthed. She reached out her hand for assistance to hop down and he took it.

"Whew. I am so glad we have stopped. I wonder if you might fetch me some water?" she requested as though she was standing fully gowned at Almacks and not here on a country lane in enemy territory, looking like a disgruntled porcupine.

He grabbed her by the shoulder, glancing from left to right. "Hush. Can you speak French?" When she nodded at him, wide-eyed, he continued in that language himself. "Then do so, for the love of god. What in the hell are you doing here?"

She leaned into his face and whispered back in French, "I had no choice. I could not return to England." She stepped back and batted her eyelashes at him. "I truly had no other option. I hoped you might be my knight in shining armor."

She looked at him, tilted her head to the side, and gave him a wide smile. "You were such a fine hero in Gravelines."

Her ridiculous attempt to manipulate him filled him with white hot anger. "You god-damned idiot! I cannot take you back. You are stuck here."

He glared at her, watching her smile falter and slowly die.

"I should bloody well leave you here in the middle of

France." He leaned forward and whispered harshly, directly into her face, "With whom we are at war, you blooming nutcase!"

"How dare you speak to me like that. I will have you know my father is a—"

"Do not say it!" he interrupted. "Saying that here will get us killed. You cannot ever say it!"

He looked directly into her violet eyes. "Get that in your head, first of all. War, my dear, does not care you think yourself a princess. You will be arrested. And after, if you live, at best you will be ransomed at great cost to your country. But they might just shoot you. This is not a game, princess!"

He glared at her until he recognized a modicum of fear in her face, noting her wide-eyed apprehension with satisfaction.

Good, let her be afraid. She should be.

Aran ran his hand through his hair and looked hard at the girl. What was he supposed to do with her? He could not take her back to Gravelines even if he wanted to. They had travelled all night and were already halfway to Paris. To turn around now would only cause suspicion. It would be a full day before he could get back to the port. Then he would have the problem of explaining why he needed entry into the restricted port when he was already loaded with goods. There was an excellent chance he would be turned away. Never mind the struggle he would have forcing her to board a ship. He was stuck with her.

He scowled at her.

This time she spoke without the exaggerated flirtations of moments ago. "I will be absolutely no trouble for you. I just need to tag along with you until I can find a way to get to Lisbon." She looked around the water stop as though searching for a task. "In fact, I can be helpful. My father always called me his little trooper. "

"Quit with the references to your father."

"Well, he will reward you. I know he will." She raised her chin.

A general's daughter, and a lady to boot. Of all the rotten luck. As much as he wanted to, he could not just abandon her here in the middle of nowhere. They would need a good cover and quickly.

"You are my wayward sister, newly widowed. Heaven knows there are enough widows in this land. You surprised me by sneaking along this trip." He looked at her. "What is your name?"

"Lady Alexis Betcher."

"Now you are Madam Alexis Garscon. We will keep it as close as possible, so you don't foul it up. I am Aran Garscon, a wealthy merchant." He looked her over. It would have to do for now. Once they were in Paris, he would develop her story. And then he would have to find some way to get her the hell out of France.

"Pleased to make your acquaintance, Aran." She held out her hand. "I will be no trouble. You will see."

She tilted her head and smiled at him.

Aran took her hand automatically, but he could not return her smile. In fact, at that moment, he felt a strong urge to put his hands around her throat and shake some sense into her. "I will see."

Keeping her hand, he pulled her around the front of the wagon.

"I have a surprise," he announced to his drivers. "My sly little sister has found a way to sneak along to Paris. Miserable wretch that she is."

They only laughed and teased him about his new problem. They were busy unhooking the horses and leading them to the trough. So far so good.

He shoved a canteen at her and roughly grasped her shoulders, turning her in the direction of the well. ""Since you promised to be handy this trip, you can start by getting me some water." He looked at her disheveled appearance. "And while you are there you might wash your face and do something with that outrageous red mop of hair."

"That I can do." She grinned at him over her shoulder as she marched barefooted towards the well. "You won't be sorry for this. I will be a dream."

What the hell had she done with her shoes?

"More like a nightmare," Aran muttered, watching her hips sway as she went to do his bidding.

Aran helped with the horses, glancing over at the well occasionally to check her progress. She had managed to fill the canteen but was struggling to wash up under the pump. Each time she heaved on its handle to get a gush of water, she was unable to get under the stream before it disappeared. Finally, two gypsy children approached and helped her. In minutes, the three of them were laughing and playing in the water. Between all the splashing and giggling, she managed to clean herself up.

His driver Manuel approached him. The two of them stood and watched the scene.

"I think you are far too interested in that little sister."

He laughed when Aran frowned at him.

"She may be a lot of things, but sister she is not." He nudged Aran and winked. "I think you impress the girls a little too much. Now they crawl into your wagons to keep you."

I will have to revise my story, Aran thought grimly. Manuel had seen through it too quickly.

He grinned. "You found me out."

Manuel laughed and slapped his back.

Maybe lover was a better scenario anyway, he thought as he watched her walk with the gypsy children to their caravan. She would make a delicious lover. He imagined her lying back on his bed with all that red hair spread across the pillow and a sexy welcoming smile on her face.

He squashed the thought. The last thing he needed was another lover. Maneuvering around the French courtesans to win their favor and have them attend his many events was trouble enough for him. But a lover would make more sense. Her background would not be linked to his, and much easier to cover. It was a better story.

Alexis approached, with a gaggle of gypsy children following her, balancing her water and several meat pies in her arms. She set them down and went to pay the children from her cash.

"No." Aran stopped her with a hand on her arm. "They will want francs."

He dug into his pocket and handed them his coins. The children ran off chortling with pride at their sale.

Alexis spread her cloak on the ground and arranged her picnic. Her tangled hair had been forced into a thick braid. Her face was clean. She had even maneuvered the cloth on her shoulder to disguise the tear. She sat down and looked up at him with the most violet eyes he had ever seen.

She is dangerous, this general's daughter. I will need to keep my distance.

The drivers joined them in their makeshift meal beside the dark waters of the canal.

Aran watched silently as Alexis tried several times to engage the drivers in conversation, but they only stared at her open-mouthed. He understood their sentiment. She was like a foreign object in their midst. Eventually she gave up on attempts at conversation and the meal was eaten in silence.

Alexis had tucked her bare feet beneath her dress. She looked quite demure once she was cleaned up, he decided.

"See," she said, smiling broadly. "I can be handy. You will soon be wondering what you ever did without me."

She popped the last of her pie into her mouth. Manuel and the others continued to stare silently at her, fascinated by her every move. And she seemed blissfully unaware of her impact. He too struggled to keep his eyes off her. She was a beautiful woman.

A horrible scream interrupted their lunch. They jumped to their feet. The gypsies were running toward the canal. A child was standing at its bank, pointing to the water and yelling hysterically in Spanish. A little girl had fallen in and was rapidly being swept away by the current.

Alexis lurched forward to the edge of the canal, pulling her gown off over her head in one fluid motion, and dove into its dark waters. It all happened so fast Aran and the others could only drop their mouths in astonishment. In the time it took for the gypsies to arrive to the banks, she had snatched the little girl from the current and was paddling her towards the walled bank.

Aran and Manuel pulled the two of them up out of the water. The gypsies dragged the little girl to safety, while Aran and Manuel helped Alexis struggle to her feet. She stood dripping on the bank. The thin cotton chemise she had worn under her gown was stuck to her body, transparent with moisture.

Aran stood stock still and stared. She looked completely naked. Her wet cotton shift clung to her breasts and gently rounded female belly. Her hips were wide, angling enticingly into long shapely legs. She looked like Venus emerging from the sea.

His reverie was broken by Manuel's appreciative whistle.

"Ooh la, la," Manuel whispered, his eyes glued to Alexis. "You have a beauty here, *monsieur*."

Aran whipped around and grabbed her cloak from the ground, shaking it out before wrapping it tightly around it. She held it together muttering a thank you. He pushed a thick strand of hair back from her face.

Still staring at her, he searched for something to say to break the spell which had frozen the enticing picture of her nakedness on his mind.

"That was amazing. You can swim," he said lamely. Women did not swim. He had never met one who could; their clothing was prohibiting for one thing.

"I can." She smiled tentatively. "More of my father's doing."

She grinned at his frown.

"He wanted me to sail and demanded that all sailors learn to swim. I never learned to be a proper sailor, but I took to the swimming." She rubbed her cloak against her sodden hair in an attempt to dry it. "I wonder if you might guard the back of your wagon while I try to change."

"I can do that," he said.

Again, the picture of her rising out of the water replayed in his head. The image was permanently etched into his mind. He tried to force it from his consciousness, but it refused to budge.

He waited at the rear of the wagon, his back to her, while he listened to her rustle into her clothing.

"That was well done. I'm impressed," he commented with his back to her. He thought of her fair skin glistening in the sun, as she pulled off her wet chemise, feeling the involuntary response of his body. He shook his head to banish the thought. Realizing his men too had watched the scene, he added, "But this time you might want to wear a petticoat. After the performance a moment ago in that wet chemise, modesty would be an excellent course."

"What do you know of petticoats?" She laughed.

"More than I want to." He grimaced, thinking about the women of Paris.

When she walked around the corner, dressed once more, she was met by a crowd of gypsies, speaking rapidly in Spanish, and patting her back and shoulders. To his surprise, she answered them in the same language as she allowed them to lead her down the path toward their camp. She spoke Spanish as well as French. This might come in handy. It was a language he too was fluent with. She was an accomplished young lady.

He and Manuel watched as she was surrounded by a mob of women. Someone brought a hairbrush and was doing up her hair. Another woman adorned her ears with hooped golden earrings. There was much laughing and giggling.

"We must be on our way, *monsieur*. It grows late," Manuel said as he hooked up the last of the horses.

"We will let her enjoy her fame for a minute more, then we will be on our way," Aran said without taking his eyes off her.

Manuel laughed, patting him on the shoulder before climbing up onto the seat of his wagon. Aran sighed before he too pulled himself into his cart.

Alexis looked back at the loaded wagons, and quickly said goodbye to her friends. A young woman placed a necklace of some sort around her neck, before she hurried to the carts.

"Up here, Alexis. You may ride with me," he called to her.

Climbing up into the seat beside him, Alexis graced him with a glorious smile and eyes shining with pure joy. He could not resist returning that smile. Deciding he would explain her necessary change in identity during the trip, Aran gave the reins a quick snap and they were on their way.

To be safe, Aran switched to Spanish to explain her new role. The drivers were unlikely to overhear them, but if they did, they would not be able to understand them.

"I changed my mind," he said. "For this trip back to Paris, I need you to be a lover who crept along on this journey. I will work out the details once I am home. Just speak Spanish or French and be secretive about your past for now."

He frowned, annoyed. She was not paying attention. Instead, she was examining the strange turquoise amulet the gypsy had draped around her neck.

"What is that?" he asked.

"The gypsy mama said it's a life. It's a gift for me." She tucked it into her dress with a pleased smile.

He sighed. She did not seem to know or care she was an enemy in a foreign land. It was going to be a difficult and dangerous couple of months.

He tried again. "So, you are a woman who crept along this trip. That is all for now. Just remember, no English and keep silent about your past."

They were passing a pasture where horses grazed.

"Yes, yes. Oh, look at the colts! They are darling." She laughed as she watched the foals race in circles around their grazing mothers. "It has been too long since I have been able to spend time in the country."

Frustrated, he closed his eyes and took a deep breath. He could only hope she would remember not to slip into English.

Their heavy wagons forced them to journey through the French countryside at a slow pace. The rolling hills, with treed lanes, and intermittent fields had a pastoral quality. Everywhere the farmers were in their fields, plowing and seeding the spring crops. Fat cows with their new calves romping at their sides littered the pastures. Alexis seemed to be enthralled with the sights. She demanded the name of each village they passed and listened intently to any information he could give her.

She is young, dangerously naïve, and still thinks she is on a holiday trip.

He appeased her, anyway. There would be plenty of time for her to regret her circumstances once the reality of her precarious situation became clearer to her. Besides, her exuberant enjoyment made the trip less tedious. He actually began to be entertained by her company.

After several hours, she became quiet. As the sun went down, she closed her eyes. She began to sway back and forth, dozing off, then jolting awake and trying to balance again on the cart bench.

Taking pity on her when she next dozed, he reached over and pulled her onto his shoulder, keeping his arm around her to hold her in place. She snuggled into him, putting her arm around his waist to anchor herself.

He looked down at her in the waning light. She had the face of a beautiful girl in her sleep, the picture of innocence. His hand rested on her shoulder where the cloth had been torn away by the sailors at Gravelines. Her skin felt warm and smooth. She shifted against him, and her hair tickled his nose. He smoothed the strands of hair on the top of her head, smelling the sweet scent of rose water emanating from her scalp.

What am I going to do with her? He sighed. Already he was feeling protective toward this irritating young woman. There would have to be a way to incorporate her safely into his life until he could get her back to England. There was simply no choice.

They stopped at an inn to get a few hours' sleep. He was able to get her a room of her own, while he bedded down with his crew in the common room. Other than suffering much teasing, and the ribald jokes about his banishment from her room, he was able to get through the night with their story intact.

By dawn they were back on the road again. He was surprised by Alexis in the morning. Expecting the prim English lady, he had prepared for a panoply of complaints. Instead, she had come down freshly washed and eager for the day. She had not even objected when he told her they would have breakfast and their coffee in the carts. She was like a child on a holiday. Again, she spent an enthusiastic morning relishing each sight.

But the closer they got to Paris, the more troubled he became. Alexis still had no sense of the difficulty she presented. Her buoyant attitude had begun to grate on his nerves. He itched to lecture her on the danger she had put both of them in. He began to answer her queries in mono-syllables. She eventually gave up on making conversation, focusing instead on absorbing the beauty of the French countryside.

For the remainder of the journey, he concentrated on creating a believable niche for her in Paris. Thankfully, her French was exceptional, with a Parisian accent. Somehow, she would have to be converted into a believable mistress.

To make matters worse, he sensed the charade he had created for himself in Paris was beginning to crack. He believed the French home guard had placed someone in his home. Believing he had finished his service in Paris, he had not been too concerned. But now that he was back on assignment, suspicions about his true identity could mean his life here was in jeopardy. Having Alexis, an English general's daughter, as a responsibility at this time could only make his position more precarious.

The Minister of Police was a man named Joseph Fouche, known throughout Europe as the master of intrigue. It was said Fouche had a spy in every household. Napoleon was interested in espionage; he had used Fouche both to successfully squash the monarchist movement in France, and to aid him in his battles across Europe. In 1804, Fouche uncovered a conspiracy to assassinate Napoleon, referring to over a thousand dossiers kept on the citizens of Paris. The extent of his surveillance had shocked the citizens of France. Though these conspirators faced a trial, many of Fouche's enemies of the state either disappeared or were found beheaded.

As a relatively new element in French society, Aran would be suspect. He had arrived out of nowhere as a wool merchant and manufacturer of French uniforms. He spent far too much time with army personnel, being forever in their midst, spending lavishly to cultivate his new friends.

Fouche had used the same tactics in conquering Austria, putting his spies in Vienna to glean information. He was not about to watch idly as Aran maneuvered in Paris. It only made sense that Aran was watched and watched carefully.

His new footman Emile was particularly suspect to him. But it could be any of his servants, old or new. And all his servants, on the government payroll or not, with the possible exception of Rolande, his valet, would not hesitate to turn him in should they discover his identity or objective in Paris. He was a secret enemy in a country at war.

Alexis would have a role to play in Paris. For both their sakes, she had better be a capable actress. Being the daughter of a high-ranking general made her a valuable bargaining chip should her identity ever be uncovered.

It was going to be tricky indeed.

Chapter Four

The coach lurched to a stop next to a dark townhouse, shaking Alexis awake. It was late. They had taken the wool to a warehouse outside of town, then journeyed here to what she assumed was his home.

She had fallen asleep in the short ride from the warehouse. Aran helped her down from the coach, then reached back to grab her satchel and heavy reticule. The house was dark when they entered.

Aran held the door for her.

"I do have servants," he said, "but they were given some valuable time off while I was away. Because I am back earlier than expected, we will have to fend for ourselves for a day or two."

Alexis could only mutter tiredly in response. He handed her the reticule and balanced her satchel while he lit a lantern. "Come on, almost there, princess. Just up these stairs and then you can sleep."

Trudging behind him up the staircase, she thought these

were the longest set of stairs in history. When they finally reached the top, he swung a door open to her right.

Setting the lantern down on a side table by the door, he said, "This will be your room." He walked a few steps into the room and swung open another door. "And this is mine."

He looked at her as though expecting a response.

Alexis was so tired, she couldn't care less about adjoining rooms.

If he expects a reaction, he will be sadly disappointed. I do not care if he puts me on a sofa and demands we share it.

She walked to the bed, a welcome sight, and sat down. Letting herself flop down on the pillow she closed her eyes and instantly fell asleep, with her booted feet still on the floor.

Alexis awoke slowly. Pulling the quilt around her, she luxuriated for a minute, snuggling into the pillow. She opened her eyes and looked around the room, feeling disoriented.

The events of the last several days came back to her in a rush.

Aran stood in the doorway holding a tray. She was in this man's home.

"Ah, there you are. Good morning, princess." Aran set a tray down on the bedside table. "I tried to rummage up something for us to eat. No tea, of course, but I managed some good French coffee."

He pulled a chair closer to the bed and poured himself a cup.

Alexis sat up abruptly, thinking to protest his presence here in what must be her bedroom. Realizing she wore nothing but her chemise, she gave a little squeak and pulled the sheet up to her throat, glaring at him.

He sipped his coffee, watching her. He was fresh, clean, and entirely at ease.

Alexis felt her face burn as she glanced down at the floor beside her. Her dress, petticoat, and boots were in a messy heap. He must have undressed her. She narrowed her eyes at him.

Following her gaze, he said, "Yes, I pulled your dress off you. It was filthy. And no one enjoys sleeping in their boots. You may thank me if you wish."

He smiled.

She continued to scowl at him. Setting his coffee back on the tray, he stood up and went to his room. When he returned, he tossed a huge robe at her.

She quickly put it on.

"You might want to wash your face. You look a sight. There is a bit of water in your dressing room." He indicated the door to the right. "When you are cleaned up, we will have a little talk about how you will survive here."

While Alexis washed, she tried to think about her predicament, but it was impossible to get past the idea that she was in the heart of France, in Paris. The word Paris felt good on her tongue. She whispered it to herself. "Paris, Paris, Paris."

She had always wanted to visit Paris. Now, she was here. It felt new and exciting.

It might be a few days before she could make her way to a port and proceed to Lisbon. She was lucky to have found this protector. It was all going to work out perfectly.

The last couple of days with Aran had made her feel at least somewhat secure. He had behaved like a gentleman during the trip to Paris and seemed to be an honorable man. She did not feel threatened; in fact, the opposite was true.

She cleaned up the best she could. Everything Alexis needed was there, a toilet, soap and water, and even a hairbrush.

When she returned to the bedroom, sitting demurely on the bed across from him, she felt presentable. "I am ready for your plan to get me to Lisbon."

To her dismay, he gave a short bark of laughter. Then he cleared his throat, looking at her more seriously. "The first thing you have to understand is you cannot get to Lisbon from here. The only way to get to Lisbon would be to return to Gravelines, and then London to board a ship." He grimaced. "And I won't be back in Gravelines for some time."

"But I must get to Lisbon!" She felt a ripple of panic. "If Gravelines has no ships travelling to Lisbon, then another port will do."

He took her hand and spoke firmly, staring into her eyes. "Forget it. You cannot. We are at war, Alexis. Even if I could get you to a French port, which I cannot, there would be no vessels travelling to a port occupied by the British. This is the first fact you must accept. You are here in Paris with me until I can get you back to Gravelines and put you on an English ship. It is your only way out."

Releasing her hand, he poured her a cup of coffee, doused it with cream, and handed it to her. "Drink this while you think about this reality. You are here for several weeks whether it suits you or not. If I try to get you out too soon, it will raise much suspicion. I am being watched, Alexis. I am a secret enemy here, and we are at war. We cannot simply head back to Gravelines having just returned from the port. We would be picked up before we even reached the outskirts of Paris."

She frowned at him.

He glowered back at her. "And know too that you are a huge burden to me. I like it even less than you do. I would like nothing better than to dump you on the streets of Paris to fend for yourself. You are here and safe at my generosity." He held his mouth in a firm line. "So, you may drop the superior attitude. Indeed, I insist you do. Here your status as an English lady, the daughter of an English general, means nothing. In fact, it is a hinderance."

Alexis let his words sink in.

He silently offered her bread and cheese which she ate as she considered her position. Her eyes began to burn with unshed tears. She had escaped Lionel, but she seemed to have landed in a situation just as precarious. She began to understand that she was indeed at Aran's mercy. If he abandoned her to the streets of Paris, she would not survive. The frightening scene on the streets of Gravelines was still fresh in her mind. She shuddered.

Each time she examined her quandary, she came to the same conclusion. There was no way out. There was no one to turn to. Whatever he determined to be her fate for the next several weeks would be her only option.

She counselled herself not to panic. It would all work out. Finally, it was the image of Lionel, with his heavy loose lips, and a lifetime spent in his presence which calmed her. Whatever her fate, it could not compare to that. She had made the right choice.

Aran watched her eat in silence. It was some time before he spoke. "Alexis, I too am English and hiding my identity. We are enemies in a foreign land. Remember that. If discovered, we will pay for it with our lives, both of us. I have a plan to help us survive until I can get you safely out of here. Are you ready to listen?"

His face was deadly serious, and his eyes seemed to bore into hers.

She swallowed nervously. "I am ready."

Indeed, she thought to herself, I have no other option.

"You are already masquerading as my mistress. We are going to stay with that. It is the only thing which will work to explain your unexpected arrival. Hence the adjoining rooms." He turned and indicated the door to his bedroom.

Her cheeks reddened.

"And that," he said, pointing at her face, "that missish blush is exactly what might give us away. Can you act, princess?"

She nodded.

He took her hand. "You must be my lover."

She looked at him wide-eyed and gasped, pulling her hand from his.

"No! No, not in reality. I promise you will be safe from me." He waved his arm to dismiss the notion. "None of that will happen here. But you must be able to pretend, Alexis. You will have to do an exceptional job."

He leaned back and took a sip of his coffee, watching her as though considering her abilities.

She looked down. She would pretend to be his lover for her time here. In exchange, she would be safe until she could get back home, and then hopefully to Lisbon. The idea was shocking. Yet there was a part of the plan which appealed to her. Once again, she would be far beyond the boundaries set for an English lady. It would be another adventure. And it did not seem to be too difficult.

He pressed on. "You will have to stay in character as much as possible. Outside of this room, you are Alexis de

Mal. At every moment of every day, you will be her. Submerge yourself in the character. Be her." A fleeting sadness touched his eyes. "You may take it from me. I am an expert."

"Even here in the house?"

"Especially here in the house. I believe there is an operative here in my home, perhaps more than one, watching my every action. But all servants talk, Alexis. You must always, always speak in French or Spanish. As of today, you know no English. It must become a habit. Even here in your bedroom, English is off limits."

He was quiet for several minutes. "Alexis, there is a man here in Paris. His name is Joseph Fouche. He is a spy master —the best in Europe. You must have heard of him?" He waited until she nodded before he continued. "He watches. His people are placed everywhere in Paris, and he knows all. He is particularly suspicious of me. I am playing a dangerous game here in Paris and you must do the same."

He looked at her as though assessing her potential. "My plan is for you to be my new lover. And you, my dear, will have to play the part, and play it well. You must be a courtesan, and never the English miss, even here in my home." He squeezed her hand lightly. "Our lives depend on it, Alexis."

She digested his plan. Her idea of a sojourn in Paris, an adventurous holiday, began to crumble. She realized that once again she had been naïve, thoughtlessly focused on her girlish dreams of Paris. Her cheeks burned as she considered her ignorance. To continue in her reckless behavior would have grave consequences for them both.

"I think I can manage it," she said quietly, and meant it. From this point on, she would take on the role he prescribed for her and do it well.

She listened intently as he described her new persona.

"Your mother will be the famous courtesan Celeste de Mal. She was a red head, Alexis, and the first woman who came to mind when I looked at you. Perhaps your hair alone will help the role be believable. She retired early, leaving for the country while she was still young. And you were born there, at your grandmother's home, far from Paris—a secret to her former associates. Celeste died shortly after leaving Paris. The timeline works. Celeste left Paris ill. Your existence means she was also pregnant. It's a scenario which makes sense. Memorize it."

He seemed pleased to see that for once he had her complete attention.

"And you must never, ever mention your father. To do so will make you a target, Alexis. Alexis de Mal has no father. I will do everything to help you with your role. I will always be in character. You will be able to take your cues from me. I will not allow you to slip into the prim English girl. Luckily, we have a little time before the servants return to practice." He sighed and raised his eyebrows in a question. "Are you ready, princess?"

"I think so."

He walked over to her and rested his hands on her shoulders. She flinched. He ignored it.

Leaning down, he kissed the top of her head. "Now then, do you have a different dress? I thought I might take my best girl out and buy her some respectable clothes."

She looked up at him with her face flaming.

"I... I have a clean dress," she stuttered.

He reached down and tilted her head up towards him. With a deadly serious face, he leaned down and kissed her lightly on the lips. "Good. I expect you to be presentable in, say, fifteen minutes."

He left the room. Alexis spent a few seconds just staring

open-mouthed at the closed door. She touched her hand to her lips where he had so nonchalantly kissed her.

The next few weeks would be a challenge indeed. She had never seen a courtesan. She had heard whispered rumors about lovers, and once or twice even the behavior of scandalous mistresses had made its way to her virgin ears, but never in her life had she thought she could become one.

She thought again about the words her aunt had used to describe her: spoilt, naïve, and helpless. Her stomach flipped as she considered the possibility that it might be true. If she made a mistake, even a small one, her life and Aran's were in the balance.

Chapter Five

As was his habit, Aran glanced behind him once again as they crossed the boulevard and entered the shopping district. For once he was not being followed. His early arrival must not yet have reached the ears of the home office.

So far, Alexis seemed relaxed and comfortable. She was doing well. He reminded himself to continue touching her with familiarity as much as possible. That it was disconcerting to her was apparent by her blushed face and stammering when he was near her.

It was probably safest to keep her tucked away in his townhouse for now. Especially until she was more comfortable in her role. He was a little uneasy with Celeste de Mal as Alexis' mother. The fame of Celeste might present a problem. But it had been twenty years; legend and reality had to have blurred by now. And keeping Alexis in his home was another oddity. A man normally set up his mistress with her own apartments. He sighed. That he could not do. Alexis was a young woman who had been taken care of her whole life. She was simply too childishly naïve to survive on her own. If it was discovered he kept a hidden lover, so be it. He was not the first man to keep a lover to himself for a few weeks.

Today she would have to understand the necessity of always staying in character. It meant becoming accustomed to his touch. Whenever she lapsed, he would subtly remind her, by pulling her close to his body, or putting his arm around her shoulders. Her face was becoming the color of that startling red hair.

He was pleased with his idea to do a little shopping. It would give her the opportunity to practice her persona publicly. She would need something to wear until she could do a little shopping on her own. Besides, it was standard procedure for a man who had a new woman. It was an accepted part of her payment. Like a new mistress, only beginning to ply her trade, she had nothing suitable for her role. The excursion would fit perfectly into their plan.

Today they would buy a few items, but she would need a complete wardrobe. He decided his valet Rolande would be a great help with this. No one was more knowledgeable of the current fashions than his outrageous valet. But until Rolande returned, they would need to find some ready-made items to get her through a few days.

He chose an expensive shop he had visited often with his friend Gigi. The modiste came to assist him. Together they chose a variety of underwear and lingerie for Alexis. He watched her face. Her cheeks were flushed, and she refused to meet his gaze. He guessed she had never said the word lingerie in her life. He could not resist grinning at her discomfort.

This is only going to get worse for her, he thought with amusement.

48

"I am also looking for two or three day dresses. Ready-made, if you have them. I will be ordering her several gowns, but not today."

The modiste turned her attention to Alexis, looking her over carefully. "I might have something for you, *monsieur*. We will see." She turned to an assistant. "Claudette, bring me those gowns from the arbor, all three. We will try those first."

She took Alexis by the arm. "Come, come."

Aran followed them into a dressing room.

"Now then, off with this dress. And step out here on this block." She began undoing the laces at Alexis's bodice.

Claudette came in, hung the dresses on a rack, and assisted the modiste. They had Alexis in her chemise in moments. Alexis's cheeks were flaming again. She glared at Aran, indicating with her eyes that he should leave. But he only smiled at her and shook his head slowly. She crossed her arms over her breasts.

"Ah, she is new to this business, yes?" The modiste looked at him and laughed.

He nodded. "Very new, but I am pleased with her. I have decided to keep her. I want only the best for my little love."

He looked at Alexis's disgruntled face and winked.

"Oh, do not be shy, girl." The madame patted her on the cheek. "You have chosen well. He is a wealthy and generous man. You will soon have many pretty things, yes?"

She cackled happily as she assessed Alexis's body.

"She has a fine form, *monsieur*. A little wide in the hips." She patted Alexis's backside. "Heavy, but very nice."

Aran could not resist reaching over and squeezing Alexis' rear. She squealed and glared at him while twisting to dislodge herself from his grip.

He rubbed her rounded bum appreciatively. "I like it well enough. A good backside is a favorite of mine."

The modiste and Claudette cackled while Alexis scowled. He looked at Alexis and smiled mischievously. Narrowing her eyes, she gave him an evil stare. If looks could kill, he would be dead now. He laughed again, deciding he was enjoying the day.

When they left the shop, with the promise the items would be delivered to their door in a couple of hours, Alexis turned to him angrily and began in English. "That was humilia—"

He yanked her to him and kissed her on the lips. This time it was not a peck. He pulled back and slid his hands up her waist to rest on her sides just below her breasts. He squeezed his warning, letting her see the anger in his eyes.

She dropped her eyes demurely, then looked up at him.

"Thank you, *monsieur*. I love my new apparel," she said in perfect French, but her eyes flashed angrily, belying her words.

"You may call me Aran, love." He tucked her arm into his and began walking.

"Thank you, Aran."

He leaned down and kissed Alexis once more, lightly. She was angry but he was relieved to see she did not blush. She was adapting quickly. He would forgive Alexis for her one mistake. He had, after all, pushed her a bit too far in the dress shop.

Later, in their rooms, he allowed her to complain to him.

"You will not ever come into a dressing room with me again!"

"But that is how it is done," he reminded her. "I am

your provider. It is only natural I get to choose the merchandise you wear. It is standard procedure."

She grabbed her parcels and stomped into her dressing room to change, leaving the door open so she could shout at him.

"It is humiliating. To be standing half naked while people talk about you as if you were not there. I hated it." She stuck her head around the corner. "I will not have it."

He only raised his eyebrows at her.

He could hear her muttering as she attempted to dress.

Alexis has probably had a lady's maid her whole life. It is doubtful she will ever be able to dress alone.

He was hungry. He had been ready to go out and eat an hour ago.

"From now on, I will be trying on dresses on my own. I get to make some ground rules too." There was more rustling from her room and a few exasperated grunts. She poked her head around the corner again. Her dress was on but flopped loosely across her neck. She raised her voice. "And for the record I do not have wide hips. That woman had wide hips. My hips are simply fine."

"You have wide hips, Alexis."

She growled in frustration and disappeared back around the corner.

After a few minutes of listening to her mutter and groan, he went to her dressing room door and leaned on the frame. She was trying to reach the buttons on the back of her gown without success. She had twisted the gown around her body in an attempt to make them accessible. She had them half done up. Her chemise had somehow gotten bunched up in the whole mess and poked out from her bodice. And now she was stuck.

He bit the inside of his mouth to keep from laughing.

He was sure if he so much as cracked a smile she would wallop him.

"Can I help you, princess?"

She tried to wrangle the dress around again. Finally, she expelled a breath, dropped her arms to her sides in resignation, and said, "Yes."

He stepped into the room and examined the muddle she had made. He was careful not to look at her face. If he saw the aggrieved expression, he was sure she wore, he would not be able to stifle his laughter.

After determining the tangled chemise was the greatest problem, Aran knelt in front of her, reached up under her dress, and tugged it down. Then he grabbed the dress by its bodice and twisted it back into position over her breasts. The bloody chemise tangled again. He reached under her dress again holding it down while he pulled the gown back into place. He maneuvered it from side to side until he thought it was laying correctly.

"Put your arms into the sleeves," he said.

He stepped back and examined the results.

"Seems right," he said to himself, satisfied with the effect. "Now turn around."

She turned obediently. There was a long row of small buttons. She had fastened most of them but had them misaligned. He had to undo them and start again from scratch.

"I don't know why they do not settle for one or two big buttons, instead of this multitude of tiny ones. It's an inconvenience." His big fingers struggled with the tiny pearl buttons.

He finally managed to button the last one.

"There. *Voila!*" He smiled at her, pleased with his success, as she turned. "You are perfect."

To his surprise, she gave him a wide smile. Her mood had done a complete turnabout.

"You realize you will have undo them all later." She laughed, apparently finding the situation amusing.

She has a sense of humor, after all, he thought.

Their first day had gone well. She would make a fine mistress. Perhaps they could get through the next few weeks without too much trouble. But then he looked at her flaming red hair and let his eyes wander the length of her body.

No, it would never be easy around her. She was dangerous. She was too beautiful, and as a lady and a general's daughter, she was off limits.

The next few weeks might be difficult indeed.

Chapter Six

Aran spent the first few days with Alexis from morning to night. He even took her shopping again, helping her to become familiar with the best locations. As a merchant who dealt at the English port in Gravelines, he was able to exchange some of her English money to francs, which had come in handy for all the shopping she had done. She bought everything from gowns to silken underwear. This time he had even stayed in the showroom while she was measured and fitted for her gowns in the dressing room.

"Unless you want my qualified opinion," he'd said with a smile.

"I think I can manage," she retorted, pleased with his capitulation on that particular point of contention.

They strolled back to the townhouse.

As they neared his home, Aran said, "When we arrive, my servants will have returned. Rehearsal is over, Alexis. From now on you must be very, very careful."

She felt a tinge of panic. The last few days had been like

a holiday. She had pushed her concerns from her mind, enjoying her trip to Paris.

He squeezed her arm. "You will manage, and I will help you when I can. Now then, you will have a lady's maid of sorts. His name is Rolande—"

"A man! But Aran, I cannot have a man for a lady's maid!"

"Rolande is a different sort of man. He does not like women the way other men do." He chuckled at her confused expression. "He chooses other men as his mates, Alexis. I am more likely to be subject to his advances than you, my dear."

Alexis had never heard of such a circumstance. She did not believe it to be possible. "But can I not have a woman in my rooms? I'll not be comfortable with a man, even if he is...not interested."

"No. I trust Rolande. I saved his life on the streets of Paris two years ago, when he was being attacked by brutes. He has been my valet ever since."

She shook her head, still shocked by his suggestion.

"No, Alexis. There is no one else I trust with you. You are bound to make mistakes, especially in the first few days. It is too risky to bring in someone I don't know." He pulled her in closer and patted her arm. "It will be a good arrangement. Rolande will be company for you. I intend to have him to act as your paid companion, as well as your maid. When you meet him, you will understand."

They had reached the gates to his townhouse. Aran paused on the step, turning to her.

"Other than Rolande, you must keep a distant relationship with my staff. I keep as few people as possible. Emile serves as a butler and footman. Colette is a maid. They will be the ones you have most contact with." He squeezed her hands briefly. "Know that either or both are agents. Then there is the cook and the kitchen staff. Keep your relations with them formal."

When Aran pushed open the door, a tall, dark man met them and inclined his head politely. "Good day, *monsieur*."

"Ah, Emile. I hope you enjoyed your holiday." Aran gestured to her. "I have a house guest, Emile. This is my friend Alexis de Mal. She will be staying in my adjoining rooms. I expect you to look after her well."

Alexis felt her cheeks burn. Her position as a mistress could not be more obvious.

Emile remained stoic, bowing respectfully. "*Mademoiselle*."

Remembering her role, she replied, "Emile. I will try not to burden you overmuch."

She smiled at him before taking Aran's arm.

Aran turned back to Emile. "Please ask Rolande to come to my rooms when he is able."

Once in her room, it was only moments before the adjoining door burst open and a slender figure came towards her.

"Ah, *mademoiselle*! I am so excited to meet you." He took her arms and pulled her in for a hug.

Alexis looked uneasily over his shoulder at Aran who stood braced in the doorway. He raised his eyebrows at her and smiled.

Rolande arched back to examine her. "And you are a beauty! My *monsieur* has found someone at last. We will have such fun together, yes?"

"Ah, yes. I think."

Rolande looked like no man she had seen before. He was outrageously handsome in a boyish style. He was her height, with a lithe frame. He had dark hair and eyes. It was his eyes which were most predominant in his face. In part because, to her surprise, he wore mascara and a black liner. He looked like an ancient Egyptian with his thick dark liner circling his huge eyes and trailing in a thick strip to his hairline. His lips were full and suspiciously dark red. She was sure he also wore rouge.

"*Monsieur* tells me you have been shopping. First, I will see what we have here to work with. I cannot imagine my master choosing appropriately. We will see." Rolande hustled into her dressing room. The sounds of parcels being opened, with much muttering, emanated from the room.

Aran, still leaning on her doorframe, looked at her and raised his eyebrows in a question. Realizing her mouth had dropped, she snapped her lips together.

"Well?" Aran asked.

When she did not reply, he added. "Remember, I have asked Rolande to be a companion to you as well as your assistant. As your hired companion, the two of you will be able to tour the city as friends. I thought it might be a better relationship for you. It will get lonely for you here, with me away at the warehouse most days, and out most nights. Enjoy his company, Alexis." He switched to Spanish and added softly, "But he cannot be privy to your secrets, remember that."

Aran retreated to his room, leaving the door open.

Alexis took a breath and strolled to the dressing room. She stood hesitantly in the doorway.

Rolande sat amongst the heap of parcels Alexis had strewn into the room after her shopping spree. She had no idea how to manage her wardrobe. The care of her clothing had always been done for her.

"Ah, come in, come in. Together we will see what can be done with all of this."

They spent the afternoon sorting and hanging her things. Rolande would slip on an item of clothing and mimic perfectly the type of woman who would wear it.

"And this one, *cherie*, this is not for you."

Rolande pulled a bonnet onto his head, fastening the thick ribbons in a huge bow, then tilted his head and batted his dark eyelashes at her.

"I am an innocent," he said with the purest little smile.

Alexis could not help but giggle. Rolande chose another hat and sat it on his head at a jaunty angle.

"Now this one, darling, is all the rage," he said in a sexy drawl.

In no time at all, Rolande had her laughing at his antics.

Rolande knew more about beauty and fashion than anyone she had ever known. At times she was convinced he was more feminine than herself. By the time she was to dress for dinner, she found she had no difficulty with Rolande as her lady's maid. Aran had been right. He was perfect.

The next morning, Aran left after breakfast. She and Rolande planned to do a little shopping, then enjoy lunch at one of the bistros.

Alexis stood at her window and looked across the back garden to assess the weather. It was going to be a sunny day, perfect for a morning outside.

A movement below caught her eye. Emile crept across the yard. He paused just before the gate. Alexis took a step back from the window, just as he turned to glance back at the house. He then slipped through the gate and disappeared behind the hedges sheltering the back courtyard from the alley.

There would be no reason for Emile to sneak away from the townhouse through the back gate. Perhaps Aran was right, and Emile was an agent. She wondered what he had gone to report. The obvious answer was Aran's changes in the household; a new lover, with Rolande promoted to lady's companion, and perhaps even their plans for the day. She shivered. The spy master would be creating a new dossier today. She was certain Alexis de Mal would now be listed in the thousands of files the man kept on the citizens of Paris.

The moment Aran returned she would share this discovery. Aran would need to know his suspicions were justified.

The seriousness of her position in France made her stomach lurch. One mistake and Fouche's suspicions would be confirmed. Joseph Fouche was famous for his ruthlessness. People suspected of conspiracy often disappeared, their bodies sometimes found floating in the canals. Clearly Emile would be watching her.

She considered her portrayal of a courtesan.

"Submerge yourself in the role," Aran had suggested.

She would take his advice. From this morning forward, she would be the daughter of the famous Celeste, a new mistress excited to have found her first lover and keeper. Each time the prudish girl she had been surfaced she would crush the thoughts. It was too dangerous to be the daughter of an English general here in Paris.

Chapter Seven

Alexis tossed and turned in her bed, feeling hot and damp. She pulled off her heavy night gown and donned a shorter silk one to cool herself down, but it did not help. To ease her restlessness, she left her room to wander the elaborate townhouse. Its ornate Louis XIV furniture had impressed her on her first morning. Having lived in Aran's house now for several weeks, she had become so accustomed to it that it felt like home.

Tonight, it was cool and dark. She ran her hand along the ornate handrail as she wandered down the stairs of Aran's beautiful home. Its address in the prestigious Marias district had taken her by surprise. Aran obviously lived well here in Paris.

Her first two weeks had passed without incident. Paris had all the luxury items Londoners craved in abundance. Sometimes Aran would not go to his warehouse. On those days, they perused the shops, strolled the streets, and ate marvelous French food in the elegant bistros which littered the streets. She loved Paris and she loved his company.

Aran was the perfect gentleman. He laughed easily, seeming to be entertained by her enthusiastic extravagance.

There had only been one tense day. They had gone out for lunch at a little outdoor café near the river. It was next to the offices of the Minister of Police.

"This is a favorite haunt of Napoleon's ministers. We will likely see Fouche here."

"But why bring me here? Isn't it dangerous? "

Aran patted her arm. "You will not be required to speak to the man. I want him to see you. If I keep you a secret, he may become curious about you. I think you will be safer if he knows you are not hidden away."

After their coffee was served, two gentlemen settled at a table across from them. She noticed Aran stiffen before he reached across the table and took her hand.

Speaking softly in Spanish he said, "Keep your eyes on mine, Alexis. Fouche has arrived, my dear. He is the elder of the two men who were just seated." Aran smiled pleasantly and leaned casually in his chair. This time he spoke in normal tones. "So, tell me, love, what is your favorite part of Paris?"

Alexis was stunned with the ease of Aran's demeanor. He was accomplished in the art of duplicity. She took her cue from him, looked down, and stirred her coffee. She added cream, concentrating on this normal activity until her heart slowed. She was determined to be Alexis de Mal and show Aran she could be as nonchalant as him.

When she raised her head, she was entirely the mistress. She looked him in the eyes and said softly, "My favorite?" She gave him a slow smile. "It would not be found here on the streets of Paris, darling. I have a more private setting in mind."

Aran laughed loudly. "You have been in the company of Rolande too long, my dear."

Alexis took a sip of her coffee and let her eyes wander to the man across from her. Fouche had a narrow face, with a thin, slightly crooked nose above a small narrow mouth. But despite the sharpness of his angular face, his most striking feature was his drooping rounded eyes. They gave him a sleepy, harmless countenance which was completely at odds with his fearsome reputation. He raised his heavy lids to look at her, his thin lips curling into the slightest smile, as he nodded a greeting.

Alexis returned his smile politely, before turning to Aran. "I am ready to go now, my love."

Neither of them mentioned the encounter until they were well away from the restaurant.

Alexis turned to Aran and spoke quietly. "He doesn't look dangerous."

"No, but being underestimated is one of his tools, " he replied.

Aran was quiet and distracted, holding her arm snuggly against him, as they strolled down the boulevard towards the townhouse. Here the human traffic had thinned. Despite the pleasant day, they met few pedestrians along the bricked walkway and only an occasional carriage clattered past.

The sun was warm against her back. Alexis found herself fighting the urge to rest her head against his shoulder. She was sad when they reached his home, and reluctantly gave up his arm.

She was beginning to feel like the mistress she portrayed. It was a strange role to play. As time passed, the lines between acting and reality became blurred.

When the servants had returned on the second day, she

noticed a distinct change in Aran's behavior. He was careful to remain at her side in the evenings. At breakfast, he would greet her with a kiss. And always, he would rest his hands on her.

When he discovered she could play the piano, he would often begin their evenings together by insisting she play for him. Aran stood beside her with his hand resting on her shoulders. At first, she had found it disconcerting and stumbled as she played. But gradually the feel of his warm hands on her shoulders became commonplace and relaxing.

The footman, Emile, seemed to be in constant attendance. She noticed he often lingered by the door, a silent sentinel, ready to do Aran's bidding. When Aran directed him to leave the room, he would slip out the door, but leave it open behind him. On the occasions he remained in the room, Aran would be particularly amorous. If he read to her, he would sit beside her on the sofa. One night she had slipped off her shoes and tucked her feet beneath her as she leaned into the corner of the couch, listening to the sound of Aran's voice as he read her a work of fiction. Whatever he chose to read, she found she would be entertained by his deep resonating tones alone.

He'd moved closer to her.

"Here." He tapped his lap. "You can stretch out your legs across me."

She had obediently laid her legs across his lap. He pulled her dress down and tucked the sides discretely around her legs. He winked at her. "There, that will be more comfortable."

She noticed that he glanced at Emile lurking quietly by the door.

After that, whenever Aran read, she cuddled into the corner of the couch, with her legs relaxed across his lap while he sat close to her. Often, she would raise her knees and rest them across his chest while she enjoyed his stories. He would use one hand to hold her legs tight against his chest, while the other balanced the book before him. And though she knew it was all a ruse to convey the intimacy of new lovers, she relished those evenings. They were a scene of domesticity she had never experienced.

Her mother had died at birth. As an only child, she had often felt alone and isolated, especially with her father frequently away serving his country.

And oddly, on these occasions with Aran, it was the pleasant smell of his closeness she came to appreciate the most. Aran smelt of a spicy cologne, combined with his own distinct manliness. Each time he moved in close to her on the sofa, she always took a deep breath, appreciating the scent of him. It felt comfortable, yet there was also a strange excitement in his nearness.

This evening, the sound of his voice as he read to her had lulled her into a languid trance. She almost dozed off, with her head resting on the back of the sofa as he read. His hand felt wonderfully warm where he held her knees against him. He began to absently run his hand up and down the curve of her legs. With each stroke, he had moved further down her legs, until his hand rested on her hips.

He stuttered in his reading, withdrawing his hand, and gripped her knees firmly against his chest once more. She stirred from her sleepy state, feeling a strange sense of loss.

"I think it is time we retired, love," he'd said, shifting her legs to the floor and setting the novel down on the side table. He had a painful expression on his face.

She'd looked at him curiously. "Are you feeling well? You look flushed."

"Ah, Alexis," he said, standing up and taking her arm,

"I think I am a little fevered right now. It might be best if you went to bed and gave me some time alone."

He walked her across the hall and glancing at Emile who lingered just outside the library, kissed her lightly at her door. "Goodnight, princess."

Alexis was not satisfied with his perfunctory kiss. She leaned forward to kiss him back, feeling a shock of excitement as he pulled her roughly against him. This time, he ran his tongue across her lips and she opened her mouth to him. It was though a current of energy flashed through her body. She grasped his shoulders with her arms to keep herself from sliding weak-kneed to the floor, overwhelmed by the strange ripples of elation coursing through her body.

Aran abruptly withdrew from her and rested his forehead against hers as he regained his breath. Finally, he whispered, "Go to bed, Alexis."

Alexis reluctantly entered her room and closed the door softly behind her, leaning against it. It was the first real kiss he had ever given her. His touch had been anything but perfunctory. Her body still trembled with her reaction. She put both hands to her lips where Aran had so passionately kissed her. They still burned from his touch. It had been both wonderful and frightening at the same time.

Now, despite almost dozing off with Aran on the sofa, she found she was restless. She prowled about downstairs. The large receiving room was dark, its only light the pale moonlight filtering in from the glass doors to the garden. Through the glass she could see Aran, his back to her as he stood outside on the patio facing the garden. She watched his still figure for long minutes.

He too must feel this strange uneasiness tonight. It seemed the closer she came to him, the more comfortable and happier she was in his presence, the more this awful wanting plagued her. She reached out her hand and touched the cool glass which separated his body from hers. Then she turned and crossed the tiled floor to the stairs, and her room, so close to his, leaving him standing alone on the dark terrace.

Alexis returned to her bed, but still sleep evaded her. She considered her existence here in Paris. The household followed a loose routine. Aran left each day to work at his warehouse, and some nights he was mysteriously absent. Often, he would spend part of the evening with her, then leave to attend an engagement. The days passed slowly. She was being left more and more in the company of Rolande.

At first there was much to see and do, but lately she had begun to feel the constraints of her isolation. The evenings in her room were the worst for her. If she had thoughts of home, she squashed them. She refused to mourn her lonely existence in London. Instead, she would celebrate her resourcefulness in escaping the future her aunt had planned for her. Every time she thought of home, the image of Lionel's pasty face would emerge, and she would shiver with relief. Yet here in Paris, she felt as though she was missing an essential element. There was always this strange yearning.

At last, she faded into a troubled sleep.

———

The next day, she and Rolande planned to visit the modiste, and then enjoy lunch. Rolande took her arm as they crossed the muddy boulevard, helping her avoid the piles of horse manure littering the road.

As they reached the bricked walkway, he extended her

arm and fluttered his free hand like a court jester, indicating the sidewalk.

"A marvelously tiled route for my *mademoiselle*," he said with an exaggerated bow.

Alexis laughed at his antics. But when he straightened, she noticed he glanced behind her with a look of concern. She turned to see what had disturbed him. A man in a dark great coat and beaver hat crossed the street behind them, but she could see nothing to worry her.

Rolande distracted her. "Today will be your final fitting for the new gown. If all is well, you shall be wearing it tonight. And then ooh, la la, my *cherie*, the *monsieur* will not be able to keep his hands from you."

"I still worry that the dress is a bit...revealing."

The streets became busier as they neared the shopping district. Rolande was occupied maneuvering them through the crowds. "Nonsense. Every man will adore a dress such as that. Aran will love it."

He winked at her with his heavily mascaraed eyes.

They arrived at the dress shop. As Rolande opened the door, she happened to look down the walk behind them. Lingering on the corner was the man in the great coat and bowler hat.

Rolande followed her gaze.

"Come my dear," he said, taking her arm and steering her into the shop.

The two of them stood near the glass display windows while they waited for the modiste to finish accommodating another customer. Alexis watched the street. The man in the beaver hat loitered just beyond the doors of the shop.

She knew with a certainty the man was following her. The knowledge made her a little queasy.

She took a breath, turning to the modiste as she approached. It was a welcome distraction.

The dress fit perfectly. Once Rolande had secured the shop's promise to have it delivered in the afternoon, they left to find an outdoor café where they could lunch. Alexis could not resist a quick scan of the street, searching for the man. To her relief, he seemed to have disappeared.

It was a lovely day, and the restaurants were busy with Parisians enjoying a meal in the fine spring weather. Rolande led her to a queue, and they waited in line to be seated.

"You must preen a little, *cherie*. If you look like someone of importance, they will rush to seat you. Despite the revolution, Parisians love royalty." Rolande flipped his hair back and batted his dark lashes. "I am the queen of Paris, darling. And you all are so honored by my presence."

Alexis covered her mouth to hide her giggle.

They were seated at a table separated from the busy street with a railing. The location provided Rolande with endless opportunities to mimic the passing people, or to comment on their fashion choices, and they enjoyed a delicious lunch.

"Oh, *cherie*, look just there. It is Madame La Fleur with her famous entourage. It is said she goes nowhere without a footman or two to do her bidding."

Alexis watched as a robust woman hustled by with several liveried young men carrying parcels in her wake, struggling to keep up to her brisk pace. Alexis smiled as she watched the woman plow through the pedestrians.

Her reverie was interrupted by a raspy voice. "Ah, it is the beautiful young woman I saw with Monsieur Garscon last week. You must forgive my interruption. I simply could not pass by without meeting you."

Alexis looked up to find Joseph Fouche himself standing at her table. Hovering behind him was the man in the bowler hat. She was stunned, staring at him open-mouthed.

"Forgive me for being so forward, *mademoiselle*. I am Monsieur Fouche, a minister of the regime." He looked down at her, his sleepy eyes meeting hers, and she saw that beneath his drooping lids, those eyes were hard and glittering.

Alexis recovered quickly, snapping her mouth closed and giving him her hand. "Alexis De Mal. Pleased to meet you, I'm sure." She smiled at him, hoping he could not hear the thundering of her heart. "And this is my friend, Rolande."

Rolande only nodded, his black eyes wary.

One of the skills she had learned as a debutant was to mask her true feelings and respond always with distant politeness. It would serve her well today. She crushed her fears and took a breath, forcing a smile onto her face, as she had done many times in the past.

Fouche returned Rolande's nod as he raised her hand to his lips. "Alexis De Mal. Hmm. The name is familiar to me. Would it possible that you are related to the famous Celeste De Mal?"

He held her hand while he waited for her answer.

Alexis gently pulled her hand away from him. "Yes, she was my mother."

"Ah, and it is so like Garscon to find such a prize as you." His narrow lips curled into the slightest smile. "I once met your mother, and you, my dear, have the look of her. She was a patriot I am told. Are you the same?"

His eyes seemed to pierce into hers.

She carefully ignored his question about her politics and focused instead on his comment about Celeste. "You have an advantage over me, sir. I unfortunately do not remember my mother. She died when I was born. I hoped that here in Paris I might learn more about her."

Alexis smiled at him, trying to look innocent and new to Paris, which was not difficult. It was exactly her circumstance.

"Sadly, I cannot help you much, *mademoiselle*. I know only the stories of her conquests in Paris, having met her only once when I was very young, just before she retired from Paris. And I had not heard that she had a lovely daughter. Very interesting indeed." He looked at her speculatively as he twisted his thin lips into a smile. "For a girl raised in the country, you speak textbook Parisian French. Now why is that, my dear?"

Alexis forced herself to give him a wide smile, while her heart leapt in her breast. "Why thank you, *monsieur*. My grandmother would be much pleased to hear that her endless lessons did not go unnoticed."

He reached into his breast pocket and pulled out his card. "Should you like to hear those tales of your mother, I would be happy to share them with you." He handed her his card. "I am available to talk at any time."

He graced her with his thin smile. "We could trade stories."

"Thank you, *monsieur*." She took his card and slipped it into her reticule. "It would be a pleasure to learn more about my mother. I may do that."

Fouche nodded. "I must take my leave. But remember, my dear, any time, I am available."

He turned and walked away.

Rolande sipped his coffee, his mascaraed eyes peering at her from behind the rim of his cup. He set the cup down with exaggerated care and played with its handle. His face was uncharacteristically solemn. "Powerful men, *cherie*.

They have no problem risking your life in their schemes. But one must remember that it is their agenda and your life."

"Rolande, I have no intention of getting anywhere near that man. He scares me."

"Come on, love." Rolande stood and reached out to her. He abruptly changed the subject, once again her cheerful friend. "I have an excellent idea for the afternoon. There is a matinee performance at the Circe de Advant. We should have a little fun, yes?"

"Yes."

They returned to the apartment after a pleasant afternoon in time to dress for supper. Rolande helped her into her new gown. It was cut extremely low. Its bodice was an almost sheer material, with embroidered designs in the darker shade of its skirt, strategically placed for a modicum of discretion. It displayed her breasts in a manner that almost made her uncomfortable. Yet in a strange way the blatant sexuality of it excited her. Rolande assured her Aran would love it. She sashayed down the stairs to where Aran waited below.

When she stood before him, he looked at her with a strange expression. Very slowly, he reached out his hand and touched the bodice of her gown.

"This, my love, is a little decadent, don't you think?" He ran one finger along the seam and her skin, tracing the outline of her breasts.

She shivered and moved closer to him. "Rolande insists it is the latest fashion. He said it is conservative compared to what is being worn."

She leaned in close to him, hoping he would kiss her, as he often did, especially when they were below stairs.

Instead, he stepped back, frowning at her before he took

her arm. "Rolande is a troublemaker. I shall have a talk with him."

At dinner, she confided to Aran about the events of the afternoon. Glancing at the closed door to the kitchens, he spoke quietly in Spanish. "Fouche suspects me, Alexis. He is far too interested in my activities here in Paris. I am beginning to think he is playing with me, letting me operate so he can ferret out my contacts. We must be even more careful, my dear. A couple of weeks and we will leave. The trick will be to get out of here before he acts. My god, Alexis, I must get you out."

"I don't believe I gave him anything to suspect."

"No, it is not you. His words today suggest he is interested in using you as another tool. He has been watching me for a while, Alexis. Lately, he has been more vigilant. Everywhere I am watched. Even at the warehouse, I feel eyes upon me incessantly. It feels as though he has tossed a net around me." He ran his hand through his hair.

For the rest of the evening, he was distracted and kept his distance, insisting they play chess. For the first time, she was able to beat him at the game.

"I did it! I have finally beaten you." She clapped her hands and grinned.

"I say you had an unfair advantage." He looked down pointedly at her bodice. "You employed a distraction."

She laughed happily, still pleased with her victory. "Tomorrow, I will come down with my breasts bare, if it means I can beat you."

She arched her back, wriggling her chest in his direction.

He suddenly looked serious. "Oh no, you will not. Stop that, Alexis. And I will definitely have that talk with Rolande." He shot her another scowl. "Tonight," he added.

She only laughed at him and thrust her bottom lip out in an exaggerated pout. "You are such a sore loser, Aran. I will have to continue beating you until you become more accustomed to it."

After that incident, Rolande complained each time he dressed her, muttering, "The *monsieur* would like you dressed as a nun."

One evening, when the cool dampness of a spring shower had permeated the house, they sat by the fireplace, where Aran read to her. On this occasion, he chose more serious material, as though the formality of their high-backed chairs loaned itself to an intellectual topic. Aran frequently chose books on the philosophy of the Enlightenment, texts which expounded the value common man, and the concept that all men were created equal. In many cases, they discovered they had a common view of the world, but sometimes they had lively debates; debates he always won. He was an accomplished scholar.

"Napoleon is a champion of the common man. Did you know his is the first army which promotes men by ability, not social rank? In the rest of Europe, a soldier who is not of the peerage cannot advance past the level of corporal. I think it is one of the reasons he has been so successful in war."

"But I thought Napoleon was your enemy?"

"I approve of his ideas on the equality of all men. But war is a ghastly endeavor, Alexis. Some of the French believe through war they will spread the idea of the enlightenment across Europe. That this message is their destiny to propagate. Since the revolution, it's been like a religion to the French." He looked at her and smiled. "But me, princess, I believe it is too high a price to pay."

He shared with her then the story of his father's enlistment after his mother died. "I believe he went to fight in Spain to relieve some of the pain of mourning. But instead of finding peace, he found more agony. He came home a broken man. He threw himself through a second story window one night." His voice cracked with emotion. "My twin Arabella and I had lost our mother. When we lost father too, it was devastating. Unbearable. It is why I can tolerate my role here in Paris. If I can end all the suffering sooner, it will all have been worth it."

Alexis's heart ached for him. She went to Aran, where he sat by the fire, and wrapping her arms around his body while he sat, tried to comfort him. He laid his head upon her soft belly and slid his arms around her waist. For long minutes, he remained still. She rubbed his back in gentle strokes.

His hands shifted down to her hips. He squeezed them lightly, before moving to cup her round bottom. He groaned against her tummy, and she put one hand into his dark hair, holding him tightly against her. His hands strayed further. He tugged on the inside of her thighs until she obliged him by shuffling her legs further apart. He began stroking back and forth between her legs. The material of her dress had bunched up in his hands as he rubbed her dress against her nether regions.

Alexis felt a flush of tingling excitement. She was glad of her lack of petticoats as the fabric of her dress chafed against her. She rocked against him, wanting. She did not know what it was she so needed; she only knew he must not stop touching her. She could hear his breathing. His face had a look which was almost painful as they swayed together to the rhythm he created.

He shifted off his chair, going onto his knees in front of her. Lifting her dress with one hand, he slid the other between her thighs. She caught her breath when she felt his hand cupping her in so intimate a spot.

"Oh god, Alexis. I have to touch you, just this once." He groaned.

His hand rubbed her, back and forth, across her silky folds. She realized with confusion she was wet and slippery to his touch. His fingers probed her until she felt them slide into her body. She gasped. Her hands dug into his shoulders, keeping him near her as he worked his fingers on her body.

He rhythmically moved his fingers, holding her tight to him with his other hand gripping her buttocks. His eyes were closed, with his cheek still pressed against her abdomen. A tingling sensation radiated through her body. Wanting it to go on forever, she rocked her body to his movements, encouraging him to continue with his ministrations. She arched her back and moaned, hoping to share with him this strange experience. There was a rush of dampness. He turned his face into her body and groaned.

His hand stilled in her. She felt wonderfully wet and slick in his warm hand. His fingers slowly left her body, then he cupped her again. He shifted; his hand slid from her behind. Flinging her dress out of the way, his hands found her bare thighs and he pushed the offending garment upwards, leaving her naked from the waist down before him.

He burrowed his head between her thighs as though he was determined to complete one last action. He breathed deeply and she could feel his hot breath on her. His hands gripped her hips, pulling her close. She stepped wider, arching further towards him with a soft moan. He kissed her moist wetness and sucked her nubbin into his mouth, then shifted forward and licked the length of her, tasting her, before withdrawing and resting his forehead on her belly. He groaned again. This time it was a painful sound. Her dress fell back to the floor. They were back in their original position with his hands around her waist and his head pressed against her, only this time he was struggling to catch his breath.

She held him to her and ran her hands through his silky hair. For once, she was at ease. It was as though her body was finally satisfied with her actions. She was gloriously happy. If he had stood, she would have hugged him tight to her.

After long minutes he said, "I am sorry, princess." He pulled away from her and looked up at her. His eyes were filled with regret. "That should never have happened."

His apology brought her back to reality. Her cheeks burned with embarrassment, but also with a sharp pain. That he should be sad over the intimacy they had shared confused and angered her. Aran, touching her in this way, had felt right. It was only the natural progression of all the caressing over the last several weeks. And it had felt wonderful. She opened her mouth to speak but could find no words.

She whirled and ran from the room.

That night, she heard him prowling around his room. Finally, she heard his door close, and then silence. He had gone out for the evening.

The next morning, it was as though nothing had happened. He kissed her cheek with his usual cheerfulness before settling in for breakfast. He kept the conversation light until Alexis once more relaxed and enjoyed his company.

But the memory haunted her. She had experienced nothing like it in her life. She had been kissed once or twice when she was being courted, but never had she allowed someone to touch her like he had. And never had she felt the way he could make her feel. More and more she craved his touch. Some days, it was an urge so strong it hurt to be near him without having her hands on him or her body against his. And even then, there was no relief.

Tonight, as they sat together while he read, her body remembered. She began to feel damp. She ached with a desire to have his fingers touch her as they had. She found herself pressing against him, where her bottom touched his thighs. Then, when she realized what she was doing, she moved away from him, her cheeks red with embarrassment. Finally, it became too uncomfortable for both of them. Each time she squirmed about, Aran would lose his place in the novel, forced to wait while she tried to find a position which suited her. His closeness was becoming unbearable. No matter where she touched him, her skin burned. His reading became difficult and stilted.

Finally, he suggested, "Shall we read by the fire?"

Then he grinned, acknowledging what had become a dreadful embarrassment to her.

"Maybe then we will be better able to get through this novel." His eyes sparkled with mischief as though pleased with her discomfort. "I have the feeling it may be the only way you will be able to concentrate on this story."

She leapt at the suggestion. "Yes, yes. I think it would be best."

She found that seated opposite him by the fire she could relax at last. The warmth of the fire made her feel sleepy. She began to yawn.

"I think I will go to bed," she said and waved off his offer to escort her as usual.

But once in her bed, she shuffled about trying to sleep.

It was impossible. She decided to go below and have a snack. In the kitchens, she found a tray of cookies, poured herself a glass of milk and sat at the long worktable while she ate. Deciding she would try again to go to bed, she headed upstairs.

Tonight, the hallway was dark but for a sliver of light from beneath the library door. She remembered she had not kissed him goodnight. She could not resist slipping into the library. She opened the door. He was at his usual place before the fire, with a book in hand. He stood as she entered.

She walked to him and rested her hand on his shoulder, kissing him lightly on the mouth before leaning into that special place where his neck met his shoulder and breathing his scent as she loved to do. Her role as his lover had become common to her. And tonight, she was feeling too alone.

"I came to say goodnight. I was having trouble sleeping." She sighed and stepped back. "I needed to cool down."

His eyes travelled the length of her body. They rested on her breasts. The chill air from her stroll through the house had made her nipples erect, stiffly jutting out from her nightgown. He reached out and touched one, lightly squeezing it before he dropped his hand and turned towards the fire.

He kept his back to her. "Alexis, I am a man. You cannot do this to me. Put on a bloody robe before you come to say goodnight, for the love of god."

Her eyes filled with tears. She went back to her room to spend another lonely night.

She lay in bed and vowed she would try harder to withdraw from him. But she relished his company and enjoyed their time together. She sighed. It was becoming almost impossible not to caress him in some manner each time they came together.

The sound of Aran's door closing alerted her. She listened to him undressing. The walls between their rooms must be thin, she thought as she listened to the creak of his bed as he settled in. It was because of those thin walls she also knew he too was often restless, sometimes pacing and rustling about for hours before he either settled or left for the night.

Tonight, she too would struggle to sleep. Living with Aran and portraying his mistress was becoming harder and harder to bear.

Chapter Eight

Alexis tried to focus more of her time and attention on Rolande. She glanced at him now through her mirror. The two of them sat at her dressing table experimenting with different shades of rouge. He chose the brightest shade of red and carefully colored his full lips.

"Now this," he said, before rubbing his lips together and pursing them, "this is for a night of love."

Alexis laughed. He looked a sight in the garish shade. "It is too much, Rolande, and you know it."

"It is never too much," he said, rolling his eyes and tossing his head like a diva.

The sound of a door closing caught their attention. They both looked towards the door which joined her room to Aran's.

Rolande wagged his eyebrows and winked at her. "Maybe you can get the *monsieur's* attention with this."

They laughed again.

Alexis sighed. Like the rest of the household, Rolande

believed she was Aran's mistress. Aran had laid out their roles. He was so insistent they keep up the pretense at home, that even Rolande was fooled.

But recently Alexis noticed that there was a change in how Aran portrayed the ardent lover. When she first had arrived, his touch had felt perfunctory. Since the night in the library when he had touched her so intimately, his kisses had been more real. He would sometimes linger with his lips on hers, as though tasting her. His hands on her body also seemed different. It was as if he relished the feel of her. She knew she too had changed the way she touched him. It had become a sweet agony for her.

Rolande was distressed by the lack of sexual relations between them. For him, their arrangement was a disgraceful waste. He alone in the house knew the couple slept separately. He was forever trying to rectify the situation. He had insisted she purchase lingerie in a rainbow of colors and sexy styles. He was constantly hinting about the night's possibilities. Alexis would only smile at him. She was committed to following Aran's instructions regarding secrecy.

Aran knocked softly at the door before swinging it open. He leaned against the door frame and smiled at the two of them. "What can possibly be so entertaining?"

Alexis pulled her dressing gown more snuggly around her and laughed. "Rolande has found the perfect shade of rouge. It suits him."

Rolande smacked his lips together and the two of them collapsed in laughter.

Aran smiled at their antics. "I wonder if you might drag yourself away from the mirror for a moment, Rolande, and help me choose a wardrobe for tonight."

Rolande hopped up to do his bidding, disappearing into the adjoining room.

"Ah, you are going out again?" Alexis complained.

He had been out every night for a week.

Aran walked around behind her and laid his hands on her shoulders. His hands felt deliciously warm through the thin silk.

He grinned at her reflection. "Does this mean you miss me, princess?"

"Of course, I miss you." She looked up at him. "I know I promised not to be a burden. I have tried hard not to nag but eating alone here every night is becoming a little boring."

It was over a month since she had entered his home. The initial excitement of her visit to Paris had begun to wane. She was beginning to feel confined.

She looked at him and asked, "Why can you not take me with you? Would I be such an embarrassment to you?"

He leaned down and kissed the top of her head. She loved it when he played his role of amorous lover. Though she knew it was all an act, he was only staying in character as he had so often advised her to do, it had become real for her. She felt like his mistress.

"You cannot, my dear. The company I keep is not for you. My friends, leaders of Le Grande Army," he said sarcastically, "would only see you as another prize. You would be a new toy for them to play with and discard."

He traced his fingers along her chin, and then lifted her face slightly.

"You're not for them." He let his hands fall to her shoulders and gave her a little squeeze. Kissing the top of her head once more, he met her eyes in the mirror and said, "I know that this is difficult for you. Tomorrow we will spend the whole night together, I promise."

She looked at his reflection and teased him with a sexy smile. "The whole night?"

He laughed loudly. "You are becoming a flirt, my dear. Be careful, I may just take you up on your offer."

Rolande peeked his head around the corner. "I have the perfect ensemble for you, *monsieur*. You'll be so hot that even I will be unable to keep my hands off you."

"Ha." Aran smiled. "You are the model of restraint, Rolande."

He left the room, closing the door behind him.

Alexis sat at her dressing table and scowled at her reflection. She had hoped to dazzle Aran with another new gown. Wiping the rouge from her lips with disgust, she flung the cloth aside. There was not much point in dressing for dinner now.

She chose a plain day dress and went down to eat another lonely supper. She wished she had acquaintances in Paris. Aran had refused to take her with him to any of the events he attended in the evenings. It was becoming too solitary an existence. She wanted to be in public. At times, she was desperate for female companionship. If she could just spend one afternoon with ladies at tea, or visit with another woman, shopping or sightseeing, she thought she might be able to endure another month. Her world had shrunk. She had only Aran, Rolande, and her imagination to help her get through the days.

Alexis had learned to never ask him about his evenings. It was as if here in his domain he wished to forget whatever life he lived beyond its walls. What Aran did not understand was this insistence on compartmentalizing his life kept her caged in only the narrow existence of his time with her.

She was curious about his occupation. He did the work of a French merchant, but she knew it was secondary to his true objectives. Those objectives were what took him away from her tonight, and the many other nights he left her.

Aran had not been forthcoming with her about his activities, and she had not asked. She knew only that he was a spy. She marveled at the word, playing with it: spy, spy, spy.

Spying was a dangerous enterprise. Alone here in his home, or on the streets with Rolande, it was easy to ignore their reality. And Aran was protecting her here. He had her in a cocoon, safe from a world at war.

All she had was Aran. If nothing else, she had definitely gotten to know him better. She grinned to herself. Maybe she would even take Rolande's advice and seduce him. She laughed aloud at her audacity. In just a few short weeks, Alexis had moved a long way from the prim young woman who had been the toast of London this season. The role of mistress might be a disgraceful influence on her by the standards she lived by in London, but Aran had left her little else to focus on.

The more she thought of her role, and her imaginary courtesan mother, the more attractive she found it. She had never had a mother. Hers had died at her birth. Madame Celeste de Mal was her adoptive parent. She wondered idly what this mother would do if she were in her place.

And then she knew. Her stomach rippled with excitement as she considered her new project. She was Alexis De Mal, daughter of a famous courtesan, and she would control her own destiny. If Aran insisted that she have only her role as a mistress to focus on, then it would be a role she would excel with. Her new project would begin immediately.

She would seduce Aran.

She had her chance to dress extravagantly for supper the next night. She chose a dark red gown. It was cut precariously low across her bosom. It was in the modern style, cinched tight across her chest, then falling to the floor. She wore no petticoats but instead reveled in the new body movement in women's gowns. Each time she moved, the dress clung to her in all the right places.

She frowned at her reflection. "But do you think that Aran will be angry, Rolande? He wants me dressed conservatively."

"Oh, my love." He pecked her cheek affectionately. "I fear we have followed his instructions for too long. Take my word for it. Sometimes a man does not know what he wants."

He rubbed the furrows between her eyes with his slender fingers. "Quit worrying. You will destroy your face with these lines. You must trust me with this. Yes?"

Alexis looked at the cleavage her dress displayed. She grabbed the sides of her dress and pulled it up a little higher over her bosom. "I hope you are right, Rolande. But sometimes he seems uncomfortable when I am a little too alluring."

Rolande ignored her concerns. "Ooh la, la, you will have him at your mercy tonight for sure." He winked at her and rotated his hips suggestively. "You will get a little hoochie-coochie tonight for sure!"

"I hope he notices me at least," she said, sounding depressed. She wanted to entice him, to have him want her. Wishing she had worked harder to learn the art of flirtation, she cursed her insecurity and nervousness. Taking a deep breath, she said, "I am going to enjoy this night. He will be unable to keep his hands off me. It is exactly what I must do."

She repeated this mantra to herself until she felt more confident.

Finally, she smiled at her reflection in the mirror. Rolande came to stand beside her and the two looked at each other through the glass.

"Good. You will do well, my *cherie*. Now go. He will be ready for you."

Aran waited for her at the bottom of the staircase. She was enjoying her grand entry and even swayed her hips from side to side in an exaggerated fashion as she progressed down the stairs. She felt like a princess. He threw back his head and laughed at her performance.

It was not quite the reaction she wanted, but at least he had noticed. Best of all, he did not complain about her sexy attire. He only smiled at her appreciatively.

At supper, she forgot to flirt. She had asked the cook to prepare a special meal and he had outdone himself. They had escargot as an appetizer and lamb chops with a cognac Dijon cream sauce. It was so delicious that she ate far too much. Aran only smiled at her, pleased with her obvious enjoyment.

Aran regaled her with stories of his life in Yorkshire. He told her of his twin sister, Arabella, who could beat him at everything including wrestling. She laughed at the picture of him held helpless to the ground by a behemoth of a woman.

After supper, they played chess. Alexis had played him several games previously but had only beaten him on one occasion. She was so determined to defeat him that once again she forgot her plan had been to try to flirt with him.

"Checkmate!" She clapped her hands together. "I got you!"

She leaned back and gloated over her victory.

"You do, indeed. I have been on the run since you took my queen." Aran looked up from the board and smiled at her gleeful grin. "I thought I would let you win a game for once. It has been hard to see you as such a loser night after night."

"Oh, you did not!" she squealed, and he laughed. "Take it back. I defeated you fair and square!"

"Yes, yes." He rose and held out his arm for her to take. He chuckled as he tucked her arm close to his body. "I admit you won the match."

"And?"

"And you won despite my best efforts." He grinned at her.

"Much better." She tilted back her chin. "It's the second time I've won! I intend to defeat you soundly on every occasion now that I know your secret maneuvers."

He laughed loudly and continued to lead them up the stairs. "It's time to get some rest, my love. We have played for hours."

Aran escorted her to her room and opened the door for her. She stood at the threshold. She had failed miserably with her scheme to seduce him. She had been too wrapped up in enjoying his company to make any of her planned moves. Her face fell.

"What is it, princess?" he asked.

"I want you to kiss me goodnight."

He is clearly not interested, she thought, feeling her face burn.

Aran scanned her embarrassed face. Then slowly, he put his arms around her and pulled her tight against his body.

He kissed her gently on the lips. It was a chaste kiss and not at all what she wanted.

Alexis put both her arms around Aran and kissed him back, pressing her body against his. For a moment, Aran was still. Then he groaned.

It was as though flood gates opened. He bent down, kissing her with a brutal urgency she had never had from him. He pushed her against the doorframe and pressed his body into hers. One hand gripped her hair, and he yanked her head back, savaging her mouth, as he held her tight to him. Never in her life had she been in such a passionate embrace. His teeth bit into her lips. She gasped as his tongue found her mouth. His hips began to move rhythmically against her. He moaned and moved against her, his swollen organ thrusting into her belly.

His mouth left hers and he began to kiss her neck, hot wet kisses, desperate in their desire. His mouth trailed down to her chest, where his hands found and gripped her breasts. He pulled her dress down below her nipples. He sucked and nipped at them. And all the time his hips rotated against her. She put her hands in his hair and arched against him. She could only hold him, basking in the rippling sensations he could instill in her.

Then he straightened, holding her head into his chest with both hands. She put her arms around him, pressing him firmly against her, not wanting him to withdraw from her.

He rotated his hips one more time before he groaned. "No, princess. This is not right for you. I am not what you need."

He took a deep breath and arched back to look at her bare chest, then reached down and cupped her breast before pulling the bodice up over her.

"Aran," she whispered, "it's what I need."

Tears of frustration filled her eyes.

"No." He pulled back, dropping his arms from her. He looked at her disgruntled face and gave her a half smile as an apology. Leaning forward, he kissed her chastely on the lips. "Go to bed. I am sorry for this. It will not happen again."

He turned and hurried to his room.

Chapter Nine

Aran pulled on his greatcoat. He closed the door behind him and began walking down to the main boulevard to hail a cab. Taking a glance over his shoulder, he saw two shadowy figures cross the street behind him. He shrugged.

Let them follow me. I have nothing new to show them.

He had to leave his house. He could not survive another minute with Alexis tucked warmly into the room beside his. Imagining her there, with her beautiful red hair spread across the pillow, wearing the silk nightie she had worn the night she had come for her good night kiss, was a painful endeavor.

For the hundredth time, he cursed himself for the night he had lost all control and touched her between her silken thighs the way he had. If only he had pulled away from her after she had comforted him, but he had been able to smell her with his head cushioned against her body. She had been so fresh and wonderful. The feeling of her close to him had been so sweet. He remembered how she had trembled and become wet in his hands. Even now his body shook with the memory of her. And the taste of her. He squeezed his eyes closed to dispel the memory.

That had been his greatest mistake. There had been nothing but trouble for him since that night. It was as though he had, from that day on, claimed her as his. Tonight, he had been so close to throwing her on the bed and making love to her.

He wondered what it was about Alexis that had him so ensnarled. He had a lover. Gigi had been his friend and mistress for almost two years. Though they were not exclusive, she was always available to him. She was a godsend at the raucous parties he threw for the officers of the French army. He always kept her on his arm to avoid the attentions of the women.

He and Gigi had worked hard to bring to these events as many available women as possible. Courtesans, widows, and even married women who wanted a night of debauchery with no strings attached attended, providing their special entertainments for the men. Some of the women wore elaborate masks. Their identity was secret even to him. Aran suspected more than one society matron had succumbed to the temptation of a night of wild revelry without consequences. How Gigi recruited these creatures he had no idea. She seemed to be always aware of the goings on in the social world.

For a spy, such as himself, she was a valuable resource. If she suspected he was more than the French merchant he portrayed, she made no mention of it. Never had she asked him to explain his motives. Nor had he questioned her motivations, though he suspected she was an operative of some sort. It had been all too convenient when she entered his life and began to assist him.

It was always better to have the least information about

each other as possible to protect them should one of them be taken. He thought of Joseph Fouche, the legendary spymaster, and shuddered, feeling the noose tightening around his neck.

He hailed a passing hansom cab, certain he was being followed. They would rush to flag down the next cab and be on his heels. Aran made no attempt to lose his pursuers. He was visiting a mistress; one he was sure they were aware of. That he kept two women would be unusual, but it fit his profile of the Parisian playboy well.

His mind drifted back to Alexis as it was wont to do. He wondered again why he was so enamored with her. It was not just her body. He loved to be with her. With her, he allowed himself to be Aran Forsythe—the only time he could do so, and those moments were precious to him. Every evening he spent with her was a relief and a treasure. Just reading to her by the fire was a delight for him. He liked her open mind. She was always interested in his ideas, even if she disagreed with them and she often did. He smiled at the memory of one of their debates.

He had said, "I rather like Rousseau's philosophy of education. It appeals to me that the young be taught to reason."

"Hmmm," she responded. "For a man it is appealing, but not, I think, for a woman."

"What do you mean?"

"Well, consider Sophie's education as opposed to Emile's. He is taught to reason, while she is taught to obey her man without question. A bit ridiculous, don't you think?"

He had laughed. "Surely you believe the man should be head of the household?"

She had wrinkled up her nose. "No." She smiled. "I think a man should believe he is head of the household."

He had thrown back his head and laughed at her very feminine take on the role of women. "You might have the right of it, princess. Sometimes I think we men delude ourselves."

But now he knew she was right. Certainly, Alexis ruled him. It was torture to be around her, to touch her and caress her and not have her. Yet he wanted to spend every minute with her. He would do anything for her, he realized with a grimace.

When he reached Gigi's apartment, he could not resist a peek to his left. Just down the street a hansom pulled over to release its passengers. He hurried to her door.

He hoped Gigi was not entertaining tonight. He was going to have her, he decided. Maybe that would ease some of the strain of being in the constant presence of Alexis. When she answered the door, he peered around her shoulder.

She laughed. "It is quite alright." She swung the door open. "As you can see, I'm all alone."

He stepped inside and plopped down on the little couch in her receiving room. "I came by to share a brandy with you."

Gigi walked to a sideboard and splashed a generous amount into two glasses. She handed one to him and joined him on the opposite side of the couch. She was wearing a robe of sorts. She pulled her legs up onto the couch and tucked her bare feet beneath her, facing him. She looked as though she had planned for a quiet evening alone.

Gigi had coal black hair, with dark eyes to match. She preferred pale make-up with dark red lips. She was slender and petite, with a tough streetwise personality which contradicted her delicate appearance.

"What is it that has you so troubled lately Aran?" She sipped her drink watching him over the rim of her glass. "You've not been yourself."

Aran shrugged. "Just bored, I think, Gigi."

She set her drink down on the side table. Slowly, she began to unbutton her robe. She undid the robe to just past her breasts. Then shifting towards him on the sofa, she raised her robe to her thighs and ran her finger enticingly on its hem as if waiting only for his approval to reveal more.

"I can help you feel better, love." She gave him a sexy smile and purred, "If you let me."

Aran let his eyes roam over her, smiling at the display of her long, beautiful legs. He looked at her for a long time before he leaned forward and chastely kissed her cheek.

"You are beautiful, Gigi, but I can't." It was strange. Now that he was here and it was available to him, he knew he did not want it. He wanted Alexis.

She pursed her lips into a little pout and tucked her legs beneath her once more. As she refastened her robe, she said, "Something is very wrong with you, my stallion. It has been a month now since you have touched me. What is it?"

He sighed. He had not been attracted to Gigi since those first few days with Alexis. All he could think of was her. She consumed him. Somehow, playing with Gigi tonight would feel like a betrayal to her. Aran wondered if he was just torturing himself. Maybe he should reconsider and take Gigi up on her offer. But then he thought of blue-violet eyes accusing him and knew he could not.

He sighed and took another sip of his brandy. "I just wanted your company tonight. That is all."

Gigi shrugged. She appeared unconcerned. "Well, I

have some news which may just cheer you up. I have a new man for your party. An especially important man."

He was instantly alert. "Who?"

"I may or may not invite him to your party. You have been so distant from me lately I hardly can call you a friend."

"Who, Gigi?"

"A general. One who has exceptionally perverse tastes. Tastes he needs to keep top secret. When I heard this, I knew he would be eager to join our little entertainments. He can hardly be public with such persuasions. Napoleon frowns on such behavior, especially from his officers."

He leaned forward. "Who Gigi? You must quit teasing me."

She gave a triumphant smile. "General De Sole. But I am not sure I will invite him for you."

Aran's heart pounded in his chest. De Sole would be the biggest catch he had ever had. To become acquainted with him, to share the secret of his perversions, was a dream. Perhaps he could befriend him. If he were ever invited to his apartment, there would be a storehouse of information for him to steal.

Gigi saw his excitement and smiled. "I am not sure I want to share him with you, Aran." Her lips formed into a pout. "You have not been kind to me lately. You know I miss your body, yet you refuse to share it with me. Maybe we can make a little deal. Yes?"

She leaned forward and ran her fingers across his chest.

Aran felt his stomach turn. "What sort of deal, Gigi?"

"I will bring him to the party. I will try to get him involved in some racy activities. From what I have heard, it will not be too hard. But you, my love, must then do something for me." She looked at him and raised her eyebrows, while she slid her hand down towards his belt.

He waited while Gigi enjoyed the suspense, knowing what she would request. He held back his anger. "What, Gigi?"

"I want to be back in your bed." She looked at his expression of anger and quickly added, "Just one night in your bed. It is not much to ask, my love."

She reached between his legs and stroked him, smiling at his obvious response.

"Would you make a prostitute of me, Gigi?" He took her hand and pushed it away from him.

"Yes. Yes, I would. Tomorrow night, after the party." She shrugged, leaning back against the couch. "Take it or leave it."

He thought about De Sole. De Sole was the shining hero of the war on the Spanish peninsula, a war that the British were heavily engaged in. He could very well be his ticket home. A marshalled general! Outside of Napoleon, no one outranked him. He would be privy to all the information Aran had been assigned to find. It was an opportunity he could not refuse.

"It's a deal." The moment the words were out of his mouth, he regretted it. He swallowed the bile in his throat.

"Do not look so sad, love. It is only me, your friend. What is a little playtime between friends, eh?" There was a brief flash of anger in her eyes. She rose and patted his back on her way to pour herself more brandy.

She tilted the bottle toward him, silently offering him another. He shook his head. She poured herself a couple of fingers and drank it back in one swig. She set the glass down and leaned against the sideboard.

"Now then, we have another problem for tomorrow

night. Our venue has some sort of sewer issue." She wrinkled her nose. "I took the liberty of informing our guests, both male and female, we will be moving it to your house. It was all I could do on short notice."

She poured herself another brandy, but she only sipped it before setting it down on the sideboard. "So that leaves you, my love, to make all of the other necessary arrangements."

"Good god." His first thought was the problem he would have with Alexis. He would not risk her being exposed to the rowdy crowd who frequented his parties. There were no options. He would have to keep her safely locked up.

"I have to go, Gigi," he said, moving towards the door.

Gigi brushed past him and blocked his way with her body. Rising onto her toes, she kissed him lightly on the mouth, leaning into his body. He stood still with his arms at his sides.

She traced his tightly closed lips with her finger. "Do not be so forlorn, my love. It is only me, your Gigi. Perhaps if we have this little tete-a-tetes you will be mine once more."

Aran turned away from her with disgust, but it was himself he was most disgusted with.

Nudging her to the side, he opened her door. "I don't think this will get you what you want, Gigi."

Gigi watched him, her face both speculative and disappointed. "It is worth the effort for me, Aran."

He smirked, slipped out, and softly closed her door. He noted the two men down the street as he hailed a hansom cab and sighed. He had not given them much information tonight. As his coach passed them, he lifted his hand in a greeting, which they ignored.

On his way home, Aran forced the agreement to sell his

body in exchange for the introduction to De Sole from his mind. On some level, he was convinced that Gigi would not follow through with the bargain. It was too sickening to think about. The word prostitution was an ugly one; one he did not want to contemplate.

Aran concentrated instead of all the arrangements he would have to make. He would keep the servants he had employed for the job, transferring them to his home. His people would be given the night off. It was an arrangement they would be familiar with. His home servants were not equipped to deal with the depraved behavior he could expect from the guests who attended. Even Rolande would leave after preparations were complete; he too needed to be protected from this crowd. All the preparations would have to be transferred, food, alcohol, and musicians. There was much to do.

He would need to think of ways to keep boisterous behavior to a minimum. And he wanted everyone to be aware of a curfew. No stragglers would be allowed to hang about after dawn, when his hired help would be busily engaged in cleaning up. There could be no signs of the revelry for Alexis or his house servants to deal with in the morning.

Aran did not even want to contemplate the problems he would have locking Alexis in her room. He had the feeling she would not take it well.

Chapter Ten

The next morning, Aran was not at breakfast. Alexis sat at the table and picked at her food. To her horror, she felt an overwhelming urge to cry. Hot tears ran down her face. She picked up her napkin and wiped them away with disgust.

Aran had made it clear that there would be no relationship between them. He wanted her, that had been more than apparent last night. She thought about his mouth on her neck and shivered with the memory.

But now she was here eating a lonely breakfast. She enjoyed her time with him. If her attempts to seduce him meant he would avoid her company, she wanted none of it. It had been a stupid idea to try to seduce him. She had been listening too much to Rolande's encouragement. The last thing she needed was to destroy their friendship. He and Rolande were all she had in Paris.

She left the breakfast room and wandered towards the stairs. It promised to be another quiet day.

Maybe I will read a good book. There must be something up there that will appeal to me.

The receiving rooms were a haze of activity. Chandeliers were being taken down and polished. An unfamiliar servant was washing the windows and two more were setting up a bar in the largest salon.

"What is going on?" she wondered aloud.

She looked down the hall past the stairwell towards the kitchens at the back of the house. When the door swung open, it was apparent the staff were engaged in preparations of some sort.

She walked to the end of the room and down the short hallway to peek. Sure enough, the kitchens were ablaze with activity.

Climbing the stairs, she was determined to find Rolande and discover the cause. They were going to entertain. It would be such a joy to meet other people at last. There would be new people to meet. It was possible that Aran too had worried about their little scene last night. Perhaps this was his way of making amends.

She could not find Rolande anywhere. Like Aran, he seemed to have disappeared. She started going through her closets of new dresses looking for an outfit to wear this evening. She decided on a soft violet gown. It was appropriate for any occasion. Not too risqué, but very fashionable. She took it out and hung it on a hook in her room next to her dressing table. She found shoes to match. She even dug through her jewelry to find a suitable piece. A diamond brooch and matching earrings would be perfect.

She decided to avoid the hassle downstairs and lunched in her room. After lunch, she ordered a bath to better prepare her for the evening ahead. She wanted to impress Aran by being the perfect hostess. She would even take a nap. She wanted to be at her best should the party drag on until dawn as they sometimes had in London.

It was almost suppertime when she finally awoke. With a ripple of excitement, she eyed her new gown. It was going to be a glorious evening. She decided to wait for Rolande to dress her. His taste in fashion was impeccable; he would have the last word on her wardrobe choice. She pulled on her robe instead, wondering idly what was keeping Rolande. Then she remembered that he too would be busy with the party.

She heard the door to Aran's room open and smiled. A minute later, he opened her door and leaned against its frame in his usual stance. She gave him her biggest smile. He did not smile back. Instead, he looked around the room, his gaze lingering on the violet dress before he met her eyes. Tilting her head, she looked back at him with an unspoken question.

Rolande burst into the room. He carried a tray and set it on the little table by the door.

"I am so sorry to have neglected you today, my darling, but it has all been such a rush." Hustling over to her, he pecked her on the cheek. "You will have everything you want there on the tray. I must be going. I have too, too much to do!"

"Lock the door from the outside, Rolande, and leave the key on my dressing table," Aran said in a deadpan voice.

Rolande gave her a pitying glance and hurried to do his bidding.

Alexis sat down on her bed and looked at Aran. "I take it we are having a party?"

He responded with a slow nod.

"I am guessing I'm not invited?"

He nodded again. She stood and began rearranging the items on her dressing table. She was shocked. All day, she had anticipated a glorious evening and now this. Her eyes filled with tears, and she brushed them away angrily.

"Is it because I wanted you to kiss me? Is this my punishment?" She picked up her brush and threw it across the room.

It hit the wall then bounced into the center of the room.

He looked at the brush, then slowly met her gaze. "No, princess. There was a change of venue at the last moment. I meant to tell you about it, but I was unsure how to explain it to you. And then I missed you at breakfast." His face was serious. "I will not have you mixing with the dregs of society because that is what will be here. Hardened soldiers and the whores I bring in to serve them."

He walked into the room and put his hands on her shoulders, but she brushed them off in anger.

"Do not touch me!" She glared at him. "To think that all day, I was planning on being your perfect hostess. I am such a fool!"

She stared at her feet and fought back her angry tears.

His voice was soft but without intonation. "I will lock you in. No one will be able to get to you here. And you will not be able to get out. Only I will have the keys. There should be no one wandering about upstairs anyway. Please do not make a scene calling for help. It might be the death of us both." He put his hand under her chin and raised her head until she was forced to meet his eyes. "It is for your safety, Alexis. Remember that."

She slapped his hand away. "Do not expect me to thank you for that. And no, I will not make a scene although god knows I am entitled to one."

He stared directly into her eyes, then leaned in and kissed her. His kiss was a question, an appeal for understanding. She refused to give it to him. She stepped back and gave him a blank look.

"You had better dress. You don't want to be late for your guests," she said, turning her back to him and waiting for him to leave the room.

The seconds ticked by like years as she felt his eyes boring into her back. Then the door softly closed, and the locks snapped into place.

The party raged on for most of the night. Intermittently, the sounds of a piano and raucous singing filtered up from below. But the noise had been distant enough for her to sleep.

It was almost dawn when something awakened her. Voices came from upstairs. Aran had assured her the upstairs would be off limits.

She sat up in bed and listened.

A shrill voice was raised in anger. "No Aran, not the library. I refuse."

It was a woman. A woman talking to Aran. Alexis got out of bed and tiptoed to her door. Not feeling a moment's conscience at eavesdropping, she pressed her ear to it and listened to the conversation playing out in the hall.

"Shh. Be quiet, Gigi."

"Why? I cannot wake you. You are here with me, silly man. And now you must fulfill your obligation to me." The woman gave a high-pitched giggle. "You have made me wait too long. It is time for you to pay your debt, my love."

"Be quiet," Aran said. "Come along. I have the perfect place for us."

"No. I demand your bed. I am not a puta to be taken on a desk. We had a bargain, you and me. I completed my task and now it is your turn to fulfill yours. What is the matter, my love? Have I lost my appeal?" There was a long pause, then another throaty giggle. "I see I have not."

"Once more, Gigi. Once more, I must implore you not to command this price of me. I can give you anything else, anything you want." He sounded so forlorn and desperate.

Alexis bit her lip, keeping her ear pressed to the door.

"Gigi, please—"

"I know what I want, Aran." The woman sounded angry, her voice demanding. "I purchased it fairly and now you must fulfill your part of the bargain!"

"Shh! Yes, Gigi, I will give you what you want, but you must be quiet."

"And in your bed." Her voice was strident, insistent.

"In my bed." Aran sounded resigned, and not at all like an eager lover. For some reason this was even more dreadful for her to hear. She squeezed her eyes shut. Her heart ached.

She heard the couple enter Aran's room, as she returned to her bed. Then there were only muffled sounds from the room next door. She was sure that Aran was making love to another woman. Right here in their apartment.

She bit her fist until her hand was bleeding. Her pillow was wet with tears. She wanted to break down the door and drag the horrible woman out. Instead, she pulled her pillow over her head to block any sound.

After a time, she lifted the pillow tentatively. All was quiet.

Then the woman spoke again. There was a distinct whining tone in her voice. "Why so desolate, my love? You enjoyed it. I know you did."

There was a rustling sound as though they moved about.

"No. You have had what you came for, Gigi." Aran sounded desolate.

"Aran...?" The woman drew out the syllables of his name in an unspoken plead.

"Please just leave, Gigi. I need to be alone." His tone flat.

The bed squeaked as Gigi got up, followed by rustling sounds as she dressed.

"You will do, my stallion. You do very well, indeed. I think you have paid me in full, don't you? A whore's wage." The woman laughed, but there was no humor in it. There was an angry, vindictive tone to her voice. "I look forward to our next bargain, darling. It is such a pleasure doing business with you. You are the perfect little puta. You could make a living at it, Aran. I can see you now, advertising your wares—for a price!"

"Please just leave," Aran repeated listlessly.

Alexis closed her eyes as a wave of painful remorse filled her. It was almost as though she felt his hurt.

"You agreed to the deal, Aran. I brought you De Sole. You received your pay. Why begrudge me mine?"

His door closed. Alexis listened dully to the silence from his room.

A long time later, Aran unlocked the door to their adjoining room. She waited, listening to the awful silence from beyond the door. She was terrified that he would come in, having no idea what she could possibly say to him. There was a soft thump on the door as though he set his head against it.

He spoke through the door: "I am sorry, princess."

She finally fell asleep. Hours later, the sound of a bath filling awakened her, and knew that Aran too was awake. She sat on the edge of her bed and debated her next course of action. She washed her face and cleaned her teeth. She sat at her dressing table and brushed her hair. Still, she could not think of what to do. It was almost as though she could feel Aran in pain. It was strange, but the emotion she felt most for him right now was pity.

She did not know why the whole situation with Gigi had occurred, but she knew it was not his choice or to his liking. She had heard the conversation. Whatever deal he had made, his payment had taken place in his bedroom. He had sold himself to that woman.

She decided to confront him. She marched into his bedroom and across to his dressing room. He was lying in the tub with his eyes closed.

"I need a towel, Rolande. I think I can face the day now."

"Can you? I am not sure I can."

Aran's eyes snapped open. He sat up so abruptly in the tub the water gushed from its sides. Then he simply stared at her. They looked at each other for what seemed like hours. This was her Aran, her best friend, her savior, and very soon her lover. He was her man. A little more than a month, that was all it had taken to know Aran was hers. But in those few weeks they had spent every day in each other's company. It was more than most courtships would have in a year.

She was not willing to share him with Gigi or anyone else. She pressed her lips together in a determined line. As the adopted daughter of the famous courtesan, Celeste De Mal, she had done a shoddy job. Her new mother would be disappointed with her.

"I see your whore has left," she said, still looking into his eyes.

He rose from the tub and stepping out, stood before her,

naked and dripping. "She might be a whore, but I am the prostitute, princess."

His eyes looked so remorseful, so damaged, she could not resist stepping forward and taking him into her arms. She held his wet body against hers and rocked him slowly back and forth.

Rolande entered the room with the towels. "Oh! So sorry."

Alexis pulled back from Aran and took a towel from Rolande's hands. She tossed it at Aran. "Rolande, Aran's bed needs to be stripped. Pillows, sheets, blankets, and all of it. I want the whole thing laundered immediately."

Rolande raised his eyebrows but said nothing.

"And see that my door is unlocked. I want to go down and meet Aran for breakfast." She walked back to her room without a backward glance and began to dress for the day. She had no idea how to handle this situation. Aran was a spy. That was apparent. That it was destroying him was also apparent. She was not going to allow it to happen. It was time for him to confide in her. If this was her man, then it was time she quit behaving like a child and began looking after him.

She grimaced. She had indeed been behaving like a child—romping in Paris while he had been carrying the burden of their dangerous position here in France.

"Well, that is over now," she said aloud, her face set and determined.

They were bloody well going to deal with this together. And then, he would bloody well be her lover and no one else's.

The proper young woman she had been just weeks ago objected to her decision as rash and inappropriate, and her stomach lurched. She squashed the thought. Instead, she cursed her protected life as proper English girl. Nothing in her former life as a debutant could help her now.

Her last attempt to seduce Aran had been a dismal failure. This time the stakes were higher—the image of his face as he rose from the bath haunted her. He needed her help. She had to be both his lover and his partner. Somehow, she would need to find the strength and the maturity to accomplish both.

Chapter Eleven

Aran dressed slowly. He had hoped he would be granted at least one boon in this disgusting situation—that Alexis had slept through the fiasco last night. But no. Obviously she had been awake behind the door and had heard everything. He could not imagine what she must be thinking now. He had tried hard to lure Gigi away from his bedroom. She would have none of it. He detested the life he lived in Paris.

Even now he felt as though he could gag. He could never do such a thing again. This job was destroying him. He could feel everything he had been, and every ounce of honor he once held so dearly, draining away from him.

I have been a pimp and now I am a prostitute.

That Alexis knew what he had done made it so much worse. She was witness to his lechery. He closed his eyes tightly. He wanted to scream or leave. But there was nowhere to go.

Yet it had to be done. Gigi had given him both an introduction to General De Sole, and the promise he would attend the party. De sole was Napoleon's major general in

Spain. Aran had to know why the man was back in Paris. Furthermore, if anyone knew about Napoleon's plans for this spring, it would be De Sole.

Last night, Aran had carefully cultivated the man. De Sole would definitely attend the next party. The sooner he found the information he needed, the sooner he could be done here. Leaving France before he lost his sanity, or his life, was his goal. And now he could add Alexis to the plan. He had to get her out safely as well.

Alexis. How she must hate him now. He ran his hand through his hair as he sat at his dressing table. Damn these thin walls! There was no doubt she had also heard Gigi brag about purchasing his body. That Alexis had put her arms around him this morning was confusing. He had needed her comfort so much; he had just accepted it.

He looked at himself in the mirror. For a second, he wanted to smash the reflection of himself he saw there. He turned and headed for the breakfast room. It was time to face her.

Alexis waited until he had finished a heaping plate of scrambled eggs and ham before she addressed him. While he ate, he noticed she merely moved the food around her plate, avoiding his gaze.

Now she set her cutlery down and looked at him.

"Aran, I need you to talk to me." She was speaking in Spanish. "I need you to tell me exactly what it is you are doing."

She stood and closed the door to the kitchens before she continued. She was being careful to keep her voice soft. "I know you are an English spy, but that is not enough. I want to know the specifics. I want to know precisely what your mission is."

Aran stared at her dumbfounded. He had expected

tears. That she wanted to know about his work now, when he knew the events of last night must be fresh in her mind, confounded him.

He scrutinized her. Alexis was not devastated as he had expected. Instead, she seemed determined. Her lips were pressed together in a firm line. This was an Alexis he had not seen before.

His mind shifted to her question. He was accustomed to keeping his secrets. Even his contacts were on a need-to-know basis. Gigi and he had worked together for two years, and never once had they shared their objectives.

"Aran, if you are discovered, I will be discovered too," she said. He noted the anger in her voice. For some bizarre reason, it pleased him. "I have a right to know. These actions of yours control my destiny. My life rests upon your success or failure."

Aran sipped his coffee and looked at her over the rim of his cup. This was indeed a different Alexis than the happy brat who had graced his home these past few weeks. She was deadly serious. Trusting her was not an issue; he did not doubt her identity or her ability to keep his secrets. He contemplated the risk to her should she be aware of his goals.

As though she read his mind, she said, "The risks are the same for me whether I am aware or not. In fact, I think the risks may actually be lower. Think about it, Aran. Should I ever bump into an acquaintance of yours, should your Gigi or even an army boy show up here unannounced, I will at least be prepared enough not to make a dangerous mistake."

Aran thought about those scenarios. She was right. So far, he had been able to keep her a secret, but it would take only one mistake and his world would learn of her presence. She would be safer knowing.

He cleared his throat and looked at the kitchen door. Standing, he offered her his arm. "I will confide in you, but not here. Come, we will go to your room.'

Once in her room, he settled her down on the edge of her bed and sat next to her. He spoke in Spanish.

"You know I am a spy. I was forced into this assignment after being caught at sea with a load of contraband. I was set up." He brushed his hand through his hair. "But that is unimportant. I was promised I would be able to complete one task and be done with it. Unfortunately, I was too good at my job. I now have another assignment."

He explained the British suspicions about Napoleon's increasing frustration with Russia. He explained too how important it was to England to know if and when Napoleon planned to attack.

"If Napoleon gathers troops to do a massive attack on Russia, he will have to take troops and experienced personnel from all over Europe. For instance, your father is in Portugal. Every couple of weeks, they make an excursion into Spain and attack French strongholds. Imagine the advantage they would have if they knew experienced leaders were not present. Or if they knew half the troops in a post had been removed."

She nodded in understanding. He pressed on. It was time to give her specifics.

"I need to befriend the French leaders here in Paris. I need to find out first if an attack is imminent and second, what troops from where will be participating. Therefore, I have worked hard to become the dream of the French military leaders. I am rich and like to party. Even better, I have parties with a wide variety of beautiful women for them to enjoy. And all the time I am casually fishing for information. When invited to their parties, I search their libraries. I read their letters or steal them outright."

"Gigi is one of those women at all the parties. She wants me. Last night, I gave her my body in exchange for having General De Sole as an acquaintance. I agreed to the bargain. My precious honor is nothing when compared to the English lives hanging in the balance." He took her hands and squeezed them, willing her to understand. "De Sole is a big fish for me, Alexis. Until now, I have only been able to cultivate corporals or even sergeants.

"But we learned that De Sole had a side of his personality he has kept secret from his peers, other generals and especially from Napoleon. He loves to party. Not the sedate parties of the upper echelons, but rough affairs where he can behave as foully as he wishes. Normally that brand of behavior is restricted to whore houses, Alexis. This public debauchery would not be tolerated by Napoleon, especially by his generals. But here, in my home, I can provide it for him. And it can be kept relatively private."

He looked at Alexis to see if his language upset her. As an English lady, she may not even have heard the word whore spoken in her presence.

Her face remained impassive. She was listening intently.

"And he has a taste for wild women. Gigi could bring me him. Gigi is a friend. Until recently, she has also been a lover. It has been convenient for me to be her lover. She brings lustful widows and courtesans to my parties." He smirked. "I had withdrawn from Gigi, which annoyed her. This time, she forced me to sell my body for her favors."

He looked down and drew a breath. "French society is more decadent than prudish England. There is no shortage of promiscuous women here, or men, it seems. My French persona included."

He gave her a half smile. "I admit their behavior was shocking to me at first. The depravity of some of the parties is more than I expected. The army men can be brutes, and some of the women are insatiable creatures." He looked her directly in the eyes. She must understand the extent of the dissipation he was portraying. "And I must play a role. I am the procurer. I must be more decadent than them all. I must become one of those creatures I often so despise. This is the man and the life I have kept you from, Alexis."

She took a deep breath. He regretted telling her what he was; he was not the knight in shining armor she may have imagined, but a despicable creature. He knew he had in many ways lost himself in the role he played. That he had become Monsieur Garscon.

"Have you had any success?" she asked, not commenting on the scandalous life he was forced to live. "And what will be sufficient for your superiors?"

Her questions surprised him. He scanned her face. She had a serious expression but was by no means appalled by his revelations.

He had expected her shock and outrage. Instead, she had accepted the explanation of his life here as though it was of little consequence, as though it was only his duty and responsibility. Perhaps it was because she was a general's daughter. Sacrifice and duty to one's country would have been concepts she had been raised on. He expelled a long breath.

"A little. I know there is an influx of trained military personnel returning to Paris. De Sole for instance is one. He has just returned from Spain. I passed that information to my contact yesterday. I need more. So far, the military has kept any plans for a spring campaign a strictly guarded secret. I am not even sure invasion plans exist. Even an idea of dates would be of help."

He looked at the floor, then gazed into her eyes. "I need the invasion to be a reality. And soon. I need to get out of here. Rouche is closing in, but more than that I need it for me ...you see, there are times when I am sure I cannot last another day. And then there are times I am afraid I have become as depraved as the man I portray. Having you here has been a redemption for me. You keep me grounded, Alexis. Through you I remember who I am."

Alexis did not reply as she studied him, expression unreadable. He prayed he had not lost her. His life in Paris would be unbearable without her.

Chapter Twelve

Alexis put her arms around him and held him, while her mind raced. She thought of his conversation in the hallway with Gigi, and his degradation later when she had prepared to leave. She squeezed her eyes shut to avoid tears. This was not the time. She would not heal him with her tears. Today would be about helping him find the man he was, her man. Aran had once saved her, and she was determined to repay the favor.

I am not the needy child that arrived in Paris a lifetime ago. I am a woman, and I will care for what is mine.

She pulled back from him and smiled. "What do you have on your agenda for today?"

He seemed relieved by her change of subject. "Nothing. There is not even a party tonight."

"Good. Because it is time you took me for a walking tour on the streets of Paris again. It has been days since I have eaten in a French bistro."

He looked at her and laughed. It was as though the

weight of the world had lifted from his shoulders. Some of the sadness left his eyes. He looked a little more like the Aran she was familiar with. She gave him an appreciative smile.

"There is nothing in the world I would rather do than spend the entire day with you. A walking tour it is then." He smiled so broadly she felt her heart twist in her chest.

They spent the day exploring the streets of central Paris. As the day progressed, he became more animated. His home in Marais was within walking distance of the Louvre. They gazed at the famous works of art. Aran was interested in the classics. He gave her the history and backgrounds to a variety of painters and their works. The extent of his knowledge surprised her.

She was surprised to note the Mona Lisa, which she had heard so much about, was just a small rendition of an Italian girl. "She looks so ordinary, so unaware she has become a legend."

Aran laughed. "Maybe that is part of her charm."

After the Louvre, they enjoyed lunch at a bistro, with a view of the Seine.

Aran pointed out Napoleon's new bridge in the distance. "It is the first of its kind, Alexis. It is the Pont des Arts, famous for its construction in iron." Aran looked serious for a moment. "And beyond it is the St. Denis district. This is where you will find the homes of the new rich. Mostly the new elite are members of the military command. War is a money maker for Napoleon and his cohorts."

"I thought the Marais district, where you reside, is the most desirable?"

"Not anymore, my dear. My townhouse is where the old aristocrats resided. The new rich prefer the St. Antoine or

St. Denis areas." He laughed at her look of disappointment. "Don't worry, my love, it's still a respectable part of town for a young playboy."

After lunch, they walked to the Palace Royal, or the Palais du Tribunat, as it was now to be called. The new name had not caught on and it was still referred to by the traditional title. Its famous gardens were surrounded by hundreds of shops, cafes, and salons. The shopping here was said to be the best in the world.

"The Duke of Orleans saved his neck from the guillotine by creating this center," Aran said. "Opening this portion of his palace up to the public made him popular to the mobs. The women loved the shops too much to have him killed."

"I can understand that sentiment. It is indeed a wonderful experience." Alexis held Aran's arm as they strolled the gardens, enjoying the view of the shopping centers with their tall windows, each filled with displays of merchandise. The famous grounds gave the illusion one was visiting the palace itself; the whole impression was one of grandeur. "I am going to come here to roam the shops on my own. I may need a week at least."

"All of the finest luxury items can be purchased here." He chuckled. "It is said Charlotte Corday purchased the knife she used to kill Marat here in the Arcade. At one time it was even a favorite haunt of prostitutes. They added new variety to the list of purchases which could be made here."

Alexis glanced at him. He looked genuinely happy.

"I think what I like best is the absence of muddy streets," she said. "Strolling along these paved walkways is much finer than battling the dirty lanes."

"It is. And you are not alone in that, my dear. The crowds love it. Every day the upper and middle classes fill the center. And everywhere in Paris it is imitated. It is what will make Paris the shopping center of the world."

They walked in silence, window shopping.

"Oh, look!" Alexis grabbed his arm. "It is a doll. She looks a bit like me."

"She does. It's all that horrendous red hair."

She punched his shoulder playfully. "I know you love my hair." She touched the curls which protruded from her bonnet. "And it is not red. I think it is darkening to a fashionable auburn."

He laughed. "Oh, god no. Your hair is red. It cannot be more red." He pulled her into the shop. "Let's take a closer look at this doll."

Once inside, he decided to purchase the doll. It was not an easy purchase. Aran haggled. For at least twenty minutes, he and the shopkeeper argued. At one point, it seemed as though they were about to come to blows. Alexis was surprised when the two of them settled on a price at last. After all that, the shopkeeper thanked him profusely and Aran shook his hand like an old friend.

Once back in the square, Alexis pulled back the brown wrapping to look at the doll. She ran her fingers over its delicate porcelain face. "She has brown eyes, not like mine at all. But she is lovely."

Aran leaned over and looked more closely. "She does. I suspect the doll is modeled on your famous mother, Celeste de Mal. We will fix that and have her look more like Celeste's beautiful daughter."

He led her to the art shop on the corner of the Rue de Valois. Once inside, he had a quick conversation with the gallerist. The man brought them to a back room where a young Frenchman was at work on an easel next to a tall window.

After a discussion which involved the artist leaning forward and gazing into her eyes as though he was inspecting a foreign object, he agreed to repaint the eyes of the doll. While the artist worked, she considered the discovery of a doll fashioned in the image of her adoptive mother and smiled. It could only be a good omen; a talisman to give her the strength she needed. In minutes, the eyes were a deep violet.

Aran was satisfied. "Now, my dear, she looks more like my princess."

After a much-needed break at a café for delicious French cheese and breads, they began to wander back to the townhouse. Alexis held his arm and leaned closer to him. It felt warm and secure in his presence.

She sighed and enjoyed their walk in silence. It had been a marvelous day. Best of all, Aran seemed rejuvenated.

Once home, Alexis prepared with care for their evening. It was time to begin the second part of her plan. She was going to seduce Aran and this time she was determined to succeed.

Rolande ran her a bath. She lay back in the tub and looked up at him. "I need your help, Rolande."

Rolande pulled his stool next to the tub. "What is it, my friend? What has you so concerned?" He looked down at her and frowned. "I admit I have worried for you since the *puta* found the *monsieur's* bed. This is not a good thing."

He shook his head with disgust.

Alexis waved her hand as though dismissing the entire Gigi incident. "No, it is not that. I need your help to seduce Aran."

He chuckled. "I can help you. I am an expert in the field of love. No one can compete with Rolande in this matter." He held up a towel. "Up, up my love. It is time to prepare."

Rolande went into action. For him, this plan of hers was long overdue.

Selecting the proper gown for supper had been a trial for him. He finally chose an emerald-green silk. "And under this, my dear, you will wear no petticoats."

"You don't think it is too much?" Alexis stood in front of her mirror. The material clung to her. "I think you can almost see my body through this silk. You don't think this is taking the body movement a little too far?"

"You are at home, *cherie*. It will be for the *monsieur's* eyes only. It is perfect. How can he resist this temptation?" He pulled back her chair. "Now we will fix that marvelous hair of yours."

He brushed out her hair and experimented with various ideas. "I love your hair. It is not the fashion, but it should be. You must never color it. The world is full of fashionable brunettes. Who needs another, eh?"

He finally decided on a loose twist, with a few curled tendrils falling naturally upon her bare shoulders.

"Very sexy," he said, standing back to admire his handiwork. "You are quite beautiful, my love. It is a gift. You must treasure it."

Alexis chewed her thumbnail.

Rolande slapped her hand. "No, my dear. You must be confident. It is *tres* important."

"I have another problem, Rolande." She looked at him with wide eyes. "I... I am a virgin, Rolande."

"Oh, my god." His dark eyes scrutinized her from her toes to her head as though the evidence could be seen on her body. She felt as though she had just told him she was a leper. "*Merde*! Santa Maria! How can this be possible? I knew something was amiss. But to be a virgin? Mon du!"

"Yes, well, we have not gotten around to it I suppose."

Rolande looked at her with renewed horror. "You have not gotten around to it? Aye, yi, yi!"

Not wanting to look like a complete failure, she said, "He wants me. He has kissed me."

Rolande widened his mascaraed eyes.

"It was a deeply passionate kiss. He rubbed his body against me, and I could feel it...you know." Her cheeks burned with embarrassment.

Rolande collapsed onto her bed and sat there completely dumbfounded. Alexis turned in her chair and faced him.

"Is it such a problem then?" she asked, concerned.

She wanted to move the relationship between her and Aran forward. She did not want him to see her as his ward, or heaven forbid, his sister. She wanted to be his lover in reality, not just in name only. The incident with Gigi had solidified her determination to claim Aran as hers in every way.

"What shall I do? Is it hopeless then?"

Rolande waved away her question. "Give me a minute, *cherie*. I must think this through."

Alexis watched Rolande as he regained his composure. Finally, he smiled. She sighed in relief. He had a plan. Any assistance he could give her with this problem would be welcomed.

"I am sure the master knows that you are inexperienced, yes?" he asked, rubbing his chin thoughtfully.

"I would imagine he does. I have not told him, of course, but he would assume, I think."

She wondered what she could confide about her life as a young English lady. Few women would be protected more from the realty of sex than the upper-class English lady. Young ladies were strictly supervised. Most went to their marriage bed with little idea of what was involved. Alexis had a vague notion about what went on but that was all.

"Yes, he would assume that I am innocent in all this. And worse, Rolande, I really do have no idea of what to expect."

Rolande laughed. "I think your virginity will be an attraction, my love. We will hope for that. I will not tell you just yet how to please him. We will save this for later. Yes? We must trust the *monsieur* with this. He cannot be a complete idiot. He will help you, I think." He looked at her and asked, "What exactly do you know about it? And do not be a miss. You must tell me."

"Well, I know something will happen with our bodies. That we will join in some way which involves his..." She gestured to her lap, feeling her cheeks flame again. "I have also heard it must be tolerated. I was given the impression it is a nasty event women endure."

Rolande slapped his hand to his forehead and groaned. "We have much to talk about. First and most important, it is to be a fabulous experience. You will enjoy it after the first time. This I must teach you. Nothing is more necessary than you find pleasure in him."

Rolande began to explain from the beginning. He told her about how it might hurt the first time and why. "But do not worry, my love. The pain will be quickly gone, or so I have heard."

He focused his talk on the importance of enjoying Aran's body. He went into great detail about the wonders of a man's body which made Alexis smile. Aran was right; Rolande loved men and everything about them.

When he began to explain the workings of a penis, Alexis laughed. "Ew, what men must put up with."

When he told her about how she could touch and kiss it

all, she burst into hysterical laughter. "It is too much." She held her belly and gasped. "This cannot be right."

Rolande went on to tell her funny stories of his experiences. The stories became outrageous. It just got worse and worse.

The two of them had collapsed with hilarity when Aran's voice interrupted them from the doorway. "What may I ask has the two of you so giddy?"

Alexis glanced down at the buttons on his trousers and burst into laughter once more.

Aran gave Rolande a suspicious look. "What exactly have you been telling her, Rolande?"

Rolande shrugged. "Only a few necessary bits of information on the facts of life. My poor Alexis had been grossly uninformed."

Aran scowled at him. "I am not sure you should have done this, Rolande."

He looked at Alexis with concern.

"Oh, he should have. It is too entertaining." She smiled as she stood and took his arm. "I will definitely be trying out this new toy soon."

She gave him a mischievous grin and brushed her body against him intimately.

"Rolande!" Aran was not amused. "You must not corrupt her!"

Alexis pulled him towards the door. "Do not be angry with poor Rolande. I insisted he tell me. And it is time for us to go down for supper." She drew back away from him and showed him her gown. "Do you like it?"

She twirled about and faced him again. She purposely pushed out her chest, knowing that the dark pigment from around her nipples would peek out from the bodice, and gave him a sexy smile.

He turned to Rolande and scowled once more. Roland shrugged and winked at Aran before Alexis pulled him to the door.

If she had her way, and she was determined she would, their relationship would be different by morning.

Chapter Thirteen

Despite her determination to seduce Aran, or maybe because of it, Alexis found herself feeling shy at dinner. For all her bravado earlier, she was at a loss. How did one go about a seduction? She took a deep breath and began. One thing they had always enjoyed together was conversation. It was a start.

"Tell me more about me more about your time as a smuggler. You have not confided much to me about it."

Alexis found he most enjoyed talking about his life in England. She knew too, she would be his sole confidant on the subject. To his new friends, his life in England did not exist.

"I was a failure as a sailor. I was caught, do not forget. But I do have one of the fastest luggers on the water."

He began to explain the variations on his ship which allowed for increased speed. It was not the topic which interested her, but the way he became animated when he talked of home.

"Its cabin was rigged with all sorts of hidden devices."

"Devices?"

"Secret compartments." He laughed. "The desk has no less than three hidden compartments. The first one is easy to find. That way a revenue man might think he has found the prize and quit his search. The other two are more difficult. You could also slide back the wall of the cabin to find a whole storage compartment. And then of course there are the hidden holds."

He looked at her and smiled. "But enough of that. What would you like to do with the rest of the evening? Shall I beat you at chess?"

She laughed. "I told you I know all your strategies now. No. I thought we might take a stroll in the garden. I know it's dark, but I feel like I could use the fresh air."

"Ah, it would be my pleasure." He walked around the table and offered her his arm. When she rose from her chair, he looked at her gown with a frown. "That dress is a bit beyond the pall, don't you think? It is almost a scandal."

The lamp behind her had rendered it transparent.

She gave him a sultry look. "I know. I thought the same. But Rolande says it is to be worn only at home. It is for your pleasure alone. A gift for you."

"Well, if it is a gift for me then I must enjoy it." He brushed his fingers along the top of her bodice, then took her arm, pulling her close. "To the garden then."

They walked out onto the terrace. The night was clear and warm. In front of them was a small lawn banked on the far side with flower beds, then a thick hedge. It felt enclosed and protected.

"It is hard to believe we are in the city of Paris. It seems so secluded and quiet," Alexis said as they walked out onto the grass. She looked up at the night sky. "And the stars are beautiful tonight."

"They are shinning for us." Aran was quiet for a moment. "Have you ever wondered how far away they must be? Science tells us the distance is incomprehensible. Tonight, they feel as though we could reach out and touch them."

She nestled closer into his body, and he slid his arm around her waist.

"Are you cold?"

"Not when you hold me close," she said and laid her head upon his chest. He held her snug against him as they stared up at the sky.

She rolled her head against his chest and breathed deeply, loving the smell of him. It made her feel safe and protected.

"My twin sister and I used to lay under the stars forever. Do you see that bright one? It's the North star." He pointed. "And just there is the big dipper."

She listened while he pointed out the constellations one by one. Some of them she had never heard of before. He showed her the seven sisters and told her the tale of its mythical origins.

"You love the classics," she said.

"I do. I think if I had had my choice, I would have been a scholar." He sighed. "But I didn't. I was instead duty bound to find a way to save our beleaguered estate. It has led me here."

"But there is good to be found here too. Today you were able to enjoy some beautiful works of art in the Louvre," she reminded him.

"This is true," he said. "There are many beautiful sights here. Not the least this one."

He raised her chin and kissed her. This time, he was gentle. He sucked her bottom lip into his mouth and grazed it with his teeth. Then he twisted her around so that she faced him squarely and pressed her body against his while he explored her mouth. His warm hands ran the length of her back. She shivered.

He arched back and looked at her face. "You are the most beautiful woman I have ever known."

She could only smile at him in response.

He kissed her lightly. "Come on, Let's go in. You are getting chilled.

She took his arm as they walked through the patio doors into his large salon. It looked beautiful with its soft amber lighting and high ceiling. The room had been designed to be used for a small ball. Carpets graced the floors along the walls, upon which sat the elegant furnishings. The center of the room, however, was tiled and sported a lovely gold and azure pattern.

Alexis let go of his arm and spun on its smooth surface.

"I wish we could dance," she said. "It has been so long since I have danced."

Aran watched her with a half-smile upon his face. He stepped forward and took her hand in his. With a perfect half bow, he brought her hand to his lips.

"May I have this waltz, my princess?"

He was the perfect English gentleman.

She grinned at him and graced him with a deep curtsey. "I would be honored, sir."

He took her in his arms and began to hum the Viennese waltz. She was surprised by his perfect beat. He was a graceful and elegant dancer. Alexis tilted her head back, enjoying every minute of it as they twirled around the room. She wished the waltz would never end.

When he finally slowed to a stop, she looked up at him. "That was the most perfect waltz I have ever had."

"I am a man of many talents." He laughed and pulled her close. "But it grows late, and I think I will take my fair maiden back to the safety of her room."

Alexis said nothing but her stomach flipped with anticipation. The hardest part of the evening was just beginning. She would have to seduce him. Despite Rolande's instructions, she still felt insecure and afraid. Somehow, she would have to be irresistible to him.

You must help me Celeste, my adoptive mother. You must send me the courage.

They reached her door.

"You are very quiet," he said. "What could have you so lost in thought?"

She turned and faced him. "Only that I have had the best of days and the most extraordinary evening."

"I am glad. It has been marvelous for me too." He kissed her chastely on the lips. "Have a wonderful night, princess."

"I hope to." She smiled at him and entered her room.

Rolande had laid out the most outrageous outfit. Alexis held up the sheer nightie and gasped. Her stomach tingled with apprehension.

If she was going to do this thing, she had better get on with it. She stripped off the gown and tossed it on the bed. After donning the lingerie, she stood and stared at her reflection.

Her body was clearly visible through the thin material. She rubbed her nipples. It was a procedure Rolande had shared with her. He had considered it a necessity in all his encounters. She watched fascinated as they swelled and jutted against the silk fabric.

She had heard Aran undress, but there was no sound now from his room. It was time. She took a deep breath before she marched to his door and flung it open. She grimaced as it smashed against the wall. Closing her eyes, she took a calming breath.

When she opened them, Aran was propped up in his bed. He was bare chested and held a brandy in his hand. His mouth was slightly ajar, and he stared at her.

He recovered quickly. "Is there something wrong, Alexis?"

She could only stand there, frozen. His eyes traveled up and down the length of her body—first once and then a second time—and then lingered on her breasts. He slowly reached over and set his brandy on the side table. He looked at her curiously, keeping his eyes on her face.

"Alexis?" His voice was soft, almost a whisper.

"I..."

There was nothing to be said. She strode around the bed and threw back the covers. Pulling the silly nightie over her head, she tossed it to the floor, and then crawled in beside him.

"Alexis, what are you doing? You cannot sleep here." He sounded slightly panicked, as he half rose from the bed, bracing himself up on an elbow.

She shifted closer to him and rubbed her naked body against him. Then she reached up and gently pulled his hesitant form down next to hers. Her head was against his chest, where she smelled his scent. She felt his smooth nakedness next to her. Her stomach clenched as she pressed herself against him, running her hands down the length of his broad back. He was hard and muscular.

"Alexis, for the love of god!" He sounded desperate and for some reason it made her smile.

She leaned back so he could see her face, and her cheek brushed against his nipple. She turned and kissed it, sucking gently until it was tight and erect. She reached down and grasped his organ. It was hard and throbbing. She wrapped her hand around it, feeling its silky smoothness.

He groaned. It was a painful sound. "Alexis, you can't do this."

"It is time, Aran," she whispered. "We cannot go on like this any longer. I am your mistress. I want all of what that means. I need you, Aran."

She took his hand and placed it on the soft red curls between her thighs. "Please help me, Aran. I don't know what to do."

He made a noise that sounded like a growl and rolled her beneath him. He kissed her, gentle at first, then slowly became more forceful. He began to kiss her cheeks and her neck. She shivered when she felt his hot breath on her. She ran her hands up and down his beautiful strong back and marveled at the play of muscles beneath her palms.

He kissed her breasts. They felt hard and swollen beneath his hands. He sucked and licked, and she moaned as she enjoyed the feel of him. His hands found the sticky wetness between her legs. She was shocked by the slippery feel of herself, worrying that Aran would be horrified, but he only groaned and muttered something about beauty.

Then he was licking and sucking her. She felt tight, aching with an incomprehensible need, and knew only that he must not stop. Reaching down, she gripped his hair, arching her body towards him and holding him tight against that warm wet place between her thighs. A wave of intense pleasure flooded her and called out his name. Her body began to spasm. It was a glorious experience. She lay back against the pillow, enjoying a sense of complete satisfaction.

Aran slid up her side, then rolled on top of her and kissed her mouth. She could taste the salty sweetness of her body on his lips. He reared above her, and she smiled a slow sexy smile at him. She felt lethargic and relaxed.

He smiled back. "It is only just beginning, princess."

He reached down and slid his fingers slowly in and out of her. Remembering their experience together in the library, she celebrated the return of those feelings she had so loved. She let herself enjoy every nuance, feeling wet and warm and comfortable. And then he replaced his fingers with his organ. It pushed slowly into her.

This will never work. He is far too big for me.

The intrusion made her body stretch and she squirmed, hoping to dislodge him. She thought of the pain Rolande had promised and began to panic.

She looked up at him, thinking of asking him to stop. Aran looked in pain as well; his face was distorted with it. He was perspiring. It seemed obvious to her that he too was regretting this endeavor.

"Hold on to me, Alexis. It will only hurt for a minute."

Her stomach clenched with fear.

He plunged into her in one hard thrust. She screamed.

He collapsed on top of her. "It is all right. It is fine, Alexis. Breathe." He brushed her cheek and held her face so that she was forced to look at him. "It will better soon."

He stayed completely still inside her. She wiggled again, desperate to have him move.

"Don't, Alexis. Please be still."

She squirmed against him again. He groaned and began to pump into her, fast hard strokes that shook her body. She could only hang on to him, gripping his shoulders.

He grasped her hips and pushed deeper into her. He let out a sound that was half shout, half groan. She felt him throb and pulse inside her. And then he was still. He fell on top of her, his chest pushing against with each heavy breath. When he calmed, he rolled the two of them to the side and looked at her.

She felt her cheeks glow and refused to meet his eyes. She remembered her scream and cringed with embarrassment. It had not hurt so much. Having built the whole thing up in her mind, her reaction had been extreme.

He put his hand under her chin and forced her head up. "Are you all right princess?"

She tried to smile but found her lips wobbled. Her eyes began to fill with tears which only added to her humiliation. He kissed her carefully on the lips, then pulled away from her tucking her up against his chest.

"It will be fine. I am told it always hurts the first time. I promise that next time it will be better." There was a long pause as he petted her back as though to comfort her. "Was it all so terrible then?"

"I liked the first part. The kissing and... and all of the touching. It was glorious. Maybe we could just do that?" She looked at him hopefully.

He laughed loudly and squeezed her. "We will do more of 'all of that', but you will learn to like the other too."

She snorted.

He laughed again. "You will. Wait and see."

He rose from the bed and went into his dressing room. He returned with a wet cloth and pulled the sheets back. She had her legs squeezed tightly together.

"Come on. Let me see." He laughed and tugged her legs apart.

She was mortified.

"There is one more task I must do." He gently wiped her body. He winced when the cloth came away red with blood. He leaned down and kissed her there. Then he cupped her with his hand and lifted her slowly up and down. Looking into her eyes, he said, "I promise to make it perfect for you next time, princess."

He leaned down and kissed her there once more. Then he slid up on the bed and held her in his arms.

She decided the intimacy was worth all the pain and bother. Maybe this was why people tolerated the whole business. She snuggled up against him, enjoying the contact of her nakedness against his strong hard body.

She closed her eyes and thought of the day they had shared. It was a beginning, but there was so much more she needed to accomplish. It was too difficult to think about, with her body so relaxed and comfortable. She drifted off to sleep.

Chapter Fourteen

Aran awoke slowly. He looked down at his chest and saw the tangle of red hair sprawled across it. The memories of last night came flooding back. He brushed the hair from Alexis's face. God, she was beautiful.

She had been a virgin. He had never made love to a virgin before. He remembered the blood he had cleaned from her, and her scream as he'd entered her. He hoped he had not hurt her too much. He wanted her to enjoy sex. Sure he had bungled the whole business, he swore to make it up to her.

Last night she said she wanted to be his mistress. That was impossible. Alexis was a lady and a general's daughter, who could only be a bride. She thought that since she was in Paris, she could change the rules, but she was wrong. She had fallen completely into her role, which was a mistake. She was Lady Betcher, and now she would be his wife.

There was no alternative. One did not take an innocent and walk away. It was not done. Even if he wanted to walk away, her father, the general, would force his hand. The general might be disappointed with him as a choice, after all he was as impoverished as a lord could be, but he was still respectable enough under the circumstances.

Smirking, Aran knew there would be no choice for either of them. He had compromised Alexis with her very presence unchaperoned in his house. Alexis had been destined to be his wife from the moment she had jumped into his wool cart. Looking down at her, he smiled at the memory. He let his fingers comb through her glorious hair and rested his palm on her shoulder. This woman was to be his wife.

He debated telling Alexis her destiny was permanently linked to his. If she wanted to return to society, and she would, then she would be forced to see reality. But she seemed to find the fantasy of being a mistress enticing. He felt no need to disillusion her just yet. Furthermore, she would be safer in her role. He decided to wait. They would be back in England soon enough.

He was unsure about his feelings towards marriage. Certainly, Alexis could not disappoint him. She was beautiful, kind, and even funny.

I like her fine.

He knew he was not being honest with himself, though. He more than liked her, but he refused to analyze his emotions any further for now.

On some level, he must have known what making love to her would mean. He grimaced. He had not worn a French letter. It had been his cardinal rule here in Paris. Never had he risked getting the French pox or impregnating a woman.

He trailed his hand down her side to her little round belly. Alexis might be carrying even now; his heart leapt before he wondered at this anticipation. He had never once contemplated marriage or children. Yet here he was. His future wife lay beside him with the possibility of a child in her belly. He hoped so. He realized with shock, he truly did.

And now it was more important than ever he get them out of France. Aran debated packing her up and leaving immediately. Fouche was closing in on them. But it was too close. If Napoleon were going to move on Russia, it would be soon. No one took an army on campaign in the winter. It was now April. He was sure to get word on it within a week or two at most. Napoleon could not keep his secret for much longer. They would try to get inside information, but even if they did not, once Napoleon was on the move, he and Alexis would be leaving France.

Alexis stirred beside him. He smiled when he thought of her tearing into his room the way she had. She would have to work on being a better seductress. A little more subtlety perhaps.

He pulled back the sheet and examined her body. She was very pale, this woman of his. He ran his hands down her back, up over the rise of her hips, and on to her round bottom. She had beautiful wide hips. He squeezed her rounded bottom then ran his hands down past her thighs. Her legs were long and slender.

She turned towards him with a lazy smile.

"Will I do?" she asked.

"You will do very well." He laughed. He moved in beside her and kissed her lightly on the lips. "Good morning, princess."

Cupping her generous breasts, he leaned down and kissed them, gently sucking until the nipples were firm and erect, then sliding his hand across her taunt belly while he kissed her lips. Slowly, he grazed the dark hair between her legs and cupped her gently.

He kept his hand between her legs, holding her while he kissed her. Gradually, he began to rub her slowly back and forth, relishing the feel of her, warm and wet beside him. He kissed her neck and breathed deeply of her soft, fresh scent, with the faintest aroma of rosewater from her hair. Holding her close, he urged her into the age-old rhythm. His hand became wet with her response to him, and he smiled at her through his kisses. Alexis was ready for him. He slid into her.

Aran felt her stiffen. He kissed her tenderly and gently until she relaxed, keeping her snug against him, while rotating his hips. He rolled with her tight against him to their sides, keeping their steady rhythm. Finally, he shifted onto his back and there he stilled.

Her body squeezed him, and he placed his hands on her hips and led her back to the slow beat of their dance. Gradually, Alexis began to understand his intent and rotated her hips against him, setting her own pace. She began to experiment, with each gentle push of her body against his.

At last, she had him deep inside her. Her breathing quickened and as her chest rose and fell against his, he tried to simply hold her close. But ultimately, he could not resist joining into her rhythm, encouraging her to be more force-ful. When his body began to reach a climax, he fought it back, wanting her to find her pleasure. Finally, her pace quickened. In her heightened excitement, she began to thrust hard against him. His resistance became a battle. Sweat broke out on his body, which only made it worse— her body slid across his, erotic and warm.

Just when he knew he could stand it no longer, he felt her muscles quiver and grip him. He grasped her hips and pulled her in tight. She tilted back her head and closed her eyes as he pumped his seed into her. He felt a strange bond fold around them, as she fell back onto his chest.

Aran ran his fingers through her damp hair and pulled it back from her face to admire her flushed beauty. Then he simply wrapped his arms around her and held her.

"You are my woman, Alexis," he said softly and rubbed her back as she caught her breath.

Gradually, her breathing slowed. Realizing she had gone to sleep, he smiled. He shifted her onto her pillow and pulled the sheet around her.

I am satisfied with this woman as my wife. Now I must find a way to keep her safe and get us home.

His stomach clenched.

The stakes were getting higher.

Chapter Fifteen

Before Alexis even opened her eyes the memories of last night washed over her. She stretched her arm across Aran's side of the bed, but it was empty and cold. He had risen long ago. She shifted to his side of the bed and burrowed her head into his pillow, breathing the tangy scent of him. She smiled. She was his true mistress at last. And she loved it. Her tummy felt giddy with joy.

She sat up in bed. Rolande was at the end of the bed with his hand on his hip.

"Well? How was it? You must tell!" He jumped onto the bed and sat cross legged beside her. "I want to hear every detail. You look a satisfied puss this morning. It could only have been very good. Yes?"

"Oh, Rolande." She threw her arms around him, kissing both his cheeks in the French manner. "It was sensational! Amazing! Perfect!"

Rolande let out a little scream and the two of them fell back on the bed laughing. "I want every detail. You must leave nothing out, *cherie*."

She told him everything. Every nuance and quiver.

"Well," Rolande concluded, "now that we have this ghastly business of your virginity done, I can teach you some real skills. Your *monsieur* will be *tres* impressed."

She got up from the bed, pulled her arms into the sleeves of her robe, and twirled about the room.

"I want to know everything, Rolande. I want to be the best mistress a man could have. A real Courtesan Rolande! And the absolute best!" She made her determined face. "He will never go back to his Gigi again."

Rolande got up from the bed and draped his arm around her. "And I am just the man to teach you. First a bath. It is step one. You must always be clean and fresh, my love. Like a fruit, so he can easily eat you."

The two of them laughed as he led her to the bath.

Once done with the bath, Rolande handed her a soft towel. "I will teach you only one lesson today. It will be difficult, and you must concentrate. But first we will dress and eat some breakfast. *Monsieur* is out for the day. He asked me to inform you that he will be back to dine with you. And then, you will take him to bed and surprise him with your new skills."

Alexis enjoyed a hearty breakfast. She was surprised to discover that it was actually well past lunch time. She wondered what Rolande would teach her. Today she would not think about her plans to somehow help Aran to acquire information from the French. Today she wanted to only concentrate on being the best possible lover.

Rolande was a treasure. He was the best friend she had ever had. She could confide in him anything. She wondered idly if he had a boyfriend and promised herself to remember to ask him. He had certainly had plenty in the past, judging by his stories and knowledge.

It was time to head upstairs for her lesson. She vowed to be the best student ever.

Rolande greeted her as she opened her door, "Ah, I am all ready for you, *cherie*."

He flung out his arm in an extravagant gesture indicating a tray on her bed table. It was covered with an array of large cucumbers.

Alexis looked at them and furrowed her brow.

"We are going to eat?" she asked, tilting her head at him in confusion.

Rolande laughed. "In a manner of speaking, yes. Come on, sit on the bed with me."

He sat in the center of her bed cross-legged and indicated that she do the same. She hopped up on the bed, tucking her feet under her dress in an imitation of Rolande. Since her arrival in Aran's home, she had discarded the notion of petticoats when lounging at home. It was scandalous, but here it felt that no one ever noticed anyway. Besides, she was in Paris.

Rolande nodded his approval and reached for a cucumber.

"Now you must imagine that this is the *monsieur*." He handed her his cucumber and grabbed another.

Alexis examined it and laughed. Rolande had even carved a head into its end.

With much hilarity and over the course of many hours, she received her instructions. By the time Rolande was satisfied with her skills, they had destroyed almost every cucumber on the tray. All that was left was one huge vegetable that she would never have been able to get her mouth around.

Rolande picked up the huge cucumber and began to regale her with a tale of one of his lovers that was massively endowed. The story of Rolande's faulty administrations had the two of them collapsing with squeals of laughter.

"Why is it that every time I come in here, I find the two of you in hysterics?" Aran asked from the doorway. "What is it you are up to now?"

He looked around the room, taking in the mound of destroyed cucumbers with a puzzled frown.

Alexis pulled herself from the bed and flipped her robe over the tray. "It is a surprise, my lord. You will love it."

She sauntered over to him and ran her hand down his shirt, letting it trail down to the buttons on his trousers. Leaning close to him, she brushed her breasts against his chest, while she reached down with both hands and held him. She looked up at his face and smiled as she felt him fill. She gave him a little squeeze.

He groaned. "My god, Rolande, what have you done now."

Rolande pursed his lips and sent him a kiss. "No worries, *monsieur*. Think of it as my little gift for you." He chuckled and went to the door. "I think it is a night to stay in for supper. Yes?"

When he received no answer, he shrugged and said, "I will send a tray up for you to later. Enjoy."

He left the room.

Alexis leaned back from Aran and began unbuttoning his trousers. Then she undid his belt and leaned in close to whisper in his ear.

"I have to practice, my lord." She licked the rim of his ear and sucked gently on its lobe in an imitation of the surprise she had in store for him. "Rolande insists that I do my homework."

Aran smiled with a barely suppressed groan.

She slid down his body, pulling his trousers down with her. She first breathed on him, then very carefully ran her tongue around the head of him without touching him anywhere else. She made sure that he could see her actions as Rolande had instructed. His organ reared and stood out eager for her touch. Rolande had told her that this was the best possible scenario. She was pleased with Aran and smiling at his prowess, grabbed his hips, bringing him into her mouth with exaggerated movements of her lips. She moved slowly up and down the length of him with her mouth, her hands grasping his hips, using them to help her find a slow and sensuous rhythm.

"Alexis," he gasped, arching his hips towards her.

His hands held her head to him, and he began to buck and moan. She felt the power that Rolande had assured her she would. She relished it. A rush of dampness between her thighs excited her even more.

When she felt him throbbing dangerously, she pulled back. Only then did she bring her hands to help her. She kept one hand on his tight scrotum and used the other to grip him near his base. He was silky and smooth. She moved her hand with the rhythm he had taught her last night, slow and easy.

Rolande had been right. She loved the taste and feel of him. He had told her that she must learn to enjoy his body. It had not been difficult at all. She kept her hands busy while she worked the tip of his organ. For whatever reason, the rim of it was fascinating to her and she could not resist gripping it with her lips and rotating it in her mouth. She kissed him lovingly, letting him see her lips full and extended around him. His body began to tremble. Aware that she must be more careful, she held him in her mouth snuggly with her tongue while she concentrated on his base. She moaned and twisted her hips. The need to have him inside her was almost overwhelming. She could feel her heartbeat between her thighs.

Aran growled deeply, a sound which vibrated through his entire body, and pulled her up. He yanked her dress up over her head, flinging it to the corner. In one motion, he scooped her up and the two of them fell into her bed.

And then he was inside her. At his first deep thrust, her body exploded. She arched and shouted his name, while he continued to pound into her. He pulled her hips high. She spread her legs as wide as possible, drawing him as deeply into her as she could. He began to thrust powerfully into her. She grabbed his shoulders and hung on, only able to make a strange keening sound as her body began to explode once again.

This time, he met her in her ecstasy, and they ground together. He threw back his head and made a sound that was half shout, half growl. She experienced an awesome joy as he pumped his seed deep inside her.

He collapsed on top of her. His breathing was ragged. For long minutes, they simply recovered. Finally, he grabbed her by the shoulders and rolled them to the side, carefully staying inside her.

She looked at him, tilting her head into an unspoken question.

He laughed. "The answer is yes, princess." He leaned forward and kissed her nose. "You are a wonder."

He kissed her nose a second time. "You know that Rolande will pout until I thank him for this?"

"He is a good teacher."

"That he is." He brought his hand up, pushed her damp hair back, and smiled at her. "But I wonder how much I have corrupted you. It has been only a few weeks since you were a prim and proper English girl. How could I have done this to you so quickly?"

He continued brushing back her hair from her cheeks and forehead.

"I think you will like this girl better, my love." She smiled. "But I am only beginning. I intend to be the finest courtesan in France."

"Hmmm. The finest courtesan in France?"

"Rolande thinks I am a natural." She laughed at his troubled expression. "Don't worry, my love. He also insists I would have learned these skills myself over time. He is only speeding the process, so he says."

She looked up at him. "Tell me that you love my new skills."

He put his hand on her head and smiled down at her, but his eyes were serious. "I love your new skills."

He began to expand inside her and purred softly as he pushed gently against her. She smiled and held him as he rolled on top of her. She was wonderfully wet and tender. Each slow stroke made her body quiver. How odd that the more of this I get, the more I want, she thought idly.

She allowed herself to relax and enjoy every nuance. Her skin and body felt wondrously beautiful. Aran created a slow and sensual experience this time. He stroked her body with his hands, but always delicately, with a loving embrace. And she did the same, exploring his shoulders and hips. She kissed his neck, enjoying the salty flavors of his body. She silently thanked Rolande for his lessons on sensuality as she felt the first soft tremors of her orgasm. She closed her eyes and gloried in it. She felt him pulse inside her and knew he had found his pleasure with her once again.

When she opened her eyes, Aran was watching her with

a curious expression. She gave him a slow, sleepy smile. He seemed concerned and she wondered fleetingly what could have troubled him before he rolled them to their sides, and she fell asleep.

Chapter Sixteen

At breakfast the next morning, Aran wondered what woman he would be sharing a meal with. The Alexis of last night had been a different creature than the girl he had so enjoyed the last month.

Alexis had been still dressing when he had come down. He did not know whether to curse Rolande or thank him. That she had promised to be the best courtesan in France concerned him. He knew the courtesans and did not particularly like them.

Rolande was determined to teach Alexis about her sexuality. As much as Aran enjoyed her awakening, he did not want it to be an obsession. He shuddered when he thought of the women at his parties. Courtesans were a heartless, insatiable lot. The last thing he wanted for Alexis was for her to become lost to her role as a courtesan. He knew about the battle to hang on to identity; it was a battle he fought every day.

But here in Paris, he had left her with little else to concentrate on. Alexis was virtually a prisoner here. She saw only he and Rolande. A walk down the street was her sole outing. With Rolande's obsession with sex, it was little wonder she had set her sights on being a courtesan. He had corrupted her enough. He would not sit idly by while Alexis lost herself in her persona. She needed something more to occupy herself.

He considered the possibilities. Perhaps if he introduced her as his special lady friend, his cherished mistress, and restricted her presence to only those events where there would be a modicum of genteel behavior, it might work. It could even be a new channel for them to get information. And for Alexis, it would relieve the days of idleness which could only be a trial for her.

Many of the officers had wives here in Paris. Women could be a storehouse of information. Men sometimes easily shared their secrets with their wives. Alexis could be the key to success. And it would only be a week or two.

Aran was pleased with the solutions he had sorted out when Alexis came bouncing into the room. She seemed very much her old self. He waited until she had filled her plate before he began his talk.

"There is something I want to share with you while we eat."

She looked up at him politely. "You seem very serious this morning."

"I am." He paused, watching her as she buttered her bread. He was not sure how to start. He decided to get directly to the point. "I meet many courtesans in my line of work. Most of them are desperate creatures. They come to my parties because they are searching for a new benefactor. My role as a rich playboy has made me an irresistible target for them. They fawn on me. I have come to almost despise them."

Alexis's mouth dropped down in shock. She set her fork down on her plate. Her face flushed with color.

He hurried on, not wanting to offend her. "When you said you wanted to be a courtesan, it concerned me. I would never want that fate for you, princess. You are too fine for that lifestyle."

She looked down at her plate.

"I realize I have left you with little to focus on. I have a proposal for you. Something to help you fill your days here in Paris."

She still stared at her plate. He sighed, realizing he may have made a mistake with his comments about courtesans. She was unlikely to listen to his new proposal until he clarified.

He walked around the table and knelt beside her. Reaching up, he took her hand. "Alexis, I would enjoy being with you no matter what your skills were. Learn from Rolande if you want. God knows I can only benefit from that. But remember it is you I want, not some French courtesan. It is Alexis Betcher I want, not Alexis De Mal."

She slowly raised her head, tears in her eyes. "It is only for you, Aran. I know you have had many women. I don't want to be one of many, and maybe second best at that."

"You could never be second best, Alexis. You are first with me." He wondered if he should tell her about their impending marriage. On some level, she must know their relationship could not last on the trek they were on. They would return to London and all hell would break loose. He would have to marry her and quickly. He wished he could do it now.

"Will you have other women again while we are here, Aran?"

"No. I promise you will be my only woman." His only woman for a long, long, time, perhaps forever.

"Even for work?"

"That part of my job is done. I do not think I could survive another round of that particular bargain. Not even for work will I break this promise to you." He snatched the napkin from beside her plate and pushed it at her as he stood. "Come on, cheer up. You may continue to practice with Rolande but be careful to remember who you are."

He leaned down and kissed her. "And remember too it is only you I want." He looked down at her with a half-smile. "And I will definitely thank Rolande this morning."

He returned to his meal.

"Now then, about this other matter," he said, and she looked at him curiously, "the business of finding you another task here in Paris. I wonder if you would like to attend the opera with me tonight?"

He smiled when her mouth dropped.

"I have decided to let my world here meet my new mistress. But only if you can stay in character and be very careful."

"Really! Do you mean it?" She clapped her hands together. "I can! I can! You will see. I shall be perfect."

"And there is more. I have decided to ask a young corporal to join us in our box. His name is Andre LaSalle. He has a new wife. Bernadette, I think. If they accept my invitation, we will attempt to make a connection with them." He watched Alexis's growing excitement, satisfied he had made the right decision. "You know what we need but be cautious, my love. You cannot push too hard or too quickly."

"I will be careful."

"If we simply get an invitation to their home, I would be

incredibly pleased. Or even if she should invite you alone to tea tomorrow. That would be a success." He looked at her and furrowed his brow. "Whatever happens, even if we are totally unsuccessful, they cannot become suspicious. Do not become impatient. There will be other opportunities now that I introduce my mistress to society."

"But as your mistress will I be acceptable?"

"We are in Paris, princess. I am single and wealthy. It is only to be expected that I have a lady friend to escort me to events." He frowned. "If possible, do not share our living arrangements." We will have to spend this afternoon preparing your story."

"I am so excited, Aran."

"Eat. Then we will go upstairs and prepare."

Aran hoped he had not made a mistake, but he was confident now that she could stay in character.

He hoped she could be of assistance in acquiring the information they needed—but that remained to be seen.

Chapter Seventeen

They paused to take in the elaborate Palais Garnier. It was the grand dame of opera houses. Its façade was a wonder. It had arched entries around the entire perimeter, followed by a level of elegant columns, and finally the sculpted frescos beneath a gold leafed roof.

Alexis took a deep breath. "It is beautiful, Aran."

"It is. The gold here is minor." He chuckled. "Wait until you see the interior."

Inside, the boxes that extended from the stage on each side were completely gilded; the curtains and chairs were a rich red velvet. The effect was extreme opulence.

Aran led her up the wide marble staircase to the third floor, to the right of the stage where they were to take their seats.

The Corporal, Andre, and his wife Bernadette were already present in the box. After the necessary round of introductions, they all took their seats. Alexis had Bernadette on her right and Aran to the left. Andre was on the far right.

Bernadette was a petite young woman with a round face and hair that was a rich mahogany brown, done up in an elaborate high bun. Her dark eyes sparkled with excitement.

"This is my first time at the Palais. It is magnificent," she whispered to Alexis.

"Mine too," Alexis whispered back.

The two of them grinned. Alexis realized she had sorely missed female company.

"May I bring you ladies a refreshment?" Andre offered. He too was young. He was a handsome fellow. Like his wife, he was dark-haired with a swarthy complexion. He carried himself like a soldier, with his shoulders stiffly erect. The overall impression of the two of them was that joining Aran in his expensive box was a luxury they had never experienced. They seemed to be slightly intimidated. Alexis smiled at Aran's insight. This could only help their task.

"I will have a punch, thank you, Andre." Bernadette smiled at him.

"The same for me, thank you."

Bernadette focused her opera glasses on the crowds.

"I heard that Napoleon himself will be attending, but I see his box is empty. Have you ever seen him?" Bernadette asked as she peered across the theatre towards the empty Royal Box across the way. "I have, but only once and then it was at a distance, when he was on parade."

"Me? Never. I was hoping too that he would be in attendance tonight."

Aran had warned her that she must be enthralled with Napoleon. He had said, "The aristocrats and those with old money find him to be an uncouth upstart but remember the army adores him."

"Look," Bernadette gasped, "they are preparing the box."

Two guards in full parade dress had taken positions on each side of the box.

"Napoleon loves the opera," she said. "I heard he attends whenever he is in town."

"How very exciting."

"And look! It is Eleanore de Montmorency." She lowered her glasses and whispered to Alexis, "She is the premier hostess here in Paris."

"Where is she?" Alexis trained her glasses on the crowds.

"Just two boxes to the left of the Royal Box, and one down," Bernadette said raising her glasses once more.

"I see her. At least I think I do. What is she wearing on her head?"

They both lowered their glasses and looked at each other.

"I think it is a turban." Bernadette choked.

They both laughed.

Bernadette continued to point out the celebrities. For Alexis, who knew nothing about Parisian society, it was all new and of great interest.

Bernadette said, "Look below at the second story box."

Alexis shifted her glasses into position.

"It is the generals. The one on the right, seated with his wife, is General Dumont. He is my husband's superior."

Alexis scanned the box. They were in dress uniforms and covered in colorful gold stripe and medals. In the rear of the box, a tall solid figure stood with his opera glasses trained on the crowd as well. He seemed to be looking directly at her. She quickly lowered her glasses.

"Who is the general standing? I feel like he is looking in our direction."

Bernadette used her opera glances to scan the generals'

box once more. "I think it is General De Sole. I met him once, but I know little about him."

The name De Sole was familiar to Alexis, but she could not think of where she had heard it.

They continued to peruse the audience with great interest. There was much to coo about. The elite of Napoleon's regime was even more extravagant and flamboyant than the old aristocrats. The gowns and jewels displayed were breathtaking.

At one point, she glanced over at Aran, and he smiled, giving her a nod of approval. Befriending this young lady would not be difficult. Bernadette was excited and exuberant. To her relief, she had not even raised an eyebrow at Alexis's obvious role of mistress. Perhaps here in Paris, it was a natural occurrence to be escorted by one's paramour.

"Yes! It is Napoleon himself!" Bernadette gasped.

The ladies were silent while they watched the action in the Royal Box. Napoleon cut a fine figure in his dark jacket, resplendent with medals and jewels. He radiated an aura of power. Alexis was surprised to see that he was not a tall man. His wife, Marie Louise, towered over him.

She too, cut a figure of opulence. She wore a jeweled tiara, which even from this distance sparkled and glowed as she moved. Her dress was bejeweled and glittered even in the dim light. It was white with red and blue, trimmed in the colors of France. Its puffed short sleeves spiked out outrageously at the shoulders, resplendent with hundreds of tiny sequins.

The crowd rose and erupted into applause. Napoleon and Marie Louise stood still, acknowledging their tribute. After several minutes, Napoleon raised his hand to subdue the audience, while Maria Louise bowed to her subjects. It was only after they had taken their seats that the applause quieted.

The lights dimmed.

As they waited for the curtains to open, Bernadette turned to her, "I am so thankful for this invitation. It is my first, and possibly only, opportunity to enjoy the opera from a box. I love it. I am forever spoilt."

She gave Alexis a hug.

"It is our pleasure. I have enjoyed it too." She smiled at her. "You are my first acquaintance here in Paris. I have so craved female company."

"You know no one here in the city?"

"I am afraid not. I only just moved from the country. You have no idea how pleased I was to hear that Aran had invited you to share our evening."

"Oh, but that is too lonely. You must come to luncheon with me tomorrow." Bernadette looked concerned. "Only I am a humble corporal's wife. It will not be the luxury you are accustomed to."

Alexis whispered in her ear, "You must remember that while my Aran has plenty, I unfortunately do not." She smiled at her and added, "At least not yet."

The two of them giggled.

For the first half of the performance, Alexis was giddy with excitement. She had done it! She had her first success as a spy. Step one was complete. Now she only hoped there would be information of value to siphon out of the invitation.

At intermission, Bernadette turned to her and whispered, "I have heard so much about the ladies' retiring room. We must visit it."

Alexis laughed and stood.

"I agree." As she and Bernadette moved towards the red

velvet curtains, she turned to Aran. "We won't be but a minute."

She gave him a wide smile hoping to communicate her total enjoyment of the evening.

The halls, though expansive, were crowded with spectators. It seemed as though everyone was talking at once as the noise was deafening. Bernadette grasped her hand so that they did not lose each other in the fray. Together, they weaved through the guests.

A solid object stepped into her path.

"Oh," she gasped, bumping squarely into the man. Her progress came to a halt. "I am so sorry."

She looked up to see an impassive broad face staring at her. He did not apologize or step out of her way, but rather looked at her with his ice blue eyes. She shivered. She had time to notice the epitaph of his shoulders indicating that he was a high-ranking official, and his chest adorned with medals, before Bernadette tugged on her hand. She was forced to squeeze around his immobile body to continue her trek. How rude, she thought as she moved forward, dismissing the incident.

The walls of the lady's room were mirrors from the floor to the ceiling. Everywhere the hardware was plated with gold. The floors were covered in lush carpet.

"I would be satisfied with the evening to see this alone." Alexis giggled.

"Oh, it is glorious. And there is one on every floor, complete with automatic plumbing. I could live here."

They spent most of the intermission enjoying the facilities. When they reentered the hall, the crowd had thinned out. They chatted happily, arm in arm, as they walked to their box.

A tall figure, a general in full dress uniform, leaned

against the wall, his square face stony as he watched their progress across the room. It was the man who had bumped into her earlier. His eyes did not leave her but narrowed as they hurried past him toward their seats.

Alexis shuddered as her eyes met his. There was something about the general that emitted an aura of evil. She was thankful it was not him she had been asked to charm tonight.

This was a man she hoped never to meet.

Chapter Eighteen

Once back at home, Alexis sat at Aran's dressing table and pulled the clasps from her hair, while she crowed excitedly about her victory. Aran lay propped up in bed. He had decreed that from now on she was to share his bed. The new arrangement suited her fine.

"What kind of information is important to me, Aran?" she asked, eager to be successful again tomorrow at her luncheon with Bernadette.

"Sometimes it is the trivial things which are the best. Listen carefully to any references to her husband's current and future work. What is his assignment and where, or how long she expects he will be in Paris. Note it all, then when you get home, we will sift through it for meaning." He watched her as she sat and brushed her hair. "When she drops a name, try to memorize it, especially if it is commander returning to France. That is sometimes the hardest part. It becomes easier as you develop your memory. Do not expect to be adept the first time.

"If you have a chance to search her husband's desk, do

so. But be careful. Take no chances. If you get that opportunity, then official orders are what you are looking for. Usually, I try to copy information so that the papers are not missed but you will not have time for that."

She sighed, braiding her hair. "I hope I get something."

Done with her hair, she turned to him. She felt strange now preparing to get into his bed.

"I will be a minute," she said, blushing, before leaving for her dressing room. He just smiled at her.

Washing her face, she thought about her latest lesson from Rolande. She had told him about Aran's displeasure with her goal to be a skilled courtesan. At first, Rolande had looked confused.

"Hmm. That does not sound like the *monsieur* I know. It is very strange." He had paced the room, stopping to look at her occasionally. "He has behaved strangely with you from the beginning. That man was always insatiable. Only think of the month he spent here next to you without touching you, *cherie*. It was not like him. Not like him at all."

Rolande continued to ponder the problem, while Alexis sat at her dressing table and tried to follow his movements around the room. He finally stopped pacing.

"I think this man may have other plans for you." He rubbed his chin thoughtfully.

To her surprise, he had grabbed the garbage container beside the bed and rummaged through it. Then, he went into the dressing room where she heard him again rustling about. Next, he entered Aran's rooms. When he finally returned, he sat down on the bed and looked at her. She turned on her chair and faced him.

"What is it, Rolande?" she asked, concerned with his serious face.

"Has the *monsieur* ever worn anything," he said, waving his hand towards his groin, "when he makes love to you?"

Her lips twitched. She imagined a tiny little sweater like the kind wealthy matrons put on their pets and giggled. "No, never."

Rolande slapped his hand on his forehead and swore. Alexis looked at him curiously.

"I have been wrong, my *cherie*. But I should have guessed. His behavior has been *tres* unnatural from the start. Do not look so worried, my dear. It is nothing. And I think this time it is his secret to tell."

He smiled at her. "I will teach you only one more thing. The rest, my love, you must learn on your own."

He winked at her with his outrageous painted eyes. Today, he had added glossy gold powder to his mascaraed eye lids. The effect was startling, and exceptionally beautiful.

He shifted on the bed so that his knees were between hers where she sat facing him from her chair. "This time, my love, I am not an expert. I can only show and tell you what I have heard." He glanced down at his body. "I do not have the equipment for this."

He continued, "I knew a woman when I worked in the theatre."

Alexis's eyes widened. She had had no idea he had been an actor, but it made perfect sense.

Rolande smiled and nodded, "Yes, I am a circus bum." He laughed. "This woman was from the far east. She bragged often about her skills as a lover. She taught them to whoever would listen. For a while, our ladies were the most sought after in Paris."

He chuckled, enjoying the memory.

"She said she could bring a man to his pleasure using

only her muscles here, and without a single movement." He touched her lower belly. "Using these muscles, you can squeeze and stroke a man without engaging the rest of your body. It is said to be an awesome experience. Me, I have of course never experienced it. But even if you never master the skill to that extent, it would be a pleasure. Yes? Do you want to learn the secrets, my *cherie*?"

She nodded, grinning mischievously. "I do, Rolande! You must teach me!"

"It will be your last lesson, as I said. But this time it will take a lot of work. Sometimes, it takes years to develop this skill.

"You must feel the muscles inside you and squeeze them." He put his hand on her tummy. "Now try it."

Alexis obediently began to squeeze.

"Good. Squeeze and release, each time. Now this is the important part, *cherie*. You must pretend you have a little staircase in your body. You must practice stepping only one step at a time." He held his hand on her while she did the exercise. "Each time you do this, you will become stronger. You must practice every day to become very good.

Alexis concentrated on her little stairway. She concentrated so hard that Rolande burst into laughter.

"That is not a good face for you. You best focus on just strengthening your muscles for now."

"No, Rolande. I want to learn this. It will be a delightful surprise for Aran. I want to know I please him above all others."

An image of Gigi flashed across her mind. She had never seen her. It was only her voice that she knew. Her mind had concocted a wonderous beauty for her to compete with. She was determined to never lose Aran to a woman such as her again.

Rolande sighed. "All right." He looked at her speculatively. "We will keep practicing, yes?"

After what felt like hours, she was able to accomplish three distinct steps. Rolande was pleased. "It is a good start. But you must practice. Cadona, my eastern friend, could do more than ten. But then she trained her whole life."

He patted her belly.

"I will. I will practice every day."

"And I will check you. That way you will keep on with your studies. You have one week." He put his arms around her and winked, giving her a little shake. "Then, we will see if you have improved. For today, it is back to step one. You must have a bath."

Now, Alexis returned to the bedroom feeling nervous. She had managed to impress Aran with her other new skill before. She just hoped she could master this last one. She was determined to be the absolute best. Knowing about Gigi made it imperative she succeeded. This whole enterprise was becoming difficult.

Aran looked at her and tilted his head to the side, with a little smile. "What is it that has you looking so serious? Are you feeling shy with me Alexis?"

Alexis decided there would be no secrets between them, especially here in the bedroom. She confided the new skill they had practiced this afternoon and concluded that Rolande had sworn this would be her last lesson.

To her surprise, Aran only laughed and opened his arms wide. "Come here, princess. I will help you practice."

They shared much amusement when he demanded she show him this latest technique. She perched up on top of him with her feet braced beside his thighs. "Don't move, Aran. I want to know if you can feel my staircase."

"Your staircase?" He laughed.

Her experiments were mostly a failure.

"Your face is so deadly serious." He laughed again and she punched him playfully in the shoulder.

"Let me try again." The harder she tried, the more he laughed. Finally, he grabbed her and rolled her on the bed.

"I have a better idea," he said. He tickled her until she was squealing and weak with laughter. "Now you look less like a scholar completing a final exam. Much better."

He chuckled and nuzzled her neck with wet kisses.

"You are a special gift, Alexis, and I love you dearly," he muttered into her ear.

Alexis had little time to analyze his statement. She could only put her arms around him and enjoy the night.

Tomorrow would be her first acts as a spy. Maybe she could impress him with that.

Chapter Nineteen

Alexis enjoyed a traditional but elaborate lunch with Bernadette. The starter was a creamy onion soup, followed by a pate, with a main course of delicious poached fish. She had been pleased to see she was the only guest. They kept the conversation light.

"Thank you for a lovely luncheon, Bernadette. It is by far the best I have had since coming to Paris."

Bernadette brushed aside the compliment. "I have an exceptional chef. It is the most important part of running a household. Do you not agree?"

"Oh, I do. Sadly, I do not have a proper household yet. I cannot even return your invitation." She looked at Bernadette and smiled. "But when I do, and I hope it is soon, you shall be my first guest."

Aran had told her she must keep their living arrangements secret. She would be required, when the subject came up, to feign embarrassment at her poverty and avoid giving her address. It seemed to work well with Bernadette.

"Not to worry. I understand. We will both hope for this

change soon." She smiled at her. "You are beautiful, Alexis. I have no doubt you will succeed."

"Thank you, Bernadette. I do hope so. It is hard to keep up appearances here in town."

"Oh yes, I understand your challenge. As a military wife, it is often difficult to maintain a proper household." She sighed and stood. "Come, we will take our dessert in the salon."

She laughed. "It is actually both the library, where my husband has an office, and our sitting room."

She smiled apologetically.

"It is lovely," Alexis said as they entered the room. And it was. Bernadette had filled the room with bouquets of fresh flowers. The room smelled of soft lavender.

The sitting room was long and narrow. One end held a settee, with several chairs and a sofa. The other had a large oaken desk in front of a window. On each side of the desk, bookshelves lined the walls. Alexis could not have been more pleased. She knew that somehow, she would have to find a way to search that desk.

Alexis again saw the wisdom of casting her as a new mistress, poor enough to appreciate Bernadette's modest home. Bernadette was able to proudly display her establishment, knowing Alexis had much less. It made for a comfortable relationship.

A petite maid served them an apple dessert with cheese. Alexis almost remarked that the French had a wonderful idea to include cheese in their desserts. Luckily, she caught herself. She must remember what Aran had drilled into her. She had been raised in the country living with her grandmother, who of course had been French. She must live the part of the daughter of a French courtesan with a Spanish father. A girl who was raised in the French countryside and only now came to Paris to make her way in the world by following her mother's footsteps.

Alexis loved her new background. Though Aran had warned her to be careful not to see herself as a courtesan, she decided that in this instance he was wrong. She was Alexis De Mal, hoping to have her wealthy playboy to herself. She played her role both in his home and out of it. It kept her safe, but most of all it appealed to her imagination and even her new reality here in Paris. Besides, it was increasingly close to the truth.

The prim girl from London was too far away. She did not know if she could find her even if she tried. In her mind, she had woven her modest existence in her grandmother's home, complete with the required lessons in etiquette and the instructions on how to be an exceptional lover, which was her destiny.

"Oh, but this is a lovely room," she repeated as they took their seats. "How ever did you find this apartment?"

Bernadette blushed with pride. "I was so very lucky. My Andre much pleased his general while in Austria. When he was transferred back home to help train the new recruits, Marshall Dumont set us up with this apartment."

She beamed.

Alexis realized that she had just acquired a piece of information. Bernadette's husband was training new recruits. Aran would be pleased. It was obvious she loved her Andre very much. Alexis decided to aim the conversation in that direction.

"Andre must be an exceptionally good soldier. Yes?"

"The best. I could not be more proud of him. Every day he goes to train his troops just here outside of Paris." She sighed. "I only wish he could be stationed here forever. But no. Army life."

She shrugged. "Would you like some coffee with your dessert? We have a fine blend. I think you will enjoy it."

"Yes, that would be lovely." Her stomach clenched with excitement. Bernadette was a storehouse of information. She knew what she was hearing from Bernadette was the collection of the insignificant details Aran had spoken of. Put together he might be able to make some use of them. It was not much, but it was a start.

Bernadette left to order a pot of coffee. As soon as she had walked out the door to her kitchens, Alexis hopped up and hurried to the desk. Unfortunately, the desk was clean. It had on its surface only a wide note pad, with a quill and ink. She slid the top drawer open. A letter embossed with a military crest lay at its very top. She quickly picked it up and slipped it into her bosom. Bernadette's footsteps sounded in the hall. Using her hip, she shoved the drawer closed as she turned to look out the window. With relief she saw before her Bernadette's groomed courtyard.

"What a lovely view. You have a garden, Bernadette!" She knew her excitement was evident in her voice and hoped Bernadette would perceive it as her enthusiasm to see the garden. "Sometimes I so miss the countryside."

"We do." Bernadette joined her at the window. "We even have a little patio. Would you like to take our coffee there?"

"I would love it."

Alexis found she did enjoy the garden.

"The coffee is delicious," she said, hoping she was not fawning too much, and deciding to tone it down a notch. Keep it natural, she chided herself. Then again, it was true that she was beginning to prefer coffee over the traditional English tea.

"I wonder, Alexis, if you would like to come to an officer's ball. Madame Eleanore de Montmorency is hosting one at the week's end. It will be a huge affair, a crush. Everyone is invited. I can ask for invitations for you and Monsieur Garscon if you wish?"

"Oh, Bernadette!" She gave a little squeal and clapped her hands together. "That would be so perfect! Oh, just think how pleased Aran will be with me!"

The two of them began to discuss the upcoming party. Alexis completely forgot she was only playing a role in her excitement to attend a real ball. It had been months since she had enjoyed a party. The ladies discussed everything from gowns to the wonders of the waltz. The afternoon passed quickly. Alexis found she was sad to be finally leaving.

"I will send you the invitations when I get them. To what address shall I send them?"

Alexis looked troubled. "I do not want you to hear my humble address," she said with a concern which was real. "I know! Perhaps you could send them to Monsieur Garscon?"

Bernadette readily agreed.

All the way home in the hansom cab, Alexis periodically rubbed her hand across her breast to remind herself she had succeeded in stealing a piece of correspondence. The crinkle of paper felt reassuring. She dared not pull it out until she was safely in her room. Her tummy fluttered with a thousand butterflies as she thought of her successes today. She had this letter. She hoped it was more than just a requisite for supplies or something equally mundane. She also had the knowledge Corporal LaSalle was training troops just out of Paris. And finally, most exciting of all, she had the invitation to an officer's ball. She giggled with excitement.

When she arrived home, Aran met her at the door.

"How was it, Alexis?" he asked.

She glanced at Emile who stood silently at the arched entry to the sitting room. She grabbed Aran's hand and tugged him towards the staircase, chattering in Spanish, "I have so much to tell you! I cannot wait!"

She took the stairs two at a time.

"Easy, Alexis." He laughed, but he ran with her to her rooms. "Now then, what has you so excited?"

She paused to catch her breath. Finally, I can see what I have, she thought as she reached into her bosom, pulling out crumpled letter.

"This!" She handed it to him. "And there is so much more."

She confided in rapid Spanish the troops who even now would be training just out of town, and the officer's ball. He listened carefully to her excited rambling, holding the letter as he absorbed her information.

"Well, my love." He kissed her cheek, his eyes focused on the letter. "You overwhelm me with your talents. Had I known you were capable of this I would have employed you the very first day."

Alexis beamed beneath his praise.

"Let us see what we have here." He sat down at her dressing table and pulled the missive from its sleeve.

Alexis sat across from him, on his bed, her eyes focused intently on him, hoping to catch some hint regarding its importance as he read. His face remained serious.

She began to bounce up and down on the bed expectantly. "Well? Is it worth anything? Is there something we can use?"

Aran looked up at her. His face was deadly serious. He gave a soft whistle.

"You must tell me! I can't stand it!"

"Alexis, you have here the corporal's formal orders from General Dumont. It is good. It is beyond good."

"Aran, what do you mean? You must explain."

"The corporal is ordered to train new recruits for a Grande Army. He is expected to have his squadron ready by the end of May, as Napoleon will be invading Russia by the first of June. This is gold, Alexis. It is signed by the general himself." He reached for her, and holding her head with both of his hands, kissed her soundly on the mouth.

Alexis smiled happily. "You are pleased?"

She needed to hear more praise.

"I am more than pleased. I am ecstatic." Aran kissed her again. "This is the best information I have had in my hands in a long while. You, my dear, have done better than my wildest dreams. We are one step closer to getting home, my love."

He stood and tucked the envelope into his pocket. "This I must get to my contact immediately. He will have it out of the country and in Admiral Hews' hands in record time." He kissed her again. "Thank you, my love. We will talk later."

And he was out the door.

Chapter Twenty

The next day, Aran decided he would take his new mistress for a carriage ride in the country. He sat at his breakfast table and contemplated the day's plan. it. He knew of a military base just outside of Paris. It had to be where the corporal was going every day to train his troops. If the commute was made daily as Alexis had reported, then it must be in close proximity to town. There was a base in a valley north of Paris, just down from the gypsy camps. It might be important to check out the scope and size of this operation planned for the spring.

The news of the Russian invasion meant he would be going home soon. Last night, he had sent the admiral the letter Alexis had discovered. That it was a formal document, signed by one of Napoleon's marshals, made it of more value. The invasion was no longer a rumor. He wondered for a moment if it was enough. He scowled when he knew the answer. The admiral would now want details: how many troops, and from where? That would be their assignment. However, once Napoleon left, on June first, they would be going home no matter what, he reminded himself for the hundredth time. In less than two months, he would be back in his beloved Yorkshire.

Home. Sometimes he felt as though it would never happen. Now the end was in sight. He was ready. When Alexis had come into his life, he had been near the end of his endurance, sure he could not survive another day. She had filled the last several weeks.

He was still pleased with her progress. And she had basked in his praise. He reminded himself that whatever happened, he would not confide to the admiral her role in the events. He grimaced. He was certain the greedy little man would find some way of recruiting her should he ever learn the truth. Never would he allow her to become as decadent and depraved as he had been forced to be. Protecting her was more important than his assignment.

His future wife was a prize in every way. The last few days had seemed like a honeymoon and in a strange way, it was. He could not get enough of her. He wanted her every minute of every day. Just thinking of her now made his body tingle, despite having just left her warm, wet, and satisfied in her bed.

And she had blossomed in the last week. She seemed as if she had more confidence. She was becoming a sensual being, he decided. It was not that she flirted exactly. Rather it was as if she was aware of her body in a way she had not been before. And she wanted him. It was irresistible. Never had he lusted for a woman more. That she was soon to be his wife made it sweeter still.

He decided to enjoy his coffee and wait for her, before beginning his meal. It should not be long now. Alexis had to bathe every morning. She absolutely would not begin her day without it. Rolande always had the tub prepared for her when she climbed out of bed. It was a habit he appreciated. She was always fresh and beautiful.

"Good morning, my love." Alexis came into the room. Her face glowed. Her hair was a thick braid which fell over her shoulder past her breasts.

His stomach tightened with just her presence. She laid her hands on his shoulders and kissed him before heading for the sideboard to fill a plate. "I am famished. I see you have a plate. Thank you for waiting for me, my love."

He let her enjoy her breakfast before telling her his plans. "I thought we should try to confirm your information," he said in Spanish. "A carriage ride might be a pleasant way to spend the afternoon."

He was thankful now that he had confided his assignment to her. It allowed them to spend more time together. Initially, he had worried he would lose the relief he enjoyed in her presence. She had been his escape. Instead, his tensions had eased. It was a solace to share ideas with her.

"But what a wonderful idea. It will be a way to enjoy our work, yes?"

He smiled at her use of the French question at the end of her sentence. Another month or two, and she would be more French than the French.

She smiled and added enthusiastically, "I wonder if we might have a picnic lunch. We could enjoy the afternoon."

"It would indeed. And what would be more natural than taking my beautiful lover for a carriage ride in the country for a picnic? You have become the perfect camouflage, princess."

They packed lunch. Aran hired a small buggy, drawn by a single horse.

"We want just the two of us," he explained. "A larger

coach means a coachman. Not what we want for a recon-
naissance mission."

The trip through Paris was a joy with Alexis at his side.
He pointed out the various landmarks along the way. They
even passed through the Arc de Triumphe du Carrousel. He
made her laugh when he explained that Napoleon had not
been able to complete it in time for his new bride, for whom
it had been intended. The princess had actually driven
through the arc not knowing it was mostly paper and plaster, slapped into place temporarily for her arrival.

At the edge of town, on the banks of the Seine, Alexis
was interested in the gypsy camps.

"They always park their wagons just here out of town,"
Aran said. "This has been their camp for centuries. They
gather here for a week or two every year. Then they will
scatter again."

"Look, Aran! See that yellow caravan? I think it is the
gypsies we met on our journey to Paris!"

"It is indeed. There seem to be many distinct groups
here right now. It is likely they are also stocking up with
wares to sell across the countryside." He smiled at her.
"That was extraordinary, that day at the canal."

She waved her hand, brushing aside his praise. "I am a
special person to them now. I still have the amulet the girl's
mama gave me."

He laughed. "Keep it. You never know when it will
come in handy."

They rode in silence. Aran breathed the fresh country
air and wondered what Alexis would think of his home on
the Yorkshire coast. He hoped she would come to love it as
he did. She had proven to be very versatile. Perhaps that
would help her adjust.

He turned left off the main road. "This trail has been

much travelled, Alexis. It is not the little grassy path it was when I first checked out this base. Look at the ruts. They have been moving equipment in here and plenty of it."

"They have, Aran. Look, they have even created another road to the right."

As they began to climb the last hill before the valley, a new path branched off to the right. It skirted the hillside, weaving at a wider angle up the incline. "It is deeply rutted. I think cannons would have an easier time climbing the hill on that angle, don't you?"

They made it up the rise and looked down at the valley below.

"Oh, my goodness, Aran! There are thousands and thousands of troops here!" Alexis gasped.

There were tents and troops, both below and off in the distance for as far as the eye could see. The valley moved, the troops working like so many ants. The hillsides were dotted with tents.

Aran pulled out his collapsing telescope and focused on the scene below. He snapped it back into place and turned the wagon around abruptly. "We must get out of here and quickly. It is a miracle we have not already discovered. Hold on, princess."

He snapped the reins and they cantered down the hill. The buggy lurched and swayed. Alexis had to grip the railing to remain in her seat. At one point, they almost flipped the buggy in their rush to leave the area. Aran kept up a brisk pace until they had reached the main road. Even then, he continued at a gallop until they were long past the army camp.

He finally slowed the horse to a trot.

"We were lucky, princess. That was close. It would have been hard to explain our presence there." He brushed back his hair and looked at her. "That, my dear, is the Grande Army. There are more troops there than I have seen in my life."

He was silent as several carriages passed them. Each was loaded with soldiers. Another group of supply wagons creaked past.

It was not until they were almost at the gypsy camp at the edge of town that he pulled off the main road onto an overgrown trail. Just a few hundred yards off the wooded path was a little stream.

"Do you like it?" he asked. "This can be our picnic area."

"It is perfect."

He hopped down from the buggy and turned to assist her. Next, he slid the basket down to the ground. "I'll let you set up while I water the horse."

He arrived back at their picnic area just in time to find Alexis bent over the blanket attempting to perfect the layout of their lunch. Looking at her broad backside he smiled and stepped behind her and rubbing himself against her. The second he grabbed her hips; he knew it was a mistake. He was lost to everything but her.

She laughed and pushed into him. Holding her hips against him, he groaned as she wiggled. Alexis wore nothing beneath her dress, and he wondered if she would be wet and wanting. He bunched up her dress and slipped his hand between her legs to feel her. She was slippery and ready. Groaning again, he used his fingers to push inside her.

She braced her hands on the ground and arched towards him, meeting his eager fingers with her hips in a slow rotation. This time, it was she who moaned and squirmed. He could wait no longer. He used one hand to undo his belt and pull his trousers apart at the fly, freeing himself.

He grabbed her by the hips and drove into her in one powerful stroke. For a moment, he was still, pressed hard into her. He felt her squeezing him. She seemed to be able to draw him more deeply inside her with her grip alone. He remembered her practiced skill, and smiled, relishing the feel of her muscles holding him firmly. But he could not remain still for long. Holding her hips, he drove into her again and again. She moaned her orgasm, but it was not enough. He wanted her to reach her pleasure again. He fought his need to release until he knew he would explode. At last, her body trembled and arched against him as he burst inside her.

He leaned back and opened his eyes to the wonders of nature around him as his seed poured into her. Closing his eyes, he gloried in the feelings that washed over him, sure he had never experienced anything like it in his life.

Slowly, he pulled out of her. He laid her down on their picnic blanket and held her beside him as they regained their breath. In that moment, her knew he would die for want of her. She was worth more than his life to him. He wondered for the hundredth time if he ever would be able to get enough of her.

He just held her for a long time. Neither of them spoke. He wanted to take her again with love and gentleness. It was the one way he could show her how he felt without speaking the words. She lay in front of him, her dress bunched up around her hips. He reached down and tugged at it until she braced herself up so he could slide it off her body. He held her naked in his arms, against his clothed skin. He kissed and stroked and held her, while he slid easily into her warm wetness. And finally, he looked into her eyes when she found her pleasure, trying with every ounce of his being to show her what she meant to him. And then he held her again.

He thought they both must have slept for a while. Alexis stirred beside him, and he nuzzled in close, pressing himself into her once more.

She laughed and sat up abruptly. "No. I am starving."

She grinned at him.

He smiled at the fine figure she cut with her thick red braid over her shoulder and her breasts standing out at perky attention. She scowled at him.

"We will have food before anything else." Marching to the basket, she flipped open a side and grabbed a small cloth. "And I will wash, while you set it up."

He prepared their lunch, then leaned back to watch her bathe. She seemed such a part of nature here. He wondered idly if she was pregnant. He smiled at the thought of her with a round growing belly. Then he thought of the dangers of bearing children for women and felt a wave of panic. Maybe it would be best if she never bore children. He was still worrying over the subject when she pulled her dress back over her head and sat down to eat with him.

She looked at him curiously.

"What is it? Why do you look so glum?" She handed him a piece of cheese. "Eat. You'll feel better."

They enjoyed their lunch together. The subject naturally turned to the masses of troops they had seen in the secluded valley.

"How many troops do you think there were?" she asked.

Aran rubbed his chin. "Too many, princess. It was even beyond my ability to calculate. If you looked down at the valley, the tents were strung out as far as the eye could see. There are masses of troops here. Over a hundred thousand, perhaps even five times that. My guess is they are pouring into the valley still."

"Do you think it is the beginnings of Napoleon's Russian invasion?"

"It is for sure. There are so many troops amassed here even Admiral Hews will have caught word of it. But we will send a report anyway."

"Who do you report to?" she asked.

"Now that I will not tell you. Should we be caught, heaven forbid, it is information you not be able to share. It will keep the others safe." He smiled at her. "Even I know only my contact. There must be many others, but I don't know them, and they don't know me. You may think of me as your contact now that you are a spy."

"Hmmm. I am a spy, aren't I?" She seemed to mull it over. "What an odd thought."

She stretched out her legs and patted her thighs. "You may rest here on my lap if you wish."

Aran lay down on her lap with his head against her warm belly.

"I am a successful spy, so far," she mused.

"You are. But you must always be very, very careful. Never take a risk. I do not think I could forgive myself if something happened to you."

"But what if something happens to you? What if that should happen and I am here?" Her fingers idly played with his hair, while she contemplated the possibility. It was a disturbing thought, but one that was very possible.

Aran considered the scenario. "It is an excellent question. And it is time we discussed it, as unpleasant as it may seem. Let's make a few rules." He cleared his throat and began in a serious voice. "To start, I will always be home by dawn. We will make it my witching hour. If I cannot get home, then I will send you a message. If you have no word from me then you will know there have been complications and you must leave immediately."

He frowned. "If I am caught, they will come for you, princess. And now comes the hard part, escaping on your own. But you are more than capable, Alexis," he said when he saw the objection in her eyes. He reached up and turned her face towards him. "You must pack only your carpet bag and your reticule. Just what you came with. In fact, tonight when we get home, I will help you pack it. That way it is done if you must leave in a hurry. Your jewels…yes, I know about them, Alexis. I searched the bloody thing."

"You searched my carpet bag? You did not read the letters I brought from home?" she asked, outraged.

"Of course, I did. I am an accomplished spy, don't forget."

"Oh, my god!" She looked at him with horror. "You know all about me! How could you?"

"Well, not all about you. Although I did get a fair idea of how lonely you were. I still am unsure about why you ran. I can hazard a guess. I am thinking that since your aunt somehow had your unposted mail, she played the villain of the scene."

"Well, you would be right. She tried to force her beast of a son on me in hopes of getting my fortune." She shrugged. "It seems so long ago."

"Yes, well, after we pack up that carpet bag of yours, we must destroy those letters. Should anyone discover your father is an English general, there will be only trouble for you."

"That makes sense."

"You must only pack practical items. Your heavy cloak, one sensible dress. Your boots, your jewels, and your money.

I will help you. I will also put in your purse my permit to enter Gravelines. Fifteen of them were granted to female entrepreneurs, so you will be all right." He smiled at her. "You are a consummate actress now, Alexis. Being one of those entrepreneurs will be easy for you."

She gently rubbed his cheek, while he gave his instructions. He could see her visualizing the scenario she would need to be a female merchant. It pleased him. She had the makings of an excellent spy.

"Your hair is your most dominant feature. We will also pack hair dye. Black."

Alexis wrinkled her nose and he grinned.

"But there will not be time to waste on dyeing it immediately. Tie it up tight and wear a bonnet. You will have to dye it on the road. Then you must leave. Do not hire a coach. If someone is pursuing you, the first search will be thoroughfares. Instead go down to the Seine, to Napoleon's iron bridge. There is a walkway there, a lane of sorts. The banks are bricked. There is an old man there who operates a gondola. For a price, he will oar you out of town."

She brushed back his hair. "I hope it never happens."

"Oh, it will happen. It is just a question as to whether we leave together or not. Let us pray we get out together. It might not be as frightening if we are not exposed, but we will leave here, without much of anything but our persons either way." He smiled at her. "Even if we go out together, you will only pack as though you are leaving on a brief business trip. Everything you purchased will be left behind, I am sad to say."

She smiled. "It will be enough to have you with me. Everything else is expendable."

He looked at her, watching her face as this new reality

settled in. "We will be leaving soon now, princess. When Napoleon pulls out, so do we. Our task will be complete."

He let that information sink into her consciousness. Alexis had lived a fantasy here in Paris. The world she had created was not her world. Here in Paris, she had been confined to the townhouse, yet she had been given a social freedom she had never experienced in England. She would have to begin to withdraw to her real world.

He sighed, continuing with the escape plan. "Alone or together, we must get to Gravelines. It will be the only way for us to leave France; the only port which can take us to England. Once clear of the city, we should be able to hire a cart at least to take us there. In Gravelines, you must go to the docks. Next to the warehouse is a lace retailer. Ask if there are any messages for Aran of the Sea."

"Aran of the Sea?" She giggled. "A bit romantic, is it not?"

"What can I say? I was an uncorrupted idealist at the time. It has been a long time for me, Alexis, in more ways than one. It does sound a little corny now." He chuckled. "But look at you, Alexis. Are you the aristocratic girl you were when you stood on the wharf at Gravelines?"

"Oh, Aran. I don't even know that naïve girl now." She was quiet, still caressing his cheek. "And if there are no messages?"

"Then you must go to the docks and find out if a ship is in port from Yorkshire. Use my name to get aboard. Aran Forsythe is my English name."

She looked at him and raised her eyebrows.

"I am an English lord, as ridiculous as that may seem here. Not much of one, I admit." He grinned at her. "Don't look too impressed, my dear. I am an impoverished member of the peerage."

He returned to the subject of her escape. "Offer to pay them well for your fare to my estate. It is near a small fishing village named Claron. They can dock there. Harwood Place sits on the hill above the village. You must tell my sister Arabella, or Jem, my overseer, that I have sent you. They will protect and keep you until your father returns." Or as long as you wish to stay, he added silently. "If I am alive, I will come to you there."

Alexis said nothing. Her hand stilled on his cheek. Her eyes were wide and glazed with unshed tears, and he knew she now understood completely their position here. The escape plans made it concrete. A pang of remorse shuddered through his consciousness. He wished he could have left her innocent of their precarious roles here in Paris.

"Now, repeat it back to me."

He listened while she recited it back, correcting any errors. When she had it perfectly, he reached up and patted her cheek.

"What about Rolande?" she asked.

"Rolande can be trusted, but never informed." He looked at her attempting to stress the seriousness of his words. "He is a Parisian, never forget."

Her chin jutted out stubbornly and he guessed her thoughts.

"No, Alexis, he can never come with us. He is a creature of this decadent city. Picture Rolande for a moment." He paused, allowing her the opportunity to do so before continuing. "He would never survive in England. Even London would not accept him. It would be a miserable and terrible existence for him."

He watched her until he was sure she understood. At last, she nodded. He released a breath and squeezed her hand.

"I do not believe he will ever betray us, but you must never put him in that position. You would be asking him to betray his country and that is too much. Love Rolande. Be his friend, but if you are his devoted friend then you must protect him. This is done with your silence, love."

He sighed. "He may help you leave if he is about, but do not give him details. He is smart enough not to ask. I am sure he knows something is very wrong about how I live, and what I do. He is always very careful to never bring it up."

They packed up their picnic and headed back to town. Their discussion had dampened the mood. Alexis sat quietly beside him, holding his arm. It was dusk when they passed the gypsy camp along the Seine and worked their way back to the townhouse.

Once home, they silently packed her bag. Each item of clothing was rolled up to take less space. Alexis insisted on removing the extra petticoat and adding shirt and trousers for Aran. He set her long-strapped reticule on top. It held money, both Francs and English pounds, jewels, and the precious permit for Gravelines. She set her boots on top and covered the whole thing with her full-length heavy woolen cloak. Together, they burned the letters in the fireplace.

When the last letter had curled into a black char, he turned to her. "Now, princess, you are ready. I will add a bottle of hair dye tomorrow." He smiled sadly. "We can only hope to leave in a civilized fashion." Or to leave alive at all, he added silently, thinking of the net Fouche had thrown around him.

Chapter Twenty-One

Aran leaned back against the frescoed wall and surveyed the club house he had hired for the night's entertainment. It was late. The lanterns had been turned down to a level which made it difficult to see across the room. The rich haze of tobacco smoke added to the gloom. The champagne and brandy had flowed freely all evening.

This was not a function to which men brought their wives. All who attended had every expectation the evening would compete with some of Paris's finest whore houses. Only less controlled and free to those lucky enough to get an invitation. It attracted the roughest of Napoleon's officers, those who had been hardened in the field. No amount of depravity was too much for them. There was only one rule. What happened here was to be kept in strictest confidence.

It was the time of night he most detested at these parties. He would find a way to slip away soon. There was every indication this event, like many of Gigi's parties,

parties he paid for, would turn into the usual orgy. It was a good exchange for him and Gigi, especially now with Alexis in his home. They had found a suitable venue. She had agreed to host the event, which he had agreed to pay for.

He had been only mildly successful at this gathering. There were officers here from all over Europe. It was not unusual for this to be the case. However, the number of senior officers in Paris currently was an interesting development. Napoleon must have pulled his experienced personnel from the furthest corners of his realm. This was a piece of information the admiral would be interested in.

He had met many men from Spain; this too was good news for England. That Napoleon was extracting his commanders and bringing them here to Paris to advance upon Russia was evident. It would certainly leave his empire dangerously staffed with inexperienced leaders. There would be another missive sent to the admiral tomorrow. He tried to memorize the names, ranks, and previous postings of each new introduction. He would need to be as specific as possible.

The center of the room, which was reserved for dancing, had deteriorated into a sexual morass. Most of the women were topless. To his right, a young officer groped his lavishly gowned partner and hung on her shoulder, all while swaying to the music in a grotesque parody of a waltz. A boisterous cheer erupted across the room; an officer had tipped a masked woman over a table occupied by his friends. He rammed into her as his acquaintances cheered him on. Their hoots and hollers had drowned out the music for the dancing, which made little difference to those on the floor.

Gigi approached him with De Sole on her arm. De Sole

CYNTHIA KEYES

was her prize. As a marshalled general, he was the highest-ranking officer in the room. Gigi wore a gown in emerald and gold, with a sheer bodice, her breasts cleverly hidden with tufts of embroidered gold leaves. The left side of her skirt was slit to her thigh. She swayed as she walked towards him on the general's arm, each movement exposing a peek at her long legs.

"Ah, my love," she greeted Aran. "Why are you so alone here?"

She slid her hand between the folds of his partially open shirt, caressing his bare chest. She looked up at De Sole. "Perhaps we can accommodate him together?"

The general laughed. It was a harsh sound. Aran was reminded of the reports of his brutality in Spain. He was partly to blame for the Spanish campaign's reputation as the bloodiest battle in history. It was documented that he had once taken a village and slaughtered two thousand of its thirty-five hundred residents: men, women, and even children. This man was conscienceless.

"Ah, Gigi, as much as that may appeal to you, I would far rather have a woman for our third partner." He looked at Aran and narrowed his eyes. "Where is the beauty I saw you with at the opera the other night? Now she is a piece of wild strawberry I could enjoy."

Aran's stomach twisted. De Sole wanting Alexis was not a development he was comfortable with. All reports of De Sole were that he was a dangerous man with unhealthy appetites.

"I could hardly enjoy the performance; my eyes were only for her. Red heads are my preference." De Sole reached down and tweaked Gigi's breast. "No offence, my dear."

Gigi trailed her hand down Aran's chest. "So my stallion

190

has a new lover. I cannot wait to meet her. You must bring her to celebrate with us." She licked her lips suggestively. "We will help her enjoy her evening, will we not?"

She looked up at De Sole and giggled.

Aran shrugged. "She is not a woman who enjoys this kind of entertainment."

"Ah, but I insist. Sometimes a little force is what these creatures need. I confess I want the woman." De Sole pressed his thin lips together. He looked at Aran, squaring his shoulders, and commanded, "It is not patriotic to keep such a prize to yourself. I demand you share her, Garscon."

His voice was harsh. He softened his order with a leer. "After all, I am willing to share with you."

He reached into the slit of Gigi's dress and squeezed her. She gave a little yelp of pain. A moment's fear crossed her face. Even for Gigi, this man was too much. If she were an operative as he suspected, tonight she may have to pay dearly for the information she gathered.

"Come, Gigi." De Sole tugged her arm.

Again, fear flashed in her eyes.

Aran felt a wave of pity for her. She had been a good friend to him in Paris. He grimaced. There was little he could do for her. She had her general, but at what cost? It was time for him to leave.

Once in the quiet relief of his room, he stood and looked down at his Alexis. She looked innocent and young as she slept. He was determined to keep her from harm while she was in Paris. Already she was in danger. She had somehow captured De Sole's attention, which surprised and concerned him. He would have to be careful with her. De Sole was not a man to be taken lightly. There were dangers to introducing her to society. De Sole was one of the worst of them.

He slid into bed and pulled Alexis against his body. She sighed and rested her head on his chest. He stroked her soft hair. He and Alexis would have to carefully avoid De Sole until they were safely out of Paris. What De Sole wanted, he got. Aran knew he would kill him or die trying before De Sole had a chance to hurt Alexis.

Chapter Twenty-Two

Tomorrow night was the party. Alexis was already excited. Rolande insisted she plan her ensemble today, trying on her gown to be sure no last-minute adjustments would have to be made. She stood before the mirror in her dressing room, while Rolande examined her for any last-minute adjustments that could be made to her new gown.

"And this time, *cherie*, you must wear a petticoat. Such a shame." He shook his head and sighed. "The *monsieur* has insisted. I informed him there would be many women there whose bodies would be displayed in such a way. It is the latest fashion, after all, but he was not to be moved."

He adjusted her skirts. "Not to worry, my love." He pulled back her train. "I have made it *tres* thin. Hardly noticeable."

Alexis looked at herself critically. She was indeed beautiful in the lovely gown. It was a soft emerald, almost creamy in color. She touched the dark emeralds that graced her neck. They had been her mother's. They were perfect for the gown. She ran her fingers over her bodice. It was cut low, but not too low. She would be glamorous.

Rolande stood beside her and admired his creation. "I'll put your beautiful hair up in a loose twirl, with just a little bit escaping to your pale shoulders. No one will be more sexy or more beautiful."

She leaned over and kissed his cheek. "Thank you, Rolande."

She smiled at him in the mirror, and he returned it with a wink.

"We have decided, yes? The dress will be perfect for the ball. And now, my love, you must change. The *monsieur* wishes to take you to a bistro for lunch."

She loved to stroll the streets of Paris with Aran. Today was an especially fine experience. The sun shone, bringing the Parisians out in droves to enjoy a patio lunch.

Aran selected an outdoor café. They were led to a table on the perimeter. It was perfect for people watching, a pastime Alexis had adopted from Rolande. They enjoyed their lunch while Alexis happily scanned the passersby.

"Look, Aran. Another turbaned woman." She giggled. "It has become a popular trend. Somehow, I cannot imagine wearing it."

"It has been all the rage since the Egyptian campaign." He smiled at her. "But you, princess, should try to never cover that glorious hair."

His eyes focused beyond her shoulders. He seemed to tense.

"Ah, Garscon. What a pleasant surprise to find you here."

She looked up to see a tall solid man with a stoic square face. He was at least forty, but his narrow eyes and serious countenance made him look older. Beside him was an orderly in uniform. A jolt of recognition tightened her stomach. This was the man who had stared at her at the Palais Garnier.

"And your lovely companion. You must introduce us."

She could sense Aran's tension. This was not an introduction he was pleased to make. She reminded herself to take care.

"My love, this is General De Sole. General, this is my dear friend Alexis de Mal."

The man reached for her hand and raised it to his lips. He held it there, just shy of his mouth, for several uncomfortable seconds, staring directly into her eyes before he touched it with his lips. She could have sworn he had licked her just lightly with his tongue.

I must be mistaken, she thought.

"It is indeed a pleasure to meet you. And one, I admit, I have looked forward to." He held her hand firmly and drew her arm to the side to examine her person. "I saw you the other night at the opera. Up close, you are even more beautiful, my love."

He scanned her body, lingering on her breasts, before returning to her eyes.

Alexis tugged her hand away, her cheeks blushing with his familiarity. It was disconcerting. She pulled her arm up against her body to block his gaze.

He watched her cheeks redden. "And shy. What a prize you have here, Garscon."

She looked at Aran, detecting a flash of irritation on his face before he smiled up at the general. "She is indeed a prize, but I fear she is not at all accustomed to our ways here in Paris."

The general reached around and dragged a chair up close to her. He seated himself so close she had to shift over toward Aran to avoid his thighs. She scooted over as far as she could. Aran grabbed her hand beneath the table and gave it a little squeeze of warning.

"Ah, but it would be such a pleasure to teach you our ways, madame." He said the words as though their meaning was lecherous.

Alexis looked at the general's cold blue eyes. There was something cruel in his gaze. Even now his eyes still roamed over her body, rudely assessing her.

Alexis was becoming annoyed. She raised her chin and replied, "It is too bad, *monsieur*. I find I have all the instructions I need at present. Perhaps later." She rested her hand on Aran's shoulder. "I am so very busy presently."

"Ah, but I have already had a little talk with Garscon, have I not?" He flashed Aran an oily smile. "He is never averse to sharing."

Again, there was a lewd insinuation in the expression.

"But sadly I am." She smiled back at De Sole. Her eyes had a dangerous glint.

The general gave an unpleasant snort of laughter. He continued to look at her, his cold blue eyes hard as he addressed Aran. "Your woman is a little too headstrong, Garscon. I expect you will teach her to be more accommodating."

Alexis felt an involuntary shudder at his words.

Aran ignored his comment. "As much as it is disappointing to have to leave your company, general, I fear we have another appointment." He looked at his watch. "It grows late. Come, my dear."

He stood and held his hand to Alexis who took it with relief.

De Sole stood as they prepared to leave. "I will look

forward to our next encounter, *mademoiselle*." He looked at Aran, his face set in harsh lines. "I am sure it will be soon."

His final words had the uncomfortable ring of a warning.

Alexis could feel the general's eyes boring into her back as she walked away. Once on the street, Aran quickened their pace.

"This De Sole is an evil man, Aran. He gives me the shivers."

"He is the cruelest creature I have ever encountered. His exploits in Spain speak for themselves. I begin to think he is also one of those men who enjoy inflicting pain, especially with women. We must be careful, princess. I am afraid he has a tendre for you."

"Ug. He is disgusting."

"Yes, but he is also powerful. You handled him well, love. But you must be careful to avoid him in the future." Aran glanced behind him as he took her arm.

They crossed the street in a direction opposite the route they must take to go home. Still moving at a brisk pace, he led her towards the crowds of the Palais Royale. He glanced behind him once more.

"What is it, Aran? Are we being followed?"

"I believe so."

Alexis went to look behind her, but he tugged her arm.

"Do not look back."

They meandered at a brisk pace across the park in Palais Royale's center, then along the paved walkway banking the many shops. It was a busy day for shopping. Aran expertly maneuvered her through the crowds. Finally, he led her to a stair beside an elegant shop. They climbed to the second floor. They entered a room through a set of elaborately gilded doors.

Aran had been silent. Alexis followed his lead. Upon entering the packed room, noisy with groups of people playing some sort of games, she could not resist asking, "What is this place?"

He weaved her through the crowds with increasing speed, intent on his destination. Without turning, he answered, "It is a casino, love. Palais Royale has several on its second floor."

They reached a rear exit. Aran pushed through the door, pulling her behind him. They skipped down a set of stairs, much narrower this time, descending into an alley. Holding her hand, Aran jogged forward, pulling her with him. Halfway down the lane, he yanked her abruptly into a narrow opening between two buildings, pushing her in front of him. They leaned against the wall, catching their breath.

Alexis went to ask him what was occurring. He set his finger on her mouth to indicate she be silent. She watched wide-eyed as two soldiers ran past. After a moment, Aran took her hand and they hurried back the way they had come. This time, they did not go up the stairs but followed the lane back into the crowds of Palais Royale.

"Is there some way to cover your hair, princess?" he asked, looking at her exposed red locks.

Wordlessly, she took her shawl from her shoulders and wrapped it around her head, tucking the ends neatly into the top.

He laughed, reaching up and adjusting it for her. "You have your turban, Alexis." He tucked a few loose tendrils back into place. "There, fashionable at last."

She laughed too. It was a relief after the hectic rush of the last few minutes. He took her arm. They continued at a hurried pace, this time at least in the direction of his townhouse, via an unfamiliar route. Aran was still careful to look behind him periodically.

"Who were they, Aran, and why were they following us?"

"They wore De Sole's insignia. Which is a surprise. I was sure they were Fouche's men." He looked at her with an apologetic smile. "I underestimated your lure, princess. There is only one reason the man would have me followed. He wants your address."

"My address? But I only just met him!"

"He saw you at the opera. He approached me at Gigi's party wanting information about you. He has decided to have you, my dear. This is a man who gets what he wants. He sees it as his right."

Alexis wrinkled up her nose and scowled.

"Gigi," she muttered. She was still feeling raw about the party. She had hated his attendance at that event, knowing now what his parties entailed, and knowing too her rival would be doing her best to lead him away from her.

Aran ignored her scowl. "My guess is the meeting today was no accident. He had men close at hand to follow us. It was planned. He would not believe you reside with me. Even here in Paris, living with a mistress is not done. It is the fashion to set up one's mistress in her own rooms. Any courtesan of value would demand it. If he could get your address, you would have an unwelcome visitor tonight."

Alexis shivered. "I find it perverted he should be so vigilant after so brief an encounter."

"He is a perverted man. But also, I think, my reputation for supplying him and his cohorts with willing women has done us no favors here. In his mind, because you are mine, you are a woman I can make available to him. He sees you as an accessible prize. He has said so twice."

Alexis realized they were directly behind Aran's town-house. They slipped between the hedges into the backyard and safely entered his home.

Aran put his hands on her shoulders. "I am sorry, my love. Now the streets are off limits to you. You cannot leave. Even the backyard will not be available to you during daylight hours. If this man should find you alone, even in public, you will be at risk." He cupped her cheek. "He will hurt you, princess. It will not be like what you and I share."

"No one shall have what you and I share. It is only for you." She smiled. "Come upstairs, my love. All this excitement has me itchy."

She kissed him briefly. "And I must do my homework. Tomorrow is a week. If I have made no progress, Rolande will be disappointed."

Despite her lighthearted tone, the glitter of De Sole's eyes stayed with her. Alexis said a little prayer, hoping the evil of this man did not touch them.

Chapter Twenty-Three

Alexis had been to many balls, but never had she been to one as extravagant as the one hosted by the renowned Eleanore de Montmorency. The ballroom had the largest dancing floor she had encountered in a private residence. Its floor was a tiled mosaic, with segments that were gold leafed. Its tall ceilings glittered with thousands of lights twinkling from crystal chandeliers. On three sides of the perimeter, arched alcoves opened to seating with glossy tables and blue velvet chairs. The head of the room was a large alcove which would host Napoleon himself. To the left, a staircase led to a balconied second floor which held the ladies' withdrawing room, a library, and sitting rooms. The entire wing of the grand palace was designed for entertaining.

Footmen in gold livery wandered through the crowds with trays holding flutes of champagne, weaving through a kaleidoscope of gowns sparkling in the amber light. Napoleon's new elite was even more flamboyant than the aristocrats they had replaced. Their extravagance bordered on excessive. It was as though they were determined to announce their successful climb to the top of the social order with displays of wealth. Alexis's treasured emeralds were insignificant amongst the volumes of ostentatious jewelry. The blue uniforms of Napoleon's officers accented the guests, and even they wore a variety of jeweled medals on their chests.

Aran led her to an alcove where Bernadette and Andre were seated.

"Ah, Alexis, *mon amie.*" Bernadette stood and kissed her on both sides of her cheeks. Holding her arm, she introduced her to the guests at the table.

"Pleased to meet you. Honored," Alexis responded to the introductions.

Just as the introductions were complete, a trumpet sounded.

"It is Napoleon," Bernadette whispered and gripped her arm. Everyone stood as the Emperor and Empress were solemnly introduced. "I have seen him now twice since coming to Paris. To be so honored!"

She was bouncing with excitement.

"Oh, he is magnificent!" Alexis contributed to the whispered praises around her. And he was. He had his Empress on his arm. The two of them glided up the floor to their alcove, her hand on his arm. They glittered with gems. Napoleon held himself with a regal demeanor, his lack of bloodline not evident in his imperious stance.

Once the royalty was seated, the room buzzed with conversation once more. The ladies began to discuss the Empress.

"Everyone says Marie Louise is not as fashionable as Josephine, but I disagree. She is glorious," Madame Clarice said.

"She is so patriotic," Alexis added. "I have only seen her twice and both times she has worn the colors of France."

"That is because she is Austrian," a thin woman with pursed lips said with a sneer.

"Oh, Oveline, be nice. She is a daughter of France now."

The music started. Eleanore de Montmorency and her partner took to the floor for a minuet to start the evening. Alexis watched the intricate moves. The couple held hands and circled, then progressed across the floor, coming together for a series of twirls, then separating for another series of intricate steps before coming together again. Other couples joined them.

The ball had begun.

Alexis held Aran's arm. The dance was similar to the English country dances, but more expansive and illustrative. Unlike the English counterpart, these dance moves were punctuated with exaggerated flirtations.

Knowing she would not want to try it without practice, she leaned close to Aran. "I will only waltz tonight, and only with you."

"Very wise," he answered, leading her over to where Bernadette stood with a circle of friends. "Can I bring you ladies some refreshments? Champagne, perhaps?"

"How very gallant." Bernadette smiled at him. "I would love champagne. Madame Dumont?"

She looked at an elderly matron at her side who regally nodded.

Aran bowed and retreated.

Bernadette was quick to introduce her. "Alexis De Mal, I would like to present you to Madame Dumont, wife of the esteemed General Dumont."

"Pleased to meet you." Alexis gave a little curtsy.

Bernadette had mentioned that General Dumont was her husband's supreme commander. This was a valuable introduction; to befriend a general's wife would be a valuable coup. She searched her brain for a way to charm her.

The band struck up a waltz. To her dismay, General De Sole was approaching her. She swallowed the panic rising from her belly.

Not now, not now, she chanted to herself.

De Sole stood before them and bowed, clicking his heels together in a military fashion. He was a behemoth of a man, his uniform stretched taunt across his wide shoulders. His face was stoic, but for his eyes which glittered icily. She and the ladies gave the complimentary curtsy.

"May I have this dance, Mademoiselle de Mal?" He reached for her hand and bowed over it. His cold blue eyes examined her person, scanning her rudely. Again, his eyes rested on her breasts. Alexis fought the urge to bring her arm up protectively across her body. The hair tingled on the back of her neck, and she concentrated to contain her shudder.

Her cheeks burned in anger. She did not want to appear rude before the other ladies, particularly Madame Dumont, but she would not dance with this beast.

"I am afraid I cannot," she replied.

Bernadette rustled nervously beside her, but Alexis dared not meet her eyes. Instead, she watched the general's impassive face tighten in anger. His eyes flashed dangerously. Her stomach turned with a wave of unreasonable fear.

He squeezed her hand painfully. She winced.

"Surely you would not be so thoughtless as to reject a hero of the wars, my lady." Her hand had begun to ache in his grasp. He leaned forward and snarled directly into her face, "Do you not appreciate the honor I bestow upon you with this request?"

Alexis swayed back, struggling to remove her hand. She stole a glance at her acquaintances. Bernadette was wide-eyed, but general Dumont's wife held her lips in a firm line.

No matter. I will not subject myself to this man at any price. And I certainly will not share the intimacy of the waltz with him.

She finally snatched her hand free. It hurt and she smoothed it with her other hand, careful to keep an expression of pain from her face.

"I cannot," she repeated. "I have promised my Aran to waltz with only him."

She hoped the waltz was considered as risqué here as it was at home in London. In England, the waltz was reserved for couples who were committed to each other. Single women risked being labeled as promiscuous if they partook.

De Sole glared at her with icy blue eyes that promised revenge. Stoically making a slow bow, he turned to leave.

There was an awkward silence, interrupted by Madame Dumont's hearty laughter. The general paused with his back to them as Madame's laughter reverberated even in the crowded room. That De Sole had heard this further insult was plain.

Both she and Bernadette turned to Madame Dumont with identical looks of astonishment. She apparently had no qualms about insulting De Sole.

"It is time that arrogant man was put in his place." She reached over and patted Alexis's cheek. "Thank you, my dear, for allowing me to witness it. It has made my night."

She chuckled. Looking at her and Bernadette, she said, "I must reward you. I am having a ball tomorrow night. Would the two of you like to attend?"

"Oh, we would be delighted!" Bernadette replied.

She looked at Alexis with her dark eyes glowing. Alexis could only nod.

"Then I will send the invites to you, Bernadette. My husband will know the address. You can manage the rest." She waved her hand, dismissing the issue, and chuckling once more, she returned to her husband's side.

Alexis and Bernadette grasped each other's arms and giggled. In her celebration, she forgot for the moment the unfortunate encounter with De Sole.

Bernadette whispered, "Madame Dumont seldom has a party. It is rumored her husband detests them. I have heard he has been known to retreat to his office and work, while the ball goes on." She squeezed her arm. "It will be a small affair but extremely exclusive, Alexis. We are honored to get this invitation."

Aran arrived and looked at them curiously. "You ladies look as though you are enjoying the evening."

He handed them each a flute of champagne.

"We are," they said in unison and laughed together.

The band stuck up another waltz.

Alexis handed Bernadette her glass. "This we must dance, my love."

Aran walked her out onto the floor. From the corner of her eye, she saw General De Sole leaning against the wall. His face was seething with anger as his eyes followed their progression onto the dance floor. She experienced a flash of fear— a deadly premonition.

Even as Aran held her in his arms, and they twirled around the room, Alexis could not shake the fear that De Sole would exact a terrible price for tonight's humiliation.

Chapter Twenty-Four

The next morning at breakfast Alexis was still gleeful concerning her invitation to Dumont ball and chattered happily in Spanish.

"There will be plenty of military there, Aran." She smiled. "This time, it is the home of a general. Maybe I will get the opportunity to search the library. A general's desk. That would be interesting. Yes?"

"No."

"No? I think it would be ideal. Only think of what could be found."

"Alexis, if anyone searches the home of the general, it will be me. I have years of experience—you do not." He caught her eye. "Do not even consider it. You were lucky with the corporal, it's true. But I will not have you even thinking of repeating the endeavor. Leave it to me."

He smiled at her pout. It was short-lived.

Her eyes lit up.

"Ah, I just remembered something of importance. I

must tell you what Bernadette shared with me. Apparently, the general is inclined to retreat to his office and work." She shook her head. "Imagine, even during a ball. Therefore, if you search his office, you best do it early."

Aran did not want her to try to snoop into the general's domain. "Hmmm, then I promise if I decide to do a search, I will have you run interference. You will have an equally difficult assignment. Your task may even be more important than the actual search. Deal?"

"Deal," she answered, clearly disappointed.

That should keep her out of trouble. He would not tell her she would be fortunate to be introduced to the general, never mind conversing with him to distract him. "Two entertainments in as many days. That must make you happy?"

"I am happy. Even Rolande is pleased with the challenge of outdoing himself in producing an elaborate ensemble for me." She grinned. "After breakfast, I have to do more fittings."

Emile entered with a letter in hand. "A message for you, *monsieur*. The boy said it was to be delivered immediately."

He handed Aran a missive.

"Thank you." Aran ripped it open and read.

"What is it, Aran?" Alexis asked.

He carefully composed his face before looking up and smiling at her.

"Not important, love." He nonchalantly slid it into his pocket. "Just work, a problem at the warehouse, but nothing for you to worry over."

He rose and kissed her cheek. "You, my darling, need to worry about being beautiful tonight."

"I do," she said with a laugh, "and it is an exhausting job."

"I will be out for a few hours, love. Then I will check your progress."

Aran got his topcoat and hat from the entry and left the building. His letter had been from Gigi. Once outside, he pulled it from his pocket to reread it. It was brief.

Aran, my love, please hurry to my apartment. I must see you. It is a matter of importance —— Gigi

It was unlike Gigi to message him at home. Whatever it was, it must be something of significance. He walked onto the main boulevard and was thankful to be able to hail a cab immediately. He hoped this was not another effort of Gigi's to get his attention. His involvement with her as a lover was over. Today, he would make clear the status of their relationship.

He knocked at her door. There was a long wait. He was about to knock again when the door opened a crack. Gigi looked at him through a narrow sliver then opened the door and pulled him inside. She was wearing a widow's veil. Black and tightly knit, it was draped over her face, covering her to the chin. The veil was out of place with the comfortable cotton robe that she wore. Something was very wrong.

She stood still in front of him. He waited.

Finally, she said, "Can I get you a brandy?"

Before answering her, he reached over and lifted the veil. He drew a breath. Her face had been savagely beaten. Both eyes were shades of dark violet. Her one eye was red, narrowed to a thin slit. Her bottom lip was swollen. She turned her face to the floor.

He gently put his hand under her chin and tilted her face to the right. Despite a thick coat of make-up, a faint bluish tinge blushed her cheek.

"De Sole?" he asked.

"Yes." She flipped the veil back over her face. "Brandy?"

He nodded.

She poured them both a drink and after handing him his, sat on her sofa, curling her feet beneath her. Aran sat down and took a healthy swallow.

"I did not ask you here to witness this or to extract some sort of revenge with you as my pawn. I want to assure you of that." She took a drink and set down her glass. "I asked you here to warn you."

Aran reached across to her and took her hands in his. "I will try to find a way to avenge you, Gigi. You must know that."

He was still in shock. The degree of damage the bastard had done was beyond what he could comprehend.

Gigi waved away his words. "No, Aran, I do not want that. I almost did not message you because I worried over what you might do. You must promise me you will do nothing."

She squeezed his hands.

Aran was silent.

"I have something important to tell you, Aran, but I will not until you give me your word you will act as though you have never seen this." When Aran was still silent, she pressed on. "You warned me, Aran. I wanted De Sole and I got him."

She took a breath, releasing his hands, and leaned back against the couch. She made a soft wheezing sound as she carefully shifted her body. "I will have your word before I tell you what you must hear."

It was apparent she had taken hard blows to her body as well. He was tempted to pull off her robe and examine her.

"Have you seen a doctor, Gigi?"

"Yes. I was able to see someone last night. I will be all right." She laughed a little. There was no humor in it. "Now give me your word of honor that you will leave this matter to me. He is too powerful for you to take down, Aran. Your word, Aran."

"Why must it always be a bargain with you, Gigi?"

"Your word of honor, Aran."

"You have my word, Gigi."

She expelled a deep breath. "I must warn you. All of this," she said, indicating her face and body, "was because I refused to wear a red wig. He insisted I pretend to be Alexis, your mistress. When I objected, he went into a rage. He began beating me. He raped and ranted and raged."

She took a drink of brandy. "He went wild. I couldn't control him. He said Alexis was loyal to you, and you were ignorant enough not to force her to share."

The glass shook in her hand as she raised it to her lips and took a hefty swig.

"When he was through with me, he sat just there on the chair." She waved towards the chair across the room. She began to cry. "I was on the floor, Aran. I was so damaged, and he did not care. That is the part which now disturbs me the most. My pain was nothing to him—I was nothing."

She shook with heaves of anguish. Aran shifted forward on the sofa and held her. Putting his arms around her, he rocked slowly back and forth while she cried. He had no words for her. He could only stroke her and coo soft sounds into her ear. In time, the sobbing stopped. Her back stiffened, as she began to revive, and she pushed away from him.

She lifted her veil, raised her head, and looked at him. He had to concentrate to avoid wincing at her ravaged face.

"You have been watched. He now knows she resides in

your home. This enraged him. He said he would have to kill you." She looked at him earnestly. "He meant it, Aran. The man will arrange your death.

"And when you are dead, he will teach your redhead a lesson she will never forget. This is what he plans." She pulled away from him, stood, and went to the sidebar to pour herself another brandy. "He could not have been more serious, Aran. The man is insane."

She indicated her damaged body with a wave of her arm. "This he can do without a second thought, without provocation. He is angry with you, and he is angry with your lover. With the two of you, it will be much worse. There will be no one to stop him. A marshalled general has only Napoleon himself as a superior. And he is without conscious. You are in extreme danger, my love."

Aran's stomach clenched. He was done. It was time to leave Paris. Alexis would never be subject to this while he breathed. It was too dangerous for both of them. All this time, he had concentrated on keeping from the clutches of Fouche, and now it was the maniac De Sole who would bring them down.

He walked over to Gigi and carefully put his arms around her. Slowly, he leaned in and kissed her on her swollen lips.

"Gigi, thank you for being my true friend. I have appreciated you." He pulled her in for a soft hug. "Please, take care of yourself, love."

He held her gently in his arms. She laid her head on his shoulder. It was several minutes before she finally pushed him back with a shaky smile.

He kissed her on the forehead. "Goodbye, Gigi."

He let himself out. As he waited for a cab, he began to formulate a plan. It was time to travel to Gravelines again and fetch some more English wool. This time, he would take his mistress to make the journey more pleasurable. That would be the cover.

They would be leaving first thing in the morning, at dawn.

Chapter Twenty-Five

Alexis sat quietly and listened to Aran explain their precarious situation. "But can he do this? How can he just have you killed? Is there no law and order in France?"

Her stomach ached with fear.

"He can, Alexis. He is above the law here." He ran his hand through his hair. "He will take care to cover his actions, to be sure. The act will be surreptitious. But think of it, Alexis, if he is implicated in anyway, the investigation will grind to a halt. He knows his power, Alexis."

Alexis stood and paced her bedroom. "We should leave immediately. We must get out of here, Aran. I am afraid for you."

"We will. Tomorrow morning at dawn, we will head to Gravelines. This afternoon, I will arrange it. We will have to take the carts. Our cover will be that we go for another load of English wool for my uniform factory here in Paris. I'll need several men and drivers." He flashed his half smile. "No coach, my love. You will go out the way you came in, princess."

"Why not leave now? I don't want to take any chances." And she did not. Losing Aran was not a possibility she wished to contemplate.

"Alexis, come here. Sit down."

She reluctantly perched on the edge of the bed, facing him where he sat at her dressing table. He took both her hands in his.

"We are being watched, Alexis. And not just by the maniac De Sole. Since I began this new assignment, Fouche has been vigilant. I know my cover here in Paris is cracking, that I am held in suspicion. We know someone is placed in my house. It may be my footman Emile, but it could be any of them. And I am being followed each time I leave the house. There are too many men assigned to keep me under surveillance to assume it is routine. Fouche is closing in. If we panic now and tear out of town, it will be suspicious. Our activities will be immediately reported to the Home Office. We would be picked up before we even got out of Paris."

"But Aran—"

"No, princess. The earliest we can leave is dawn. We will pack only for a quick trip for the supplies needed for my work. You must act as though you are thrilled to be able to accompany me on a run to Gravelines. Even dawn tomorrow will be considered short notice. Hopefully, it will pass without too much suspicion. I will send a message to the admiral that we are coming out." He smiled at her. "When they discover I am bringing out a princess of the Royal Navy, they will send a sloop at least to fetch us from Gravelines." He chuckled. "We will be sailing home in style."

Still holding her hands, and serious once more, he looked into her eyes. "We will behave as normally as possible. Rolande will pack a chest for the two of us as usual. And do not tell him anything, Alexis. Remember what I told you. He must remain innocent of our activities."

"I understand, Aran."

"Tonight, we will go to the party as planned. All must be as though we have no concerns. To do anything else will not only be suspicious to the home office, but it could also drive De Sole into a hurried attack."

"Oh god, Aran, I do not know if I can. To go to a party and attempt to be gay is impossible for me." Her eyes burned. She wanted nothing more than to throw herself on the bed and cry. Or to hide forever from the world in her dressing room.

"You can, princess. We will do it one step at a time. You know our schedule for the next twenty-four hours. Leave it be now. Concentrate only on your excitement to join me on this trip. Believe it. Live it as you lived the role of my mistress."

She shook her head.

"Yes, Alexis. It is not an option. You are Alexis de Mal. You are going to a ball tonight. And then tomorrow your lover has promised to take you with him on a business trip. It is a coupe for you. You could not be happier." He squeezed her hands. "You must not fail."

Rolande entered the room.

Aran smiled a welcome. "Ah, just the young man I need to see."

Alexis watched open-mouthed as Aran portrayed his role perfectly. Once again, as he had done when she'd arrived in Paris, he was helping her stay in character through his example. "

I know you are busy planning to make my princess as lovely as only she can be, but I have another task for you."

He leaned down and kissed the top of Alexis's head. "I am leaving for the port tomorrow. I have just asked Alexis to join me. I wonder if you could add a few things for her to my trunk?"

Alexis took a deep breath. If he could do it, then so could she.

"This I can do." Rolande looked at Alexis. "But how exciting for you, *cherie*."

Alexis bit back her panic and rose to face him. "Yes. I will be going along this trip."

"You do not look too pleased, *cherie*."

"Oh, Rolande." She smiled and took his arm. "I am only thinking of all the dust I endured on my journey here."

She laughed. It sounded brittle to her ears.

Aran nodded. "Good. I will leave you two to it. I am afraid I must go now to make our other arrangements." He pulled her back from Rolande and placed a quick kiss on her lips. "I will see you later, my love. Make yourself beautiful for me this afternoon."

"I will be breathtaking, Aran. You will be proud of me." She knew Aran understood this was her assurance she would succeed with her deceptions.

"I do not doubt it for a minute," he replied. He patted her cheek with a wink and left the room.

I wish I could be as nonchalant as him, she thought grimly. She would concentrate on one thing at a time as Aran instructed. For now, it was packing.

"What shall I take, Rolande? I know this time we must pack for comfort." She made a face with an exaggerated pout. "There will be no glamorous gowns for this trip."

"True. But then we can compensate with some truly racy undergarments. Yes?"

She laughed. "You are outrageous, Rolande. How ever would I exist without you?"

Rolande finally settled on a few comfortable day dresses. "We will need a warm cloak for you. Who knows what the weather will bring, eh?"

He glanced down at the warm, full length black one covering her carpet bag. He began rooting through the closet. She realized with shock that Aran was right. Rolande knew something was not quite right. That he had chosen to ignore the perfect wrap for the journey was evidence enough for her.

She wondered what he thought of her escape luggage. Maybe he only thought she was prepared should Aran and she quarrel. She dismissed it from her mind. She had other concerns.

All day she worried about Aran. At any moment he might be fighting off an attack—she squashed the thought. She would instead look forward to the party, as Aran had instructed. She was Alexis de Mal, his lover, excited and pleased to enjoy her success as an accomplished mistress.

Rolande insisted she have a warm bath, followed by a nap. "You must be at your best for the party. We cannot have you yawning over midnight lunch. You will be at your finest this way, my dear."

Alexis was surprised when she awoke from her nap. She had been sure she would not be able to sleep. But it had been hours since she had crawled into her bed. She was glad. It was going to be a long night, and another long day tomorrow.

Rolande dressed her with care.

While he was working her hair, she said, "I think I would like tight French braids rolled into a bun." She looked up at him in the mirror. "I want something off my face, and so tight it will hold for days."

And something which would be easily covered with a bonnet, she added silently.

She expected Rolande to protest. She looked at him in her mirror. Rolande would not meet her eyes.

He knows something is wrong. Her stomach clutched.

She took a deep breath and tried to relax. She must be confident that if he had surmised all was not well, he would keep it to himself.

She watched as he made a series of tight French braids, starting at her hairline and progressing to the crown of her head. They were so tight she could feel her scalp pull. He made at least twelve. Then he wove them together into one large braid which he curled into a bun. It was brilliant. Her hair would hold for days. And it looked sophisticated and elaborate enough to impress at the ball.

She reached back and held his hand. Her face was serious.

"Thank you, Rolande," she said quietly.

Finally, he met her eyes in the mirror. Concern filled his eyes, then the look was gone.

"You are beautiful, *cherie.* You will be the most beautiful woman at the ball," he said with exaggerated aplomb.

She decided what she would do.

"Wait here, Rolande." She ripped a sheet of writing paper from the pad on her dressing table. Then she ripped off several more and grabbed the quill and ink. She rushed into her dressing room.

Reaching into her reticule, she pulled out her mother's emeralds. She could not give up her francs; she might need them for her journey. English pounds would be of no use to him. Unlike Aran, he did not have a permit for Gravelines and would have no reason to be in possession of them. Jewelry was all she had for him. She wanted him to have a special piece. The emeralds would do nicely. She sat on the floor and scribbled a quick note.

Dearest Rolande,

This gift is a token of my appreciation for your guidance and friendship at a time in my life I needed it the most. I will be forever grateful. I have learned many things from you, not the least of them being how to love you. And I have loved you dearly.
But this gift is also more. Think of it as your pension, one neither I nor Aran are able to provide for you at this time.
I will not be back. Please take my things. Everything which was mine is yours. Wear it, sell it, gift it, it matters only that it is yours to do with as you will.

Thank you again my dear, dear, friend
Alexis

Alexis wrapped the note around the necklace, carefully twisting the ends to hold it in place. She did the same with two additional sheets of paper. Then she bounced back into her room.

"I have a gift for you, Rolande." She held it in her hands and smiled at him. "First you must promise not to open it until at least noon tomorrow."

Rolande laughed. "Noon tomorrow," he repeated, then he looked at Alexis with his huge eyes serious. "I promise, *cherie.*"

She handed him the crudely wrapped gift. "Do not forget. Noon."

Aran stood at the door to his adjoining room. "Are you ready, princess?"

He held out his hand. She took it.

It was the beginning of a very long night.

Chapter Twenty-Six

Alexis stood in the receiving line with Aran. They would be greeted by their hosts, then announced before they entered the ball.

When it was their turn, Madame Dumont took her hand and turned to her husband. "This is the young woman I told you about. I am so glad you were able to attend, Mademoiselle Alexis de Mal."

Alexis sunk gracefully into the required curtsy. When she rose, the general looked at her with a twinkle in his eyes. He had the countenance of a kindly grandfather.

He took her hand and kissed it. "Honored, my dear."

He appeared truly delighted to meet her. Alexis wondered if the incident with De Sole could have pleased him so much.

They progressed into a ballroom smaller than the one which so impressed her at the home of Eleanore de Montmorency, but the guests were no less ostentatious. With Parisian society in transition, the leaders in Napoleon's

France were vying for the top social roles. Part of the competition was a display of wealth.

Alexis felt a shiver. She looked up. Near the exit De Sole stood, staring hard at the two of them. "Aran, it is De Sole, just there by the doors."

Aran scanned the crowd until his eyes settled on the man. He put his arm around Alexis. De Sole narrowed his eyes into an evil glare. It was so filled with malicious intent, her body clenched. The general spun around and stormed through the exit. Alexis sighed in relief.

"He is gone now. The night will be an easier one for you." Aran pulled her close and shook her a little, whispering, "Relax, enjoy your last ball in Paris. Tomorrow we will be gone. Safe from his machinations."

Alexis worked hard to take his advice. With the threat of De Sole gone, she found she was indeed able to appreciate the evening, even enjoying a round of dances with Aran.

All the latest fashions were on display. Alexis stood with Bernadette, taking in the room and pointing out the more extravagant gowns. The party was a rainbow of colors. Every imaginable shade was represented in the room. On the dance floor, a minuet was being executed by the dancers. Again, she admired the flirtatious movements of the French rendition. Dancers came together, spun in each other's arms, then separated. After a series of steps were completed, the man took the woman's outstretched hand and moved forward in a flurry of intricate steps to complete the routine again. When the dancers twirled in unison, it was a breathtaking kaleidoscope of color.

How appropriate my last night in Paris be amongst this stunning extravagance, she thought with a smile.

"Look, it is Eleanore," Bernadette whispered to her,

"and she is wearing another turban. She certainly embraces the new fashion."

"Oh, but note the sapphire pin which secures it. I think I too would wear a turban if I had such a piece to display," Alexis said.

The ladies laughed. A party of guests behind them stood and strolled to the adjoining sitting room where a buffet of delicious food was being served.

"It must be close to midnight." Alexis said, "if the food is being served."

"Yes. It has been a wonderful evening. I think I will find Andre. I want to try some of the treats they will serve." She tilted her head. "Would you like to join us?"

"No. I think I will rest here for a moment and wait for Aran." Alexis indicated the newly vacated chairs. "If I do not sit down now, I may not get another chance in this crush."

The ladies laughed again.

The orchestra played a soft waltz. Couples began to take the floor. Alexis sat, letting the music wash over her, and watched the elegant staircase to her left. Aran had gone upstairs. She knew he would not be in the upstairs games room, set up for guests to play cards or dice. He would be searching for the office of the general. It would be his last opportunity to gather information about the upcoming invasion of Russia.

The music played on. She began to become impatient. It had been almost an hour now since Aran had gone upstairs.

The general returned from the receiving room where the food was laid out. He headed towards the stairs. Alexis' heart thundered in her chest. She remembered with a rush what Bernadette had told her about the general's habit of abandoning his wife's entertainments to work in his office.

Alexis rose from her chair. She had to somehow distract the general before he reached the stairs. Her stomach rolled as she made her way across the room as briskly as she dared. The general was fast approaching the stairs. Intent only on his progress, she increased her pace, weaving through the crowds as guests returned from the dance floor with the completion of the set. To her relief, the general was waylaid by a gentleman and began a conversation at the foot of the stairs.

Now she had to find an excuse to approach the man. He had greeted her at the door, but they had not been formally introduced. Even if they had, Alexis had no idea of what she might say to him to delay him long enough for Aran to safely return from upstairs.

A footman walked by with a wide tray of champagne flutes. She snatched one from the tray. The general was just turning away from his conversation when she stepped forward and bumped into his shoulder, dropping her glass.

She let out a little squeak and stepped back from the splattering champagne.

"I am so sorry," she gasped.

The general took her arm and pulled her away from the shattered glass. Two servants rushed over to clear the mess.

"I hope you haven't been splashed, my dear." He smiled at her. His face was kindly, but she noticed a mischievous glint in his eyes and wondered if he saw through her ruse to address him.

"I am so sorry, sir. That was exceedingly clumsy of me." She reached down and brushed her skirts. When she looked up, the general was still smiling at her.

"Mademoiselle de Mal, is it not? Well, then, this is a

stroke of luck. I was hoping to be able to speak to you tonight." He looked at her with a twinkle. "If I were younger, I would ask you to dance, but alas, it is beyond me these days. But I wonder if you would allow me to take you for a stroll around the room. I do want to talk to you, my dear."

"I ...I would be honored, sir." Alexis smiled. Whatever the general wished to speak with her about was perfectly fine with her. Anything to delay him from his progress up to his office. She set her hand on his arm. They began their promenade.

The general got directly to the point. "I knew your mother, Celeste. She was a very dear friend of mine."

Alexis felt a tremor of excitement. "Did you? But you must tell me about her! She died when I was too young. I know so little about her."

He smiled at her. "You have the look of her. Like you, she was beautiful, with red hair, but I think brown eyes. She was the loveliest woman I have ever known." His eyes were distant for a moment. "And she was brave."

Alexis squeezed his arm to encourage him. She wanted to know everything possible about her adoptive mother. They continued their slow stroll around the room.

"I met her during the frightening days of the revolution. There were times when her life was endangered. I was only a young corporal then and a King's man to boot, thus I too had my moments of terror." A sadness flitted across his face. "One night the mobs had gone wild. It was not just the guillotine where lives were taken in those days. To have even the appearance of wealth was cause enough to be murdered on the streets. It was challenging times, for all of us."

He paused, lost for a moment as though recalling the memory. "We escaped through the streets together. I had been shot and wounded. She never abandoned me, though for her own safety she should have. She never faltered." He shook his head and chuckled. "We must have traversed most of the lanes to the river that night. She saved my life. After that fateful night we became friends. I was privileged to have known her, Alexis. I am so sorry you did not. But she was a woman to be proud of."

Patting her hand, he said, "I am sorry you have had to listen to the ramblings of an old man. Alas, it was long ago."

"Oh no. I wish to know everything about her. I am so pleased to be able to know of her in this."

He looked at her and smiled. "I am sure she would be proud of you too. You are a beauty. If you have even a small piece of her character, you will be a woman to be reckoned with. I was devastated when she was taken from us so young. And had I known you existed, I would have come to meet you long ago."

They had made their way back to the staircase. Aran was standing at its threshold looking at her with a perplexed expression. She flashed him a smile.

"I see your man awaits you," he said as they approached Aran. "I hope we have an opportunity to talk again. I will look for you, my dear, and then we will have another chat."

He set her hand on Aran's arm. "I have returned your girl to you. Look after her, young man."

Aran did a little bow. "I will, sir."

The general progressed up the stairs without further comment.

"How in the world did you manage that?" Aran said.

Alexis laughed. She could not refer here to their occupation or their task. She only said, "He knew my mother, Celeste."

The music began another set of the waltz. "We will have one last dance, princess. And then I fear we must retire. I find I am exhausted from all the work today."

"Productive work, my love?"

"Very productive."

Alexis whirled around the glittering ballroom in her lover's arms. Beautiful Paris would be lost to her, maybe forever. This last dance would be her farewell.

Their escape was now only hours away. She prayed they would accomplish it.

Chapter Twenty-Seven

At home, Alexis allowed Rolande to help her undress. "Thank you for waiting up for me, Rolande. We will leave my hair. I can handle it from here. You best get some sleep."

He kissed her cheek. "Good night, *cherie*."

She wondered where he would go, and what he would do when she and Aran were gone. He had never spoken of a family here in Paris; she was sure he was an orphan.

"Do you have a boyfriend, Rolande?" she blurted out.

He stood in the doorway, his hand on the knob. He looked at her with sorrowful Egyptian eyes and smiled. "I do. He works in the theatre."

He blew her a kiss and left. She let out a breath. Rolande would not be alone here; he would survive without them.

She walked into Aran's room. He had changed from the tuxedo he had worn at the ball having donned instead the sturdier clothing reserved for his work at the warehouse. He was writing a note at his dressing table. She waited until he had finished. He carefully dusted his work, held it up for a moment, then pulled a roll of missives from his inside jacket pocket. Next, he rolled the letter he had written around the others, then tied it with a string. Finally, he used melted wax from his jack to seal the letter, pressing a coinlike button onto the soft wax. He slid the neatly rolled letter into his inside pocket and turned to Alexis.

"You are going out?" she asked. "Now?"

"Yes, princess. I have vital information here. It is what we wanted. All the details we needed are here. Napoleon is putting together a grand army to invade Russia. I have the names of the commanders and troops pulled from Spain. There will be six-hundred thousand men, Alexis: the largest army in recent history! It is outrageous! Only Napoleon would do such a thing!" He grimaced. "It took me forever to copy it all from the general's office. But we did it. We have the final pieces of the puzzle."

Alexis looked at him. His eyes shone with excitement. "Must you go tonight?"

"I must, Alexis. I need to get this to my contact."

"But could we not just bring the information out with us?" she asked, struggling to shake the ominous premonition she had about him leaving. A shiver ran down her spine.

"I must get it to my contact. Whatever route they have to get this information to the admiral, it is quicker by far than what we can do." He walked to his dressing room, then returned with a long greatcoat. He pulled it onto his shoulders. "Do not worry, love. My contact is within walking distance. I will be there and back within an hour."

He gave her a quick kiss. "It will be one last delivery. Then we will be on our way." He grinned and added, "Soon, we will be home, princess!" as he went out the door.

She wanted to run after him and hold him back. Had it done any good, she would have.

But what can I say? Can I say I have a premonition of danger? He would only laugh at me, then send me to bed. Maybe it is just my apprehension about the day to come.

Alexis tried to sleep. It was impossible. She continuously checked the little clock on Aran's dressing table. Twenty minutes, thirty, now forty-five. Fifteen minutes and he would be home. He had told her an hour. With Aran, that would mean it was less than an hour. He would error on the side of conservatism.

He should be here any minute, she reasoned.

It had been an hour. No Aran. She got up from the bed and paced. She had no idea where his contact was, or even in which direction he would go to find him. There was nothing she could do but wait. There was no chance of sleeping, not with her stomach so knotted with worry.

She rooted through her closet and found a comfortable cotton day dress. It would be perfect for a long trip. She pulled off her nightie and slipped on a thin chemise. She took as much time as possible selecting stockings. The longer she took, the greater the chance Aran would arrive and interrupt her preparations.

She tugged her dress over her head. She then spent at least fifteen minutes debating the benefits of a petticoat, finally choosing to wear one. Still no Aran. She wandered back into the bedroom and looked at the clock with despair. He was now almost an hour late. Each moment dragged slowly by. Where could he be?

Carefully lighting a lantern, she went down the stair-case, and through the eerily quiet parlor toward the kitchens. Pausing at the entry, she imagined the maniac De Sole barging into their home to claim his prize. It would mean Aran was forever gone. She shuddered.

Once in the kitchens, she found a little leftover chicken

in the icebox and ate it all. She filled herself a glass of milk. On a stool, parked in the center of the long worktable, she sat with the glass in front of her next to the lantern. She just sat. And waited.

Finally, she picked up her glass and walked from the kitchen through the dining room to the stairs. In one horrible instant, she registered that she had forgotten her lantern and worse, she didn't need it. The room was no longer black with night. Soft shades of dawn had begun to enhance the room. The sun would soon rise.

Slowly, she sat on the bottom step of the stairs, setting her glass down on the floor. She squeezed her eyes tightly shut.

Breathe, Alexis.

"I cannot panic now," she whispered. "Aran will have survived."

He will have survived, and he will be confident I will too. He would be so disappointed in me if I fail. Especially if I give up without an effort. Alive or dead, he would never forgive me.

Thinking of what the general had told her of her adoptive mother helped to still her pounding heart. *She was brave, he said. She would be proud of me, he said.* Leaving her milk at the bottom of the stairs, she stood and raced up to her room.

The wool wagons would pull up at any moment. It would be so easy to climb up into the wagons.

This I will not do. She chided herself to stay focused. *I have a plan. It is more difficult, but it is much safer.*

Hurrying into the dressing room, she found the carpet bag and reticule neatly covered with her black cloak, just as they had left it.

"Thank you, Aran, for having the foresight to pack this bag. I would be far too rattled to do so now," she said aloud. She put the long strap of her purse around her neck.

After putting on her boots and wrapping the cloak around her, pulling its wide hood up over her head, she opened the carpet bag for a quick look inside. A huge dark gray bonnet was placed on the top. She smiled. Aran had thought of everything. She dashed back the hood and pulled it on, tying it snugly.

Picking up her carpet bag, she surveyed her room one more time. There was nothing else to pack. She noticed the amulet hanging from the corner of her mirror and carefully removed it, placing it around her neck. It was the only memento of France she would bring home. Walking through Aran's room on her way out, she noticed the small knife he had used to cut his wax for the letter laying on the dressing room table. She snatched it up and slid it into her pocket.

It was time to leave. She decided to go out of the back. As she stepped through the backdoor, pulling it softly closed behind her, she allowed herself only a brief moment of farewell. Her time in Paris, Rolande, and most importantly Aran had all been precious gifts in this apartment. She had grown to be a woman here in Paris. The childish girl who had arrived here thinking only of a grand adventure was so distant she could no longer conjure her up even if she wanted to. And that was a good thing.

I will surely need my strength and confidence to survive this night.

At her back gate, she scanned the lanes. All was quiet. No one stirred. It was still the gentle light of predawn. *Good, the dim light will help me get away undetected.* Pulling her hood up over her bonnet, she worked her way to the main boulevard, keeping to the shadows at the edges of the alley.

She glanced behind her intermittently. Nothing moved.

Whoever had been watching the house, and she was sure they had been under surveillance, must have followed Aran because no one pursued her now.

She crossed the boulevard. Scanning its wide length, she shivered. It was too open. There was too much chance of being detected should she think to use it to make her escape. She chose instead to use the narrow side streets to journey to the river. These streets wound their way to the river. It would take longer. They were dirty, narrow, and filled with sewage and mud, but much safer than the main roads.

She scurried through the dark streets. Each time the familiar panic rippled through her body, she focused on her adoptive mother. She may have traversed these very streets to escape her captors.

Give me strength, Celeste. Let me have your courage.

She refused to contemplate her goals beyond getting to the river and the bridge. She was tempted to fear her arrival at the river. If Aran were not there, what would she do? She pushed her worries aside. Aran had taught her to concentrate only on her current task. It had helped her to get through the ball, and it would help her with this next step of the journey.

She looked up. It was impossible to determine if the sun had risen. The buildings towered above her, leaving only a narrow strip of sky. Lines of clothes strung across the opening, further impeding her view.

A garbage can to her left crashed down into the street. She shrieked and leaned against the stoop of a derelict building. A mangy dog skittered from the can's mouth and fled up the street. She took a bracing breath and moved forward.

She remembered to check behind her periodically as Aran had done. It appeared her escape from her home had been successful. She had not been followed. No one was on the streets as of yet. It was a blessing.

She quickened her pace. If Aran were alive, he would come to the river. Perhaps he was already there and waiting anxiously for her. This revelation gave her the energy to continue. She held the carpet bag against her and jogged down the maze, fighting her tangling petticoats, intent on reaching the Siene as quickly as possible.

She burst through an alley into the light, at the river at last. A sharp breeze off the river brought with it fresh clean air, a welcome relief after the stench of human waste from the alleys. She paused and let the wind clear her head. Up ahead was the dark iron of the Pont des Arts. It was the bridge. All along the river the lane was tiled. The pounding of her boots echoed in the dawn. It became so loud to her heightened consciousness, she debated taking them off to eliminate the sound.

She was nearing the bridge. A row of delipidated buildings clung to the lane on her right, with the river on her left, its banks reinforced with brick as Aran had described. A two-foot wall protruded from the bank, then fell straight and steep into the dark waters of the Seine. Here it would be deep enough to launch a boat, or a gondola.

A little craft was tied to a protrusion on the wall, floating in the water below. A piece of the wall had been removed and a set of three steps carved into the bank. It was here they must load into the gondola. No one was around.

Hoof beats sounded in the distance. She whirled around. A man had staggered from one of the alleys into the lane, not fifty feet behind her. She squeezed into a channel between two buildings, peeking out to watch. The man continued towards her. He seemed injured or exhausted.

Is it Aran?

She gripped the brick corner of the building as she leaned out to watch his progress.

Please be, Aran.

Two horses broke into the lane behind him. She held her breath, as he began to run. He was only ten feet from her. He raised his head. Their eyes met.

It was indeed Aran. He pulled a rolled letter from his inside pocket and tossed it aside, where the breeze took it and it skittered across the bricked walk to rest against the building. Jerking his head to indicate that she move back into her hiding spot, he turned and faced the horsemen, his body sagged and exhausted.

She forced herself to lean back between the buildings. Laying back against the wall, and panting her terror, she listened as the horses approached.

Chapter Twenty-Eight

Aran looked into the violet eyes of his Alexis; her face was shrouded by the oversized gray bonnet. He sagged with relief. She had made it to the river and would survive. Reaching into his pocket he tossed the letter towards her. It would be her mission now.

Keeping her safe will be my life's most important accomplishment.

He swung his head to get her to retreat into the security of her hiding place. When she was safely out of sight, he turned to face his destiny.

They will kill me now, he thought without emotion, standing still as the riders approached.

It had been a long exhausting night. Upon entering the alley behind his home, with the missives tucked into his pocket, he had been followed. He had crossed the boulevard and tried to lose them in the maze of streets leading to the river. But always they pursued him. He passed the darkened home of his contact, Louis. He could not go there now. It would be the death of both of them.

He circled back again into the dark streets, trying to think of a way to deliver his information while keeping ahead of his tail. He decided he must somehow alert Louis to his presence. In the past, they had often met on the street, bumping into each other and cursing, while they transferred the letters.

He needed to somehow get the man awake and out into the street. In an alley, beside a heap of trash, he found what he needed. He grabbed two pieces of broken brick from the pile of rubble and scurried away. He would have to circle back twice more. An hour had already passed. Alexis would be beginning to worry.

At least his tail was not yet openly pursuing him. For now, they seemed content to keep him in their line of vision. He tried again to lose them to no avail. No matter how many times he squeezed into the tight lanes between the rows of houses, or how often he doubled backed and turned in opposite directions, they managed to always stay close. Twice he was sure he had lost them, and by sheer luck they picked up his trail.

The gods are against me tonight, he'd mourned. But he had gained enough time to scrape the word, *outside*, into the larger brick. It would have to do.

Whoever the pursuers were, they knew these streets. It was an arduous journey before he returned to the front of the contact's home at last. He tossed the brick at his front window, and the glass shattered.

There was no time to wait for Louis. He sped off down an alley at the corner. He would have to circle again and hope that Louis had gotten the implied message. The sky was beginning to lighten. Dawn was approaching. He thought of Alexis, wondering if she was awake and preparing to leave. He hoped so. With a sinking feeling, he realized these men would never have let them load up onto the wool carts and leave town. They must be De Sole's lackies.

Their only option for escape had always been the river. These were not Fouche's men; these men were hired to kill him. How ironic that after two years of avoiding suspicion and capture by Fouche, it was instead the maniac De Sole who might take him down.

Even if he managed to transfer the information, these men would pursue him. To go home would be to be caught, and if he allowed that to happen, Alexis would be at the mercy of De Sole. He prayed Alexis would be able to make the necessary trek. She was no longer safe in his home.

"Please, Alexis," he chanted to himself as he jogged down a muddy lane, "leave the apartment and go to the Seine. Please be at the river."

He finally reached the street his contact's home for the third time. With relief, he saw a man shuffling down the street.

Before he had traversed five strides, two uniformed horsemen appeared at the end of the lane.

He looked over his shoulder. His pursuers were standing in the center of the lane behind him. He had no choice but to veer off down a narrow alley to his left. His stomach turned. That De Sole's men had been joined by two men on horseback meant the chase would be in earnest. There was little chance now of reaching his contact, instead he must concentrate on staying alive.

He ran up and down the twisting streets, weaving his way to the river. Always they were behind him. When he could slip between a space too narrow for the horses, he did. But one rider would guard his place of entry while the other veered around to attempt to beat him to the exit. There was no escape. At one point, he was sure he had lost them, but they had been quick to catch his trail, and the chase began again.

His mind began to blur as exhaustion became his enemy. No longer able to think clearly, he simply ran. He ran for the river where he hoped his love would be waiting for him. He ran until he became dizzy and disoriented.

Finally, he sprang forward into the bright lane along the river. The iron bridge spanned the sparkling waters of the Seine. His heart leapt when he saw the gray bonnet peeking from between the buildings ahead. Despite his exhaustion, he experienced a rush of elation.

His Alexis was here. She was safe.

The horses entered the lane behind him. He used the last vestiges of his strength to run toward Alexis, wanting only to see her eyes one last time. He got his wish. He looked into their violet depths for a lifetime before he tossed her the letter, and only then did he indicate that she withdraw behind the building to safety. He turned to meet his fate.

The men slid down from their horses. He stood, slumped and panting.

"We have our gutter rat now." The tallest one laughed. "You gave us a merry chase. I quite enjoyed it."

The second man pulled his cutlas from his belt. It hissed as it was removed, catching Aran's attention. He stared at it, emotionless as the man held it high where it caught the early morning light, glittering ominously.

"We have a message for you from General De Sole." He sneered. "He asked that you receive it with his best regards."

He stepped forward and plunged his sword into Aran's body.

Aran had time to only turn slightly with a crouch. It saved his life. The cold steel entered his right shoulder.

The man pulled back on his sword. Both men laughed.

Aran used his last ounce of energy to fling himself over the wall and into the water.

Chapter Twenty-Nine

Alexis pressed her back into the wall and prayed. She heard the soldiers attack her Aran, then laugh with glee at his demise. She squeezed her eyes shut. The sound of a splash echoed through her mind. Her eyes shot open. Carefully, she leaned ahead and looked out into the lane.

The two soldiers were standing at the brick embankment staring at the water.

"He has sunk like a stone," the nearest soldier said.

"We'll wait. The general wants him dead," the other replied.

"I gave him a death blow. He will not live even if he should surface."

Alexis quietly reached down and pulled off her boots and set them on top of her carpet bag. She removed her cloak, her bonnet, and the strap of her purse from her shoulder, then grabbed her dress and wiggled it over her head. She left it all in a heap on top of her bag. Standing in her shift, she peered back into the lane. The men were mounting their horses.

She leaned back against the wall. The seconds crawled by.

Alexis let out a breath when she heard the horses canter away. Leaning out from her hiding spot, she watched until the riders turned off into a street. Then she ran across the road and dived into the canal, trying to enter at the exact location where she had last seen the soldiers.

The water was dark. Beneath its surface, she could see no more than a foot in front of her. Frantically scanning before her and flailing out her arms to find Aran, she reached the bottom. Nothing. When her lungs were about to burst, she broke to the surface and gulped the air.

Just as she was about to go under again, a flutter of bubbles arose from against the wall. The water around them was tinged with red.

"Aran!" She plunged down again, this time keeping her hand on the brick embankment as she dove to the bottom. Her hands touched a soft form. Aran had anchored himself to the bottom under a shaft of scrap metal, discarded here during the construction of the bridge.

She tugged him free, and they rose to the surface. When they broke into the air, she pulled him to the wall. He began to cough. He was alive. Holding him while he sputtered, she closed her eyes, thanking the gods for his life.

She paddled them to the gondola and the break in the brick wall. Forgetting about his wound in her eagerness to get him safely from the water, she pulled him up the stairs by the shoulders. He groaned, as his head fell to the side. He was unconscious. Alexis looked down at his body. Where she had grasped him by the shoulder, an expanding mushroom of deep red blossomed on his chest. She swore. She had thoughtlessly pulled him where he was injured.

"Stay here, Aran. Don't move. I will be right back," she

said to his inert body. Needing something to stop the bleeding, she ran for her carpet bag. The rolled letter had blown to the base of the building next to her things and she snatched it up and stuffed it into her bag. Bundling her belongings into her arms, she hurried back to his side.

Kneeling beside Aran, she dumped her things to the ground. The petticoat would make a fine bandage. Her hands fumbled as she used her knife to cut a long piece of cloth, folded it, and held it against his wound. It seemed to be working. The blood flow had eased. She began to cut strips from the garment. By the time she was done, her first bandage was red with blood. She removed it and looked at the injury. The cutlas had sliced the skin in a long gash, before ending in a deep puncture wound. She rolled him to his side. Thankfully, the sword thrust had not penetrated completely through his body. The wound still dripped blood, but it was not the steady flow it had been.

He began to tremble.

I must wrap this wound then get him warm. Her heart was beating wildly.

One step at a time. First, she would take the wet shirt off and then wrap the wound again.

There is no time to panic now. Later, I will allow myself to panic.

She had him wrapped. She was thankful he was still unconscious as she struggled to get his dry shirt on, not bothering with the sleeve near his injury. When the job was complete, she looked at him. His body still shook with cold. She yanked off his boots. They came with a rush of water. She removed his wet stockings and pants and used what was left of her tattered petticoat to rub his legs dry. She kept rubbing until she was sure she had warmed him at least slightly. His pants and dry stockings were easier to put on than those she had taken off. She threw the wet boots and clothing into the gondola. Finally, she wrapped her heavy woolen cloak around him. It would have to do. It was all she could do for now.

Realizing she was still in her wet chemise, she looked up and down the lane. Thankfully, it was still early, and no one was about. She grabbed her dress and pulled it over her head, then the reticule, her stockings, and boots. She wound her braided hair into a bun and pulled the awful, oversized bonnet back over her head and tied it.

"It is good that you remembered to cover those red locks, princess."

She turned sharply to look at Aran. He was conscious again. His dark eyes watched her. He even tried to smile.

"We have made it this far, princess. I am sorry for this." His eyes indicated his body beneath the heavy cloak. "It will make it much harder for you."

"Oh, Aran, you are alive. That is all that matters to me. Whatever you do, you must not leave me now. Promise to stay with me, Aran." She crawled over to him and knelt by his head, putting her hand on his cheek. "Promise me, Aran."

"I promise, princess." His voice sounded weak. "Get the admiral's letter Alexis—"

"I have it Aran."

"Good girl. But now you must hurry. Go to the faded red house just there. Get the boatman."

Alexis scrambled to her feet and jogged across to the red shack. She pounded at the door.

An old man swung it open. "Aye? What can I do for you?"

He was a grizzled character, in a flat sailor's hat. He wagged a bushy gray beard at her, then looked around her to see if she was accompanied.

Alexis understood his silent communication. He was not interested in dealing with a woman.

"My husband asks that I fetch you to take us upriver."

He peered around her again, seeing Aran by the wall. He had sat up.

"Oh, aye." He now seemed eager for the business. "That I can do. I will just get my bag."

He shut the door again.

Alexis returned to Aran's side.

"Help me get into the boat, Alexis. I do not think I can manage it on my own."

She went to the side of his good shoulder and helped pull him up. With her assistance, he was able to struggle to his feet. He groaned and rested his head on her shoulder. Together, they eased down the three steps. Alexis pulled the small craft parallel to the launch and he climbed in, carefully making his way to a reclining chair in the bow.

Alexis put together her scattered things on the bank and joined him on the gondola. A tattered cushion lay on the seat, and she slid it under his head. Aran lifted his legs onto the bench across from him and closed his eyes. She wrapped the cloak around him once more.

When the old man arrived, he glowered at the two of them. "It is twenty francs, before you even get into the boat," he said, perturbed that they had already boarded. "Where is it you want to be going?"

"The gypsy camps," Alexis blurted without thinking.

The old man looked around her at Aran. He still lay with his eyes closed.

"My man drank too much," she said. "Now we need to get home."

He narrowed his eyes at her. It was clear he didn't trust

the gypsies. She wondered if she had said the wrong thing. Maybe he would kick them off his boat.

"I have the money for you. How much is the fare?"

"Forty francs. And I want it up front."

Alexis remembered the smuggling captain from Gravelines. She opened her reticule and counted out thirty francs while he watched. "I will pay you thirty. Twenty now, and ten when we arrive."

The old man grunted.

"Deal." He indicated the bag he had tossed on the deck. "I have water, bread, and cheese. It will cost you five more if you want it. And you will pay me now."

"Deal," Alexis replied, digging in her purse for another five francs. She handed it to him. "And I will give you five more if you make good time."

She sat at the bow next to Aran, watching the old man's back as he steered his craft, using the current to propel them forward. The gondola glided past the islands. Notre Dame with its grand steeples came into view, then receded.

Goodbye, beautiful Paris.

The sun was climbing high into the sky by the time they had meandered past the St. Dennis district. It must be almost noon. She turned Aran's clothing which she had laid out to dry. At first, she had worried that De Sole would somehow discover their mode of travel, that a craft would approach them and haul them away. It had not happened. She silently thanked the wisdom of Aran's escape plan.

She looked down at Aran. He slept. She pulled back his shirt. Spots of red had appeared on his shoulder. He had started to bleed again. She reached into her carpet bag and took out another strip of petticoat. She rolled it into a thick pad and slipped it under his bandage, pressing it onto the wound. She held her hand firmly in place. He had lost a lot of blood. She chewed her bottom lip, not knowing what else she could do for him.

The canteen lay on her lap. Each time he awakened, she urged him to drink.

She glanced up at the old man. He steadfastly worked his oars, never once turning to look in their direction. If he had guessed their plight, he was uninterested.

The houses began to thin out. They were gliding through the warehouse district. It would not be long now.

Alexis realized she had been thinking of the encampment as their salvation. What if her troupe were gone? Maybe the yellow wagon would be nowhere in sight. Her stomach turned. One step at a time, she reminded herself.

The gentle rocking of the boat, and the warm sun on her face, made her sleepy. She leaned back and closed her eyes.

The jarring of the gondola onto the muddy shore woke her. She sat up quickly and turned behind her. They had reached the camps. She peered into the arrangement of wagons. Her heart leapt when she saw a bright yellow one near the perimeter.

A group of gypsies gathered on the riverbank, curious to see who had arrived as the old man jumped from his boat and pulled them up onto the slope of the shore. There was much curious chatter in Spanish. Alexis saw the mama of the little girl and waved frantically in her direction.

The woman looked at her without recognition. Alexis's heart dropped. She pulled the amulet from beneath her dress and fingered it nervously. The gypsy woman had told her it was a life.

Undoing her bonnet, Alexis pulled it from her head and shook out her red braids. She prayed the troupe would

honor the agreement of the amulet; she needed that
life now.

Chapter Thirty

The young mother, Siska, let out a shout of recognition and hurried to the gondola. In moments she had appraised the situation and recruited a group of men to help move Aran into a wagon. It was small compared to some of the others, with a light gray canvas cover. Aran was placed on a mattress, which fit snuggly between two benches on each side. There was much chatter and debate as several of the women contributed sheets, a woven blanket, a quilt, and cushions for the comfort of the wagon. Aran was soon resting on the makeshift bed.

An old woman with a face so weathered and wrinkled she resembled a dried prune arrived with a little cloth bag. She shooed the women away and climbed into the wagon to examine Aran. Alexis climbed in behind her. The other ladies remained just off the back of the wagon, speaking in hushed tones.

The old woman pulled back the colorful quilt which had been draped around Aran and opened his shirt. She clicked her tongue and muttered her dismay as she removed the blood-encrusted bandage. Turning and pulling wide the cloth curtain at the back of the wagon, she said, "Boiling water, a needle, and thread. And salt. And Kiera, bring me some bandages."

Alexis helped her remove his shirt. Because Alexis had been unable to get his right arm into the sleeve, it slid off easily.

"There is trouble here, *gringo*," The woman said, feeling his forehead. "You have stopped the bleeding but already he is hot. I may be able to help him, but maybe not."

"He will be fine. He has promised to survive."

She looked at Alexis and nodded. "That is good. It will help."

After washing him with salt water, she opened her cloth bag, pulled out a pungent brown cream and applied it carefully to the ugly gash. Then she meticulously stitched the wound, and wrapped a bandage around his shoulder and arm, rather than his chest.

"Easier. It will hurt him less when we remove it." The woman pulled the sheet up over him. She left the quilt pushed down by his feet. "You may use this if he gets the chills. When he is hot, cool him with water."

She looked over at the canteen the ladies had filled for her. "And give him water whenever you can." She leaned back on her heels and surveyed him. "He will get very hot. If he can come through it, he will live. If not..." She shrugged.

She left the cream, salt, and bandages and crawled out of the wagon.

"Aran, you will have to battle," Alexis said, rubbing his cheek. "I will help you, but you must not forget your promise to me. You cannot leave me."

She cursed the polluted waters of the Siene. To have his

wound saturated in its foulness could only have made the injury worse.

He moved his head slightly and opened his eyes. He smiled.

"Alexis," he muttered.

For three days, his fever raged. Alexis alternately bathed him with cool water and covered him with a quilt when he shook with chills. Sometimes, she was able to get him to take a little water, but most of the time he would twist his head and spit it away.

"Drink, Aran. Please, just a little." She would tip the canteen into his mouth.

He always managed a swallow or two before he turned his head away.

But his eyes remained wild and unfocused.

Over and over, he muttered, "Alexis. Alexis, you must go to the bridge,"

"Yes, Aran. Yes." She tried to reassure him. He was forever stuck in the moments before he was stabbed. Sometimes, he would smile at her and whisper, "It is good to look into your eyes one last time."

And then she would fight back her tears.

She would remind him of his promise not to leave her. "Aran, you must fight to stay with me," she would say. "You gave your word of honor. Fight, Aran."

She was never sure if he understood her.

Alexis found she was afraid to leave his side for even a moment. She lay beside him and slept only in brief intervals. She lost track of day and night. The time blurred into one long interlude. When she awoke, she would always experience a moment of terror before she heard his slow breathing.

Several times each day, the old woman would come and

check his progress. She would cluck unhappily over his wound and mutter to herself as she changed his dressing. When Alexis asked about his progress, she would only shake her head.

Siska and Kiera helped her to survive. They would drag her protesting from the wagon to come to the fire and eat, while the old woman changed his dressings and checked his wounds.

"You must eat, *gringo*. You will be of no use to him if you become ill," Siska would say.

Now while sitting at the fire eating her oats and coffee for breakfast, Alexis watched a platoon of soldiers ride up the adjacent road. The sight of soldiers heading to the valley was not unusual, still she pulled up the hood of her cloak to cover her hair.

Siska hissed as they swerved into the gypsy camp. Alexis had to force herself to breathe as a score of men from the camp went over to talk to them.

Alexis peered at them from beneath her hood, wishing she had worn her gray bonnet. But even the bonnet would look out of place here. Most of the women wore colorful bandanas or scarves, or kept their heads bare. She said a silent prayer as she squinted toward the troops, hoping to discern the badges on the uniforms. She had the sinking feeling they would belong to the general's personal guard, but it was too great a distance to be sure.

The soldiers dismounted and her heart sank.

There was little she could do except wait and hope that these people would not reveal her presence. In a panic, she glanced at the wagon, thinking of making a hurried escape into its dark interior.

Siska grabbed her arm.

"Do not move, *gringo*. Drink your coffee." Siska kept a

grip on her arm with one hand, while nonchalantly eating her porridge with the other. "Be natural. They will soon be gone."

A gaggle of children chased each other, running between them and the campfire. Siska let loose a string of admonitions. The normalcy of the scene calmed Alexis. She took a deep breath and raised her mug to her mouth. Siska relaxed the hold on her arm.

Siska wore a blue scarf. It covered her hair like a kerchief which she tied at the nape of her neck.

She removed it and smoothed out the silken material. "When I stand in front of you, tie this scarf around your head. The hood is too foreign here. Too noticeable."

Alexis felt her heart pound. Her hair was the one aspect of the plan she had neglected. Once in the gypsy camp, she had been too focused on Aran to remember it. Aran was right. It would be her defining feature. Every soldier De Sole sent out would be watching for her red gold hair.

Siska stood in front of her. She quicky tied the scarf around her head and knotted it at the back as the gypsy girls did. Then she pulled back the hood. Her hair was still coiled into the tight braids Rolande had fashioned for her days ago. Though a few wispy hairs had escaped, the braids had held, pulling her hair back cleanly from her face. Alexis said a silent thank you to Rolande for his foresight.

Siska smiled, pulling off her hooped earrings and offering them to her. "Here, complete the look."

She waited until Alexis had them in her ears before she sat down.

The soldiers were searching the camp. Alexis's stomach twisted with fear as they dismounted and drew back the curtained tarp at the rear of the first wagon. She remembered the letter in her carpet bag. Once they discovered

Aran, if they did not kill him outright, that missive would be a death sentence for them both.

The old woman was with Aran. Alexis wanted to turn and look at the wagon but knew that to draw attention to it would be an end for them. Siska stood and refilled her cup with coffee. Her silent message was clear.

At this time of the morning, the wagons were empty. The people had risen for the day. There were several camp-fires ablaze, where families were finishing breakfast and, like Siska and Alexis, were enjoying the strong campfire coffee. Children roamed the campgrounds, running and playing with new friends from other gypsy families. The presence of the troops affected only the adults, who had become silent, moving slowly about their chores, or sitting still and wary beside their fires.

The soldiers moved systematically through the camp. Alexis kept her head slightly lowered. When two men pulled back the tarp of the yellow wagon, nearest their campfire, she noted the signa of De Sole on their chest. Rage burned through her. If she could have cut them all down, she would have.

As De Sole's men approached the dull gray wagon, Siska reached over and gripped her arm, anchoring her to her seat. Alexis closed her eyes and said a brief prayer. Her heart pounded in her throat as she turned to the wagon and awaited the inevitable.

They yanked back the tarp. An outraged scream, then a stream of curses in a raspy Spanish voice, blared from the wagon. A bottle of cream was flung at their heads. The soldiers ducked, dropped the canvas curtain and leapt back. Curses still emanated from behind the drapes. The men stood as though stunned, then burst into laughter.

"A naked woman just for you, Francois." One of them

laughed. "And she is just your age. I hear you like mature women."

He slapped his partner on the back.

His partner grinned sheepishly. "A little too old even for me." He chuckled. "My eyes will never recover from the sight."

The soldier rubbed his fists into his eyes in exaggerated distress. The two of them laughed and moved on.

Alexis released a breath, gripping her hands together to still her trembling fingers. She looked across at Siska who wore a broad smile.

"Never underestimate an old woman," Siska whispered.

The two of them sat sipping their coffee as the men finished their search of the camp. When the soldiers finally mounted their horses and rode back toward Paris, Alexis raised her head and expelled a long breath. She reached behind her head to return the scarf.

"No. Wear it. You look like a proper gypsy girl in it." Siska laughed, rising, and took her arm. "Now we must tease the old woman about her attempts to seduce those soldier boys."

Alexis laughed with her as they walked together to the gray wagon.

When they pulled back the tarp, the old woman was tugging on her dress, having just pulled it over her head. She reached into her bodice to adjust her long thin breasts, glaring at Alexis and Siska with her crumpled ancient face.

Siska gave her a cheeky grin, rested her arms on the end gate of the wagon, and said, "Well, Grandmother, I see you are using your body to entertain the troops once more. And here I thought you had given that up."

Alexis expected the surly old lady to sling something at

Siska, but to her surprise the woman cackled with delight. "It is good to use this old body again."

They both laughed. Siska helped her from the wagon.

Alexis was not sure how to compliment her. "That was astounding. You tricked them well."

She patted Alexis on the cheek, then her expression became serious. "I have changed his dressings. He is the same. It will go one way or the other soon."

Alexis spent the day cooling Aran by wiping his body with cold wet cloths. She had borrowed a needle and thread from Siska, and when Aran slept, she sewed a pocket in the hem of her gown, just large enough to slide the incriminating letter securely into the fold. It would not do to have it so vulnerable to discovery again. She pressed it flat and examined the result. Unless the dress was carefully examined it would not be found. When Aran recovered, they would find a way to get to Gravelines, where they and the letter would be safe from discovery.

Sometimes, she was sure Aran was improving; he seemed to be able to sleep for an hour or two, before he would begin restlessly fighting the fever which heated and chilled him alternately.

When Siska and Kiera came to relieve her and take her for supper, she was almost too exhausted to go. But Kiera tugged her from the wagon, while Siska stayed to watch over Aran.

Alexis ate the thick stew offered sitting by the fire. Looking around the clearing as she chewed, she noticed something was different. The community was thinning out. Many wagons had left.

"Is everyone leaving?" she asked Kiera.

Kiera too looked at the vacant campsites. "It is near the time for us to leave. This morning, the troops searching the

257

camp made some of the families nervous. Soldiers are not trusted here. They decided to go a little early."

Alexis ate in silence, afraid to ask the obvious question, but she needed to know the answer. She cleared her throat. "Did the soldiers say what they were looking for?"

Kiera looked her in the eyes. "They were searching for a flame-haired young woman. They said she is the general's woman and sadly she is missing. There was no mention of her man."

Alexis took a deep breath. So, De Sole was searching for her. That he had gone to the extreme of searching the gypsy camp told her he had already scoured the city. Aran would be assumed dead. What kind of story had De Sole concocted about his death? That he had fallen into the Seine and drowned? Certainly, he would have been at the house the moment the news of Aran's death had reached his ears. She smiled when she thought of the general's surprise when it was discovered she was not to be found.

She wondered if Fouche would believe the tale. If so, maybe it would improve their chances of getting out of the country. If Fouche was in doubt about Aran, and as Aran suspected, had only held off arresting him hoping to capture his contacts, then getting into Gravelines might have been where they would have been caught. But if he believed him dead, they would not be waiting for him at the port.

Rolande would have been questioned along with all the other servants. She was thankful now to have followed Aran's advice and kept all the information from him. He and the other servants would be able to offer little assistance to De Sole.

Kiera interrupted her thoughts. "We too will be soon leaving for the north. We wait only for your man. Our old woman says he cannot travel yet, but it will only be days before we know if he lives or dies. And so, we wait."

She shrugged.

Alexis had no way to thank the gypsies for all the trouble she had put them through. She only hugged Kiera before crawling back into her wagon.

On the morning of the fourth day, she awoke with a start. Something was different. She leaned over to check Aran. He was breathing in long slow breaths, not the painful gasping of the last few days, and seemed more peaceful somehow. Reaching over, she placed a hand on his forehead. It was cool.

Elation surged through her, and she bit down on her lip to contain a scream of joy. He had made it. He had survived! She had to stop herself from shaking him awake. Instead, she eased from his side and left the wagon to share her news.

There was much celebration and excited chatter. Alexis knew that this was in part because they had become impatient to leave. She did not care. It was a pleasure to have people share in her happiness.

She pulled Siska to her and gave her an exuberant hug. "He made it, Siska. I know we could not have done it without your help." She lifted her amulet from her neck and put it around Siska's. "You have given me a life, Siska. We are even now."

Siska lifted her black hair and let the amulet fall onto her breasts. Her dark eyes shone. She reached down and grasped her hand.

"And I also have made a new sister," she said with a smile.

"Sisters," Alexis repeated.

Together, they went to the fire to have some strong black

coffee, and the cooked oats that awaited them for their breakfast.

Alexis sipped her coffee. *I will never prefer tea again.* She smiled to herself as she looked around the campsite. Already the gypsies were breaking camp. Pots and pans and even chickens were being loaded into the covered wagons or attached to their sides. The old woman climbed up into her wagon.

Alexis gulped down the last of her coffee. Taking her tin bowl and cup, she washed them in the basin provided as she had seen the others do. Then, she placed them on the stack of clean dishes.

She smiled as she thought of how much she had changed in the last two months. It felt like a lifetime ago since her arrival in France. Gone was the English girl who had known so little about life outside of the restrictive cocoon of her upper-class existence. The girl who had climbed into Aran's wagon had never washed a dish in her life.

I like this woman better, she thought.

When she returned to the wagon, the old woman had braced up Aran's head and was spooning a thin broth into his mouth.

"That is enough for now," she said, wiping his chin. She looked at Alexis. "He will sleep."

Alexis crawled up to the front and laid her hand on his forehead, brushing the hair from his eyes.

He looked at her, and his mouth curved into the remnants of his former smile. But his eyes were clear. She felt her heart swell.

"Good morning, princess." His voice was raspy from disuse.

She laughed and leaned down to kiss him. "Good morning, my love."

"Enough now," the old woman said. "Let him sleep. You must get busy hooking up the horse. We will be leaving soon."

Aran looked at her and raised his eyebrows. He knew she had never hitched up a horse in her life. He smiled again. "I will get down and help you, princess. I seem to have overslept a little."

Alexis laughed. "It has been four days, Aran."

"Four days?" He flinched with pain as he attempted to sit up.

The old woman put a hand on his forehead and eased him back onto his pillow. He was too weak to resist even that slight force.

"No. It is too early," she said. "There will be no getting up today. Tomorrow for a little, maybe."

She shifted to the back of the wagon. Before she left, she announced. "I will check him at noon when we stop to eat. Sleep now."

Alexis watched Aran fight to keep his eyes open. He lost the battle. She smoothed his hair before she too left the wagon to learn her new skills.

Kiera sent her husband Raoul to show her how to hitch the horse. He put the yolk around its neck and began to fasten the harness. It soon became apparent she knew nothing. Once they were set up, he turned to her. "I will return."

He walked over to Kiera and had an animated conversation with her. At one point, he threw his arms up into the air. The other wagons were beginning to move.

She climbed up into the wagon seat and looked at the reins looped onto a horn beside her. Never in her life had she held the reins in a carriage or anywhere else.

Raoul came back to her wagon and hopped up into the seat next to her.

"I will ride with you only a few minutes until you learn. It is simple. Take up the reins. Keep them even. Better," he said, watching her concentrate. "Now, you only give them a little shake and say *hie*."

She tried it. The horse didn't move.

"Again, but more firmly. Like this." He took the reins and gave them a brisk shake. "Hie!"

The horse began to plod forward.

He handed her the reins. "Now pull on both and say *whoa*."

She did. The horse came to a stop.

"That's it. Pull one rein only in the direction you wish to turn if that's what you want to do. The horse knows what to do," he added. "Now go."

She gave the reins a firm snap and said, "Hie!"

The horse walked forward. She smiled with satisfaction. Raoul nodded, pleased, and hopped down from the moving wagon.

She had no further trouble managing to drive the wagon. She spent most of the morning preening with pride in her accomplishment. Determined to never allow herself to be so helpless again, she promised herself that she would learn to drive even a coach before the year was out.

To her relief the wagons were heading North. That they were moving in the direction of Gravelines was enough for now. When Aran was well enough, they would have to make plans. Periodically they would meet long lines of soldiers, and she would keep the scarf tightly wrapped around her hair, though it was unlikely they would be searching for her. They would be joining the mass of troops in the valley just out of Paris.

And the gypsies ignored them, moving silently through their midst. Gypsies did not trust soldiers.

By midmorning, the glow of her feat in mastering the skill of handling the reins had worn off. By evening, it was a chore. After two days of travel, she could also unhook her horse and water it. She was able to harness the shaggy beast, feed it and even brush it down at night.

The gypsy train continued meandering northward. They branched off to stop at many villages along the way, selling their wares, or entertaining for coins.

Each day, Aran improved. At first, he was startled by his condition.

"Four days? And I thought it was only a night." He looked at her with pride. "You did very well, Alexis. I am not surprised, but I am thankful. I owe you my life, princess."

"Aran, you owe me nothing. You repaid me when you lived." She kissed him lightly on the forehead. "It is all I wanted from you."

By the second day of the journey, he was spending much of the day sitting up. He had opened the flap between the driver's bench and his wagon so that they could enjoy the trip together. And though he still took long naps in the morning and afternoon, Alexis enjoyed his company. By the third day, he was eating solid meals. He began to join the troop by the fire.

That first night at the fire she noticed him in deep conversation with Raoul. She saw Aran pull out a bag of coins and give it to him.

When she asked him about it later in the wagon he replied, "I paid for two things. First the help we were given and second, I need to get closer to Gravelines. If we can get to the village of Fondelac, we will be a day's journey to Gravelines."

She nodded. She would be much more at ease with her new friends knowing they were no longer a burden but had contributed to the troupe. But a smile died on her lips with the mention of Gravelines. England seemed far from her reality in France. It was too hard to think of a return to England. She blocked the notion from her mind.

It had been a week since they had left Paris. Aran was still weak, but every day he became more and more like the exuberant man she had known. They began to take turns at the reins. He had even begun to help her with the horse.

Now he crawled out of the wagon to sit beside her as she held the reins.

"You are doing a respectable job, my dear, but it is my turn to drive." He grinned at her. "Besides, we need to talk. We will soon reach Fondelac. At this time tomorrow, we could be back in England."

Alexis was surprised by the jolt of pure fear that flooded through her at this announcement. She did not want to consider the possibility she would soon be home. If it meant keeping Aran by her side, she would have been happy to stay with the gypsies forever. She knew she loved him with her whole heart. Once in England, his task to protect her would be over. He might easily drop her at her aunt's and go back to his beloved Yorkshire.

"I don't feel ready to go home Aran. Not yet."

"Alexis we must get the admiral his information. Already we have taken much too long. The admiral will know that you are coming out with me. They will be waiting for us in Gravelines."

Alexis reached down and smoothed her hem where the letter was tucked away. It crinkled beneath her fingers. The letter was their reality. Her hopes were second to the mission they had to complete.

Aran watched her, and when she met his gaze, he nodded. "It is more important than either of us Alexis. And we have one more hurdle to cross. If De Sole is still searching for you, he could well have someone at the ports, including the gates of Gravelines. His obsession and anger are boundless. Your hair, Alexis, will be our downfall. At Fondelac we will dye it."

"Ah, must I?" She wrinkled her nose. "I know you are right, but can we at least go with a shade of brown? Black hair feels too foreign to me."

Aran laughed. "You are vain my love. Brown will do if we can find the dye in the village. We will hire a room at an inn to prepare for the crossing." He paused. "De Sole is only one of our problems. We will have to hope Fouche has not sent an alert for me."

"Would he not think you dead?"

"He might." He laughed. "This time his talent for gathering information will work against him. He will have a report from the soldiers at the Siene, both of whom will insist on my certain death."

For several minutes they rode in silence. Aran appeared to be lost in thought. Finally, he looked at her with concern. "Alexis, I know about your problem with your aunt and her son. And I have a solution."

She waited, feeling as if her entire life was about to shatter before her eyes.

He gave her a half smile. "When we get on board an English ship, I will ask the captain to marry us."

Alexis's mouth dropped.

"Later in London, or wherever, we will do it up right in a church before God, if it is your wish."

She looked down, feeling his eyes burning into her as she processed his words.

Tell me you love me. Tell me you wish to spend your life with me.

He said, "It is the only way, Alexis. You have spent almost three months with me. Do you know what that means?"

"I know what it means, Aran," she replied in a dull voice.

Still feeling his eyes on her, she refused to look up.

He continued, "Alexis, you are Lady Betcher once more. You cannot spend three months as a mistress, then return to your life as you knew it. You are an unmarried woman. There are rules which cannot be broken."

When she did not reply, he pressed on, "I owe you my life, Alexis. It is only right that I marry you now."

It was too much. She could hear no more.

He owed her, and he was just making another of his elaborate plans—another solution where he would play his role. He was so good at it, after all. It was his talent.

He did not love her. She knew she should say no. It was the honorable thing to do. She should not force this beautiful man to permanently attach himself to her. When she opened her mouth to speak, she had no words. She wanted him too badly. Never could she turn down an opportunity to be with him forever.

I am a selfish woman, with no honor. I should try to do right by him.

Instead, she found herself simply nodding.

Her eyes burned with unshed tears. He had not spoken of love. He had said nothing at all about his feelings for her, only his duty and his plan.

Without a word, she climbed through the flaps into the

wagon. Laying down on their mattress, she buried her head into the pillow and cried.

She thought about their escape. Having saved his life, Aran would naturally want to help her—to repay the debt. How ever she tried to quelch the thought, it reared back into her mind. He owed her. Marrying her to save her from her fate was his responsibility. Yet even with this knowledge of his motivation, she could not let him go.

At night in the darkness of the wagon, she removed all her clothes. Aran lay on his back, as he had since his injury. She lay on her side beside him, reaching down to take his silky smoothness in her hands. She stroked him until he groaned.

Then she braced herself above him with her feet anchored on each side of his hips. Wordlessly, she eased him into her body. She began to use her body as Rolande had taught her.

She reached out her hands onto the bunk on each side of his body, arching so that no other portion of her body touched him. Rising onto the balls of her feet, she began to ride him, moving up and down the length of him, clutching him inside her, slowly at first, then with increasing speed.

He held her hips.

"Alexis, my princess," he moaned, attempting to meet her thrusts.

"Lay still," she said. She made love to him, her body only touching his organ, and then finally his groin as she pushed him further inside her with each thrust.

Feeling him begin to throb inside her, she used her muscles to pull and hold him. He gave a long growl and attempted to raise his hips to her. Alexis arched and plunged hard into his body. Again and again, until he burst inside her. She held him tight in her body, thinking at this moment that even Rolande would be amazed at her strength. He trembled and moaned his appreciation beneath her.

She lowered her feet, then carefully pulled away from him. Wet tears streamed down her face.

At least I can give him this, she thought in agony.

She used the sheet to wipe away her tears before she slid along his body in the darkness to take her place at his side.

I will never let him go. There is no honor in me. If he must spend a lifetime in the unhappy role of my husband, then so be it—if there was a lifetime for them to live. Tomorrow, at the gates of Gravelines, their future would be determined.

Chapter Thirty-One

When they arrived at Fondelac, in the early morning, they had to leave their gypsy family. He had watched while Alexis said her tearful goodbyes. It was the only emotion she had shown since he had announced their impending marriage.

Aran rented a room at an inn, where they could spend a few hours making the last-minute preparations. They were able to find the hair dye and some readymade clothing that would help them portray their role as merchants. After much needed bath, and a change of clothes Aran went to purchase a pair of horses and a cart, leaving Alexis to complete her tasks, including sewing a pouch into her dress for the missive. He would need the cart to get into Gravelines with his permit. The security at the gates would be expecting a merchant to come prepared to pick up goods from the ships or warehouses inside the walls.

Alexis remained silent and distant as they began the short trek to Gravelines.

Now, as they approached the high walls of Gravelines,

her face was stoic. She wore an expression he had been forced to become familiar with over the last twenty-four hours. His announcement that they would marry had not been received as he expected. He sighed. Alexis had no choice but to marry him.

He had hoped Alexis would want to marry him. His heart ached with his love for her.

I will make her happy. I know she cares about me. She has come through hell to help us be safe.

But seeing Alexis so obviously unhappy left him bereft and confused.

Aran thought about how she had made love to him last night. He had hoped it might remind her of how they could be with each other. Since the injury, he had been too weak to attempt it. And last night, when she had taken him the way she had, he had been sure she would be happier. But if anything, she had become even more distant.

They reached the gates. On his previous excursions there had been only two soldiers at the city walls. Today there were four. Not a good sign.

"Your papers?" a uniformed man asked. As he reached into his inside pocket to retrieve the permit, two mounted soldiers circled their wagon. His stomach lurched. The insignia on their jackets was indeed De Sole's. He should not have been surprised to see the lengths to which the maniac would go to find Alexis, but he was.

He stole a glance at Alexis. She wore the ugly gray bonnet, completely covering her hair and tied tightly beneath her chin. One of the soldiers aligned his horse to her side of the wagon and scrutinized her. Alexis kept her head down and her hands folded demurely in her lap.

Aran concentrated on handing his permit to the gate-keeper without trembling. The soldier only glanced at them, checking the insignia on the document, then handing them back to him.

But the soldier next to Alexis was not so disinterested. He looked at her suspiciously, "Your name madam," he demanded. "And remove your bonnet."

Aran's heart sank. He had been distracted by Alexis' reaction to his proposal and had spent the last twenty-four hours focusing on her sadness. They had not discussed a background and names to be used at the gates should they be questioned. He had truly not believed De Sole would go to such lengths. It was a mistake.

As she began to untie her bonnet, he realized he had not asked her to show him her hair. He held his breath. For a horrible instant he was sure her vanity had overcome her better judgement, and she would reveal her flaming red hair.

She untied the ugly gray bonnet and pulled it from her head—chestnut brown, thank god. He let himself take a breath.

Alexis answered the soldier in a small voice, "It is Claudette sir," she said lowering her head shyly.

The soldier stared at her bowed head for a moment before responding with a grunt and reining his horse away. He waved them forward without a word. Aran was quick to snap the reins and move through the gates. Neither of them said a word until they had safely reached the streets of Gravelines.

"Well done," Aran said quietly. Alexis only nodded.

Aran parked next to the lace shop. "Wait here. I will only be a minute."

She smiled. "No problem, Aran of the sea."

He chuckled; glad she had regained some of her humor.

The lace dealer was familiar to him. When he went to say his password, the man waved his words away.

"There's a ship waiting for you in the harbor, docked. A sloop. You can't miss it—it's the biggest there. I don't think we've had one in the port before. The admiral himself waits for you. But you best hurry. I have word they're leaving today."

Aran nodded. "I will leave you my rig then. It's tied to your rail out front."

"Good. It'll be a little extra pay for me, eh?" He reached out his hand.

Aran shook it and left the shop. Another acquaintance permanently lost, he thought. His life here was unraveling at last.

He reached up and offered Alexis his arm. "As promised, a sloop awaits us in the harbor."

She ignored his arm and braced her hands on the cart to hop unaided to the ground. He grinned. It would be a while before she dropped her gypsy ways and became the proper English lady.

He grabbed their light carpet bag. It seemed strange that this was all they had left of their life in France.

In minutes, they were up the gang plank and on board the mighty sloop.

As soon as they reached the deck, the admiral came charging towards them.

"I had given up hope! We received word of your troubles in Paris, and were afraid you had met a grim fate, but here you are at last."

Alexis leaned down, flipped the hem of her gown, pulled out the crumpled letter and wordlessly handed it to Aran who set it in the admiral's hands.

"Our final report, from the desk of General Dumont.

The letter contains the number of troops Napoleon has arranged for his invasion of Russia. You will also find the names and ranks of the officers, and their previous assignments." It was everything the admiral had requested. He waited, watching the admiral's face as he digested the information.

The admiral looked down at the tattered papers in his hand and raised his eyebrows. His expression was incredulous, before he broke into a slow smile.

He grabbed Aran's hand and heartily shook it. "You have done an excellent piece of work. Excellent. I have been congratulating myself on my choice of you as our man. You could not have done better."

The admiral glanced down at the papers once more before he met Aran's eyes. His eyes twinkled. "Your father would be pleased, young man." He assessed Aran from head to toe. His brow furrowed. "You look a bit slumped?"

"I received a rather large saber wound to the shoulder as a parting gift." He looked at Alexis. "But thanks to my mistress..."

He paused, wanting the admiral to understand the depth of his relationship with Alexis. The admiral raised his eyebrows once more, then turned to Alexis with a concerned expression.

Aran continued, "Thanks to my mistress, I survived it."

There was a moment's awkward silence as he watched the admiral process the information. Hews would know who Alexis was. In his last missive, Aran had informed him that General Betcher's daughter would be coming out with him.

Alexis took off her ugly gray bonnet and smoothed her hair, merely smiling tentatively back in Aran's direction, content to let him do the explanations. The admiral caught the exchange.

"And you, missy, I assume are General Betcher's daughter. It puzzled me when you turned up in Paris with Aran. You will have to share that story with me, my dear." He surveyed her. "I sent a message to your father, promising to retrieve you. He will be relieved, I think, to hear you are safe in England."

Alexis only nodded.

"Alexis and I thought to ask you a favor."

"And what might that be?" The admiral glanced at Alexis curiously.

Aran took a breath. "I want you to marry us. I believe it is what her father would want. I am a Lord, an impoverished one to be sure, but still a respectable choice. And you know as well as I that my lady cannot reenter society under any other circumstance."

He looked pointedly at Alexis's belly. "Indeed, it may be vital we marry as soon as possible."

The admiral too stared down at Alexis's midsection. "Is this what you want, young lady?"

"It is," she said quietly, gracing the admiral with a composed smile.

Aran looked at her curiously. It was not like her to be so formal.

The admiral sighed with relief. Aran knew that had he not offered, the admiral would have had to force his hand.

"Fine. I can do that. As a captain and an admiral, I have the authority. And I can say with some certainty, that it would be the wishes of her father." He clapped Aran on the back with a pleased smile, ignoring his painful wince. "The boys are already taking us out of the harbor. We will have a fine wedding at sea.

"Now then," the admiral said, looking at his watch, "this sloop will have us in London in less than an hour. I will give you fifteen minutes to go below and freshen up. Then we will have our happy celebration, eh?"

In fifteen minutes, everyone but Alexis was gathered on the deck. Another fifteen minutes passed. Aran began to shift uncomfortably. Whatever could be keeping her? They were now only thirty minutes from docking.

Finally, the admiral barked to his cabin boy, "Go below and see what is keeping her. Tell her we are running out of time."

The lad hurried to do his bidding.

It was another five long minutes before he returned. He looked at Aran. "She wishes to speak to you, sir."

Aran hustled below to the captain's cabin. He knocked softly, before letting himself in.

Alexis was sitting on the bed. Her beautiful chestnut hair had been combed out and lay in curls over her shoulders. Her eyes were filled with tears. Aran sat on the bed and took her hands.

"What is it?" He scanned her tearstained face. "Is marriage to me so appalling then?"

"Oh no, Aran." She threw her arms around him. She cried against his shoulder in great gulping sobs.

He held her and rubbed her back. "What is it then? You don't have to marry me, Alexis. If you don't want me, we can find another way. It is fine, love."

He felt his heart break. Without Alexis, he was not sure he wanted to go on. There would never be another woman for him. But still he rocked her and told her she could give him up. She began to calm.

At last, she leaned back and looked at him. "Aran, I will never love another as I love you. I am sure I could die for love of you. I know this is just a duty for you. I want you to have everything. I want you to have the chance to love as I do. To tie you to me in a loveless marriage would be wrong. I thought I could be selfish, but I cannot. I love you too much."

A smile slowly replaced his anguished face. He wanted to shout with relief.

"I cannot force myself on you, Aran. I tried. I wanted to just selfishly take you. I know you made this plan. After everything that has happened, you must feel honor-bound to do right by me. I'll not have it."

He knew what he would do. He slid down to his knees in front of her, taking both her hands in his. "I love you dearly, princess. If you agree to be my wife, I will be the happiest of men. There is no other woman on this earth for me. I promise I will love you today and every day until I draw my last breath. Say you will marry me, Alexis."

He looked into her eyes. "Say yes, Alexis. You must know I have loved you for a long time. Since the day you crawled into my load of wool, I have thought of nothing but you. You are my destiny, Alexis. My life is nothing without you."

Alexis gave a little squeal and pulled him into her arms. He flinched as she yanked his shoulder.

"Oh, I am so sorry!" She drew back as he stood, patting his injury. "Oh, Aran."

She slid into his arms and hugged him. "I will make you happy. You will never be sorry. I will be a dream, wait and see."

"Now where have I heard that before?" He chuckled and kissed her lightly on the lips.

"I will! Let's do it, Aran!" She chose his left arm and pulled him to the door. "Let's do it right now!"

He threw back his head and laughed as they ran up the steps to join the admiral on the deck.

Epilogue

Twenty-five years later

Aran held Alexis' hand as they walked along the waters of the Seine. The Pont des Arts was directly in front of them. Behind them, the towers of Notre Dame stood out against the twilight sky.

"I am so glad we were able to take this trip together." Aran pulled her hand up onto his arm as they promenaded down the lane together.

Alexis laughed. "Our last daughter is finally wed. After all the turmoil Bella caused us, I think we deserved it, don't you?"

He smiled and pulled her close. "She took after her mother is all."

"Look, Aran. There is still a gondola here."

They both looked down at the launch with its three stairs carved into the bank. It was a different gondola, blue this time. They stopped, both lost in those memories from so long ago.

"Whatever happened to De Sole? We have never spoken of him in all these years," Alexis asked quietly.

"I asked the admiral once. It was when I still craved revenge. But De Sole had already died. He died along with the five-hundred thousand other troops of Napoleon's Grand Army. The Russian invasion is one of history's greatest calamities. It was De Sole's death and Napoleon's downfall."

They stood for another minute watching the gondola gently rise and fall in the water, before turning away to continue their walk.

The sun was setting. They reached the corner of St. Antoine's. A boy was standing on the street handing out playbills for an entertainment in the theatre behind him.

"There is still time to get a seat," he hollered, his youthful voice breaking into a shrill honking tone. "The most beautiful female impersonator in the world. The famous Alexandria herself will perform tonight! Music and dancing! Acrobats like you have never seen!"

Behind him was a colorful poster depicting all he had announced.

"Oh, Aran! Let's go in. I would so love to see a show tonight! "

"Are you sure? It might be a little racy."

She gave him a mischievous grin. "I have always liked my entertainments a little racy."

"That you have, my dear." He slid his arm around her waist. "Anything you wish, princess. It is your holiday."

They entered the darkened theatre. Alexis was pleased a box was still vacant on the second floor just left of the stage. They had the premier seats.

"It is as though it waited just for us." She smiled at Aran.

They got to their seats as the lights dimmed. There was a full house. The show was glamorous, entertaining, and colorful. Performers of a wide variety took to the stage. At intermission, Aran went to get them champagne.

He handed her a glass. "It seems we have chosen the right night to attend, my love. The buzz downstairs is that the final act will be a performance by some sort of legendary singer. There is much excitement. But do not be too shocked. I heard he is a female impersonator."

"Oh, how delicious. Only in Paris."

The lights dimmed again. The stage was soon occupied by a series of tricksters and comedians. Alexis looked at Aran. He was enjoying the evening. She was pleased.

"And now the moment you have all been waiting for, the Empress of the stage, the Grand Duchess of Entertainment, the Legend of Paris … Alexandria!"

The crowd roared.

The orchestra began to play. The curtains at the back of the stage parted. A woman in an outrageously tight ball gown of dark red stood dramatically posed with one leg exposed through the slit of her dress. She had a feather boa draped over her shoulders. Her slender leg was exposed to her feet which were adorned with extravagant heels.

She sauntered to the front of the stage, swaying to the music, and began to sing. The crowd cheered so loudly it was possible to note only that she varied from sweet high notes to a rasping sexy base. It was the movements of her dance which most entertained. She was at one moment delicate and ladylike and the next magnificently sexy. Alexis was completely enthralled.

As she watched, she began to feel there was something familiar about her. Her eyes were enormous. They had been outlined in black liner and the eyelids glittered with golden paint.

Her dress was cut low. Alexis looked at the jewels she wore. They were emeralds.

She gasped and reached for Aran's hand. "It is Rolande! Oh, Aran, it is Rolande! I am sure of it!"

"No."

"It is, Aran. I am not mistaken."

The crowd demanded an encore. The music began again. Rolande would do another number.

Alexis watched every nuance of the performance. "And he is fabulous, Aran."

"I am beginning to think it is him. And he is indeed fabulous."

"Can we go backstage?"

"We can try. We will give the stage manager our name. But watch his next performance, love. It would be impossible to push through the audience now."

Alexis sat mesmerized by two more encores. Rolande had survived and thrived when they had left. Nothing could have pleased her more.

After the performance, they gave their names from long ago to a stagehand. They were escorted backstage, where they waited in a sitting room for Alexandria to change.

Rolande entered the room. There was a moment's pause while they examined each other. He looked almost the same. He had aged well.

"Oh, Rolande, you are magnificent." Alexis walked towards him and held out her arms.

They hugged. Rolande kissed both her cheeks then held her at arm's length.

"But you are beautiful, *cherie*." He turned to Aran and executed a little bow. "*Monsieur*."

"It is good to see you in fine form, Rolande." He looked at him from top to bottom. "You are an enormous success. How ever did you choose this illustrious career?"

Rolande shrugged. "Alexis left me her clothes. I was heading to the theatre. It was an obvious choice." He looked at them. "But the two of you are still together after all these years, yes?"

Aran gave an exaggerated sigh. "We are. I have had a life of nothing but women, Rolande. Three daughters and my beautiful wife." He leaned ahead conspiratorially. "You would have hated it, Rolande."

"Do not believe it, Rolande." She took his arm. "He has loved every moment of it. Now then, do you have a boyfriend?"

She smiled at him, thinking about that last night. "Because if you do, maybe the four of us can go out for a late supper."

Rolande laughed. "I do and we would love to."

It was the beginning of a lovely evening. Alexis was pleased to spend it with the two men she had loved so well while she had grown from a girl to a woman, in Paris.

Author's Note

The Napoleonic Era was the golden age of espionage. Joseph Fouche, the French minister of police in France, held his position for three administrations. He was thorough and ruthless. Known as the executioner of Lyon for his merciless work supplementing the guillotine during the revolution, he is credited for the death of over eighteen hundred rebels. Later, Napoleon was able to crush support for the monarchy during the turbulent politics of post-revolutionary France with his assistance. The network of spies he commanded, both international and internal, is said to have never been matched even during the cold war of the twentieth century.

I have tried to accurately portray the city of Paris in the early nineteenth century, including famous landmarks such as Notre Dame Cathedral, the Louvre, and Napoleon's famous Arc de Triomphe (which was indeed half finished when Marie Louise unknowingly rode through its plaster and paper arch). The Pont des Arts, the bridge of iron, was constructed during the reign of Napoleon and is said to have been the forerunner of the Eiffel Tower. And the Palais

Royale was the shopping center so enjoyed by Parisians. However, I could not resist including the fabulous opera house, the Palais Garnier, though it was not constructed until later in the century. My apologies; it was simply too beautiful to resist!

Another point of interest was the record of licensing issued for Napoleon's smuggling port of Gravelines. That fifteen of the eighty-five permits were issued to female entrepreneurs was enlightening. The popular impression is that women of the Regency era were confined to domestic roles; clearly, this is evidence to the contrary.

vinci-books.com/the-heiress

She wants a business partner. He wants forever.

When shipping tycoon Jem Brigg is murdered, the business world
is stunned to learn the true owner is his young heiress, Eleanora
Pembroke. To fend off fortune-hunting suitors, Eleanora proposes
a sham engagement to her dashing new manager, Eliot Sparks. But
Eliot has his own agenda—winning Eleanora's heart for real.

Turn the page for a free preview…

The Heiress: Prologue

It was late. The office staff had long since retired for the night. Jem ran a hand over his ancient, scarred face and examined the figures again. He straightened his once massive frame, now shrunken with age, and laid a palsied hand over the evidence of embezzlement before him. *I have failed you Arabella, but perhaps there is still time to right this wrong.*

A long jarring creak broke the silence, interrupting his thoughts. Jem looked up from his work in alarm. Someone was prowling around the office. He glanced at the wall safe across the room, his pistol inside. Not the handiest place to keep it, he acknowledged with a grimace.

Taking a calming breath to settle his beating heart, he lifted his nib pen from its holder and scrawled a quick note into the account book before closing it and sliding it toward the heap of files on his desk. Placing the stopper onto his inkwell with exaggerated care, he rose and silently moved toward the safe. His fingers trembled as he tried to complete the combination. The door burst open, and he froze.

"I knew I would find you here, old man," a rasping voice sounded from the doorway.

With his back to the intruder, Jem tried unsuccessfully to keep the fear from his voice. "What is it you want?" He straightened to his still intimidating height and turned to face him, keeping one hand resting on the dial of the safe. The intruder took a step into the room. Though the man had cloaked his face in the black hood of his domino, Jem knew who he was.

"I want it all. But you know that, don't you?" He laughed, a loud grating sound that echoed in the silent office, as he reached into the folds of his cape and pulled out a pistol, levelling it at Jem's chest. The clicking of the hammer being pulled back on the pistol had Jem gritting his teeth to keep from flinching.

"You had to snoop, then you could not leave it be. And now you'll pay the price. But first let's finish what you started. Open the safe."

Jem tried once more to calm his fumbling fingers while he negotiated the combination. He visualized the gun lying atop his papers. If he could reach inside there was a chance he could get his hands on the revolver.

But it was not to be. The second the safe door swung open; the roar of a pistol reverberated in the room. An icy cold shiver pulsed through his chest as he slumped to the floor.

The Heiress: Chapter One

"Today is the day, Claudia. I admit I am a little nervous about the reading of the will this morning. Are you sure you won't change your mind and come with me?" Eleanora asked.

"No. This one is all yours I am afraid. Besides there is still plenty of unpacking to keep me occupied." Eleanora made a face, and Claudia chuckled. "I am sure it won't be as bad as that."

It had been a week since Eleanora and Claudia arrived in London. Eleanora had been pleased when Claudia agreed to accept the job as her assistant and join her on the journey to London. The first week had been a busy one—hiring staff and settling into the townhouse. The house had once belonged to her grandmother Arabella, and though it was a modest home when compared to its neighbors, its address in the prestigious Mayfair district made it accessible to both the parks and the offices of Pembroke Industries. Facing a small inner-city park with established trees, it gave one the impression of a country home. It was the perfect location and size for two ladies of business such as themselves. Eleanora smiled to herself at the apt description. The friends were indeed beginning what she hoped would be rewarding careers in London.

The breakfast room was her favorite. This morning the sun shone through the windows overlooking the garden, promising an end to the dreary fog and drizzle of the last few days. But despite the promise of a sunny day, Eleanora sighed. The business of reading the will played heavily on her mind. "It is just that I get the impression from my correspondence with Jem's sister, Amelia, that the family is unaware of my business arrangement with Jem. I don't think I could stomach a scene." How wonderful it would have been to spend this sunny day exploring London.

"I wouldn't worry. Mr. Jem Brigg was a power in the shipping industry for a generation. I am sure there will be enough money to satisfy the family...more than enough from my point of view. And it's not like the heirs are his children. He had a sister-in-law and a niece. They should be quite satisfied."

Eleanora smiled at Claudia's no-nonsense attitude. She had been friends with Claudia since her arrival in America more than a decade ago. Eleanora had come to live with her grandmother, Arabella, devastated by the death of her parents. Arabella had immediately found her a companion, Claudia, the daughter of a widowed captain in her employ. After accepting Claudia as her ward, Arabella immediately set about educating the girls, both in the traditional studies of the school room and in the shipping industry. "You need a passion Eleanora, something to keep your mind from your troubles," her grandmother had declared. Ships were Arabella's passion; thus the girls received the unorthodox addition of an internship in her shipping firm as part of their education. Of the two young women, Claudia had shown an aptitude for the financial side of the business. Had she not decided to join Eleanora in England, she would have certainly been offered a position in Arabella's firm in America.

Jem Brigg was given a twenty-five percent share of Pembroke Shipping in London. The same branch of the industry previously owned by Eleanora's mother, and he was assigned the task of managing the business. Jem had been a big man, both in stature and as the dominant force in an industry which had shaped the world. He was a legend on the docks. That he had kept the actual ownership of the company to himself would only have added to the power he exuded in the London markets.

Though she and her grandmother, Arabella Pembroke, were aware of Jem's declining health over the past year, the latest word from him had been that he was recuperating and had even returned to work. The news of his violent death during a robbery had been a shock. Jem had been Arabella's lifelong friend and protector. Her grandmother was heartbroken when word reached them in Boston. Though Arabella declined to make the taxing journey to London, she determined it was long since time her grand-daughter returned to England and took up a role in her business.

Eleanora set her teacup down. "I suppose you are right, Claudia. Jem would certainly have provided for his niece, Crystabel. She was his only family after all." It was time to face the day.

Eleanora glanced around the small parlor of Jem's London home, where the family had gathered to wait before joining the other minor beneficiaries in the library for the reading of the will. Above the fireplace was a portrait of the man she had always lovingly referred to as Uncle Jem. She smiled at the imposing figure that glared down at them from above, his scarred face so forbidding and unlike the gentle man she had known as a child.

Jem had never married, but after his brother Marion's death, he had taken Marion's widow, Amelia, and her daughter, Crystabel, to reside with him in his home. Crystabel had been Jem's pride and joy. When Eleanora left London, Crystabel had been a debutant, just emerging on the social scene, and now she was married, with a daughter of her own. Today, Crystabel, along with her mother Amelia, and her husband Lord Hargrove, had gathered to hear Jem's will.

"Eleanora, do come sit with me." Amelia bustled over to her and led her to the small settee, where she settled her bulky frame, arranging her skirts. She was a rotund woman, appearing even larger in a day dress covered with bows and flounces. Eleanora was forced to perch on the sliver of seat Amelia had left for her.

"We waited so long for your arrival, and you are home at last. You must tell me all about America."

"We have waited." Stephen Hargrove, Crystabel's husband interjected. Slender and elegant in an impeccably tailored suit, he was the model of the aristocratic gentleman about town. His pale face, too long to be considered handsome, reflected the bored countenance of so many of his set. "Hughes and Barnum refused to read the will until you appeared, though it has been over two months. Apparently, our Uncle Jem has left you a little stipend, and the lawyers insisted we wait for your arrival."

"Yes. I apologize for the delay." Eleanora shifted uncomfortably on the settee. Hargrove's comment added to her growing suspicion that Jem had kept the business of Pembroke and the details of its ownership, to himself. This morning's revelations were sure to be an unpleasant surprise to the family. She contemplated confiding the business arrangement she shared with Uncle Jem, but decided against it. Perhaps the other reveals in the will would soften the blow. "As I intend to make my permanent home here in London, there were my affairs to attend to. Then I was unable to book a steamship passage, thus the journey took longer than I anticipated. I hope you were not too inconvenienced."

"Not at all my dear." Amelia replied, "We are only pleased to have you back once more, is that not so Crystabel?"

"Quite right mother." Crystabel smoothed the folds of her navy silk dress. Dressed in the latest style, with her blond hair pulled back into an elegant chiffon, Eleanora could not help but admire the picture of perfection Crystabel had become. She was a beauty.

Amelia continued; her round face animated, "It will be so exciting to have a single girl to take under my wing. The season is just beginning, and I have made plans for us my dear. I must say I was dismayed to hear that you had not yet found a husband."

"Amelia, I am not interested in—"

Amelia raised her hand to block her objections and quickly carried on. "I can only imagine that finding a suitable man in Boston was impossible. But not to worry.

Twenty-five is a difficult age to be sure, but Crystabel and I will be here to assist, and all will be well." She reached over and patted her hand, while Crystabel nodded her agreement. "You are not on the shelf yet, my dear Eleanora, and you are not to give up hope. I vow before the season is out, we will have you nicely settled. Now, there is the minor matter of the period of mourning, but as Jem was only an uncle, we can correctly re-enter society. And as we have almost reached the required three-month period, all will be well..." She took a breath. "Look at Crystabel, with a fine husband."

Amelia paused and looked up at Lord Hargrove appreciably. Eleanora smiled at the pleased expression on the woman's face. That Crystabel had married into the aristocracy would have been a great boon to the family. After all Crystabel, though an heiress, was the daughter and niece of a merchant. The subject of her admiration ignored the conversation. He rested his arm against the mantle of the fireplace, impatiently waiting for the summons to the library and the reading of the will.

Eleanora took the opportunity to interject. "Thank you, Amelia, but I rather thought I would concentrate on Pembroke Industries for the—"

"Pembroke?" Her statement roused Lord Hargrove from his ennui. "Why would you be interested in Pembroke? The business is hardly your concern Eleanora," he scoffed. "Pembroke is in good hands. Though as a gentleman I could hardly be expected to submerge myself in trade, my man Matheson and I have had the place running smoothly for the past year, while Jem Brigg was so indisposed. It was a burden to be sure, but I take my responsibilities seriously." He smiled down at her. "No, my dear. You should concentrate on more feminine matters. Though it is a trial for me, I will continue to serve the family."

Crystabel nodded. "Stephen has indeed dedicated himself to the business. Why hardly a week went by without him going into the office. Uncle was so thankful, and I could not be more proud. He has been such a treasure."

"He certainly has. A treasure indeed." Amelia smiled at Stephen once more, who acknowledged her praise with a cool nod. "And a wonderful father I might add. Stephen dotes on the child. My little granddaughter Anna has been spoiled rotten," Amelia said proudly. "Is that not so Crystabel?"

"Quite right mother."

Amelia turned back to Eleanora and frowned. "That grandmother of yours has done you no service at all, Eleanora. Why, you could have children of your own by now. All this nonsense of putting you through training in her operation over there. Look where it has gotten you... twenty-five and no prospects. And you, a relative of the Earl of Pembroke, and a lady in your own right. And why she thought an education in shipping would benefit you in any way is a mystery to me." She shook her head rolling her eyes before continuing. "I would have thought it would have been a simple task to arrange a decent marriage for you. Why, I would have had this taken care of years ago." She shook her head again, this time with a tut-tutting sound. "It is beyond understanding. Arabella was not much for society, but I never thought her so capable of neglecting her duty to you, my dear. Concentrate on business? Huh," she snorted, her double chins trembling with indignation. "I never heard of such a thing. But you mustn't fret my dear, all will be well. Crystabel and I will take you in hand, won't we Crystabel?"

"We certainly will mother." Crystabel answered as though by rote. Eleanora got the impression that Crystabel did not pay much mind to Amelia's constant chatter. She, however, was relieved to have Amelia fill the room with her talk, even if she was not thrilled with the topic.

Amelia cleared her throat, prepared to continue. But before she could, Speers, the butler, announced from the doorway, "The beneficiaries are to assemble in the library. The lawyer is prepared to begin." The family followed Speers into the library, where two rows of chairs were set out, the back one filled with Jem's friends and employees. The family took their seats in the front row.

Eleanora sat quietly in her chair, twisting the strings of her black reticule. She had a fair idea of what would be contained in the will. She could only hope the disclosure would not be too unsettling for the small gathering in the library.

Crystabel slid her chair next to hers and leaning in close, whispered, "I have never been to a will reading. It all seems too serious. Uncle Jem is sure to have left some of his fortune to Stephen and me. Stephen is so very nervous about it, and I have to say I am—"

The solicitor cleared his throat, interrupting her. He sat behind a huge mahogany desk, surveying the double line of chairs symmetrically laid out before him. "I see I have all the beneficiaries assembled here. I am Mr. Hughes of Hughes and Barnum, the solicitor of the late Jem Brigg. Without further ado we shall begin the proceedings. The will is a recent document, and I personally can attest to Mr. Brigg's sound mind at the time of its creation."

After the initial legal formalities, he started with the minor stipends and pensions for Mr. Brigg's staff, both those from his home and office. After each pronouncement, a ripple of appreciation was murmured from the back row.

"And to my dear friend John Noyes, I leave my four

matching grays. He has coveted them long enough." John gave an appreciative chuckle, before the solicitor continued. "To Samuel Marsh I leave my stallion Hercules, a sturdy sire he will prize for his herd."

"Quite right. And I will at that, Jem. May you rest in peace." Samuel nudged his friend John beside him and the two of them shared a grin.

"And now for the bulk of my estate," The solicitor paused.

Eleanora glanced around the room. In the front row Crystabel sat beside her, adjusting the elaborate lace on her cuffs. Next to Crystabel was her husband Stephen, Lord Hargrove, who reclined nonchalantly in his chair, his legs extended and crossed at the ankles. And finally, Amelia, silent at last, sat shifting her heavy form uncomfortably in a narrow, straight-backed chair.

"I leave my home and its contents to my sister-in-law Amelia, together with a pension of 1000 pounds per year for her lifetime, to ensure her continued comfort." The solicitor looked up and nodded at Amelia, who smiled in return, before continuing.

"To my great niece, Anna, I leave the sum of 5000 pounds to be used as her future dowry. The money will not be accessible and held by my barristers until the day following her wedding, or the date of her thirtieth birthday.

To my niece Crystabel I leave the remainder of my liquid assets, a sum of 50,000 pounds, to be administrated as an annuity, with interest paid annually to a maximum of 2000 pounds. The principle is protected and locked to ensure her future security. The details of the arrangement can be explained more thoroughly through the offices of Hughes and Barnum."

"Ah," Crystabel smiled and nudged her husband, who

slowly straightened in his chair, the frown lines between his eyes deepening.

"And finally, unbeknownst to all of you, I have never owned Pembroke Industries, though I have had the privilege of managing it since the death of my dear Arabella Pembroke's daughter, Faith Pembroke-Nyles. Seventy-five percent of the business has always been under the control of Faith's daughter, Eleanora, who graciously granted me my shares when I took over management more than a decade ago. Thus, to her, I return my twenty-five percent share. It is my hope she will be pleased with the assets I have incurred during my guardianship."

An awkward silence filled the room. Beside her, Crystabel could not contain her gasp. Stephen sat up straight in his chair, his shock clearly evident on his paled face. Only Aunt Amelia seemed unaffected, still smiling, and pleased with her inheritance.

Crystabel grasped her arm. "But I had no idea, Eleanora. Did you know about this? Why you are an heiress, you have always been an heiress!"

"I...ah—"

Stephen sprang to his feet. "But this is outrageous! It cannot be! Why was I not informed?" He looked from Eleanora to the solicitor. "Something must be done. I was led to believe Crystabel was the heiress."

Grab your copy...
vinci-books.com/the-heiress

I wish I could say that I wanted to be a writer my whole life, that it was my dream. But it wasn't. I fell into it on a whim and discovered to my surprise that I enjoyed it. What I always have been is a reader. I will read anything. During the times I could not afford books, I read whatever sat on the shelves of the secondhand store. Sometimes it was History, sometimes Romance, and sometimes it was how to make macrame hangers.

But I am getting ahead of myself. I grew up in Brightsand Saskatchewan, in an immigrant family with six siblings. We were a hard-working troop, scraping a living out of a rocky mixed farm. I look back on those busy years fondly. I have plenty of stories about walking through miles of snow to school, uphill both ways!

I went to the University of Saskatchewan, studying History and English, which I converted into a career in teaching. I love my job. I teach a wild crew of junior high students. There is never a dull moment. It has been a passion of mine which has truly made life worth living. Much of my time is committed to coaching. I can be found most mornings in the gym by six thirty, spending time with my teams. We have had some memorable seasons, winning basketball districts against all odds.

I was lucky enough to marry the love of my life. My husband and I share another passion, gardening. He does the vegetables and I do the flowers. Together we spend many peaceful evenings, enjoying the beauty and bounty we have created.

I squeeze my writing into the bits and pieces of the day that remain. In many ways it is my personal time. I have been surprised by the writing process. Though I start with a plan, my characters always surprise me with their antics. I look forward to every new book, with its host of characters leading me into places unknown.